Love

IS A BLAST

Jane Hale

ISBN: 978-1-940586-56-4

9/24

Acknowledgment

Thanks to Claire Applewhite; Smoking Gun Publishing.

Thanks to Mary Ward Menke - WordAbilities and
Vicki Cox for editorial help.

Thanks to Lois Mans - Big Ideas Studio, cover and interior design.

To Robert Vaughan, Ellen Gray Massey, and the
"Write on the Beach" gang.

To my family and Pyro family, who in their own
way have contributed to this book.

Dedication

"Write what you know," they told me at all the writers' conferences, workshops, and guild meetings I attended while trying to learn the art of writing. Thanks for the advice, fellow writers. This book is for you.

To all of my friends and family who listened patiently to the reading of this book while it was in progress. Thanks; this book is for you.

To all those who know me as the Firecracker Lady and are a part of my world of pyrotechnics, this book is for you.

And to those who passed through my life and left memories: if you believe you find yourselves in these pages, ENJOY! This book is especially for you.

Chapter 1

"I'm Supergirl—I'm everywhere…" Jeannie Day Jonson lip-synced the words of the song blasting from her CD. Swaying to the music, she rotated her head from side to side relaxing the stiffness caused by hours of cramming for Hale University finals.

"How about it, Shutterbug Max? You think I've earned a night out?" Jeannie picked up the frame holding her ex-husband's picture. "Yeah, yeah, I know. Every night is a night out for you. The bartender probably has a Crown Royal with your name on it when Jeers opens." Jeannie pressed Max's photo against the fullness of her breast, closed her eyes, and imagined his head resting there. It had been a year since their divorce. Twenty-four-seven-studying was a lonely lover.

Jeannie placed the frame back on her bedside table. She should pack it away, but she just couldn't. Not yet. Did that mean she still loved him?

Jeannie laughed. "I never stopped loving you, babe. That was never our problem."

"I'm on a roll—I'm in your head…" Jeannie lost herself to the rhythm of the song. Releasing her coil of blonde hair twisted into a careless ponytail, she shook it free.

Snatching her cell phone from the desk, she held the make-believe-mike to her lips and crooned the lyrics. "Three, four, let me tell you what's in store…" Jeannie slammed the cover shut on the volume of Shakespeare and produced her own video. "Eat your heart out, Mr. William S…" Sensually, she caught the hem of her Hale U sweatshirt and pulled it over her head. Grabbing it by the collar, she tossed it over her shoulder and strutted toward the bathroom, stripping as she pranced to the music. Bra on the chair, jeans on the bed, panties on the floor, she ran naked into the tiny apartment bathroom. Peeking around the doorframe, she leered at the empty room and moaned, "I'm a perfect disaster!"

Chapter 2

An hour later, Jeannie fell in step with the Monday night party crowd pushing toward the entrance of Jeers. Enjoying the jovial atmosphere, she prided herself on the knowledge that Halesville, the third largest city in the state of Missouri, expanded its population during the month of May when high school and college graduations merged with Memorial Day weekend to become the first holiday of summer.

"For God's sake, leave the study stats at home," Jeannie muttered, pausing to take a deep breath. It took a lot of courage for her to walk alone into a nightclub like Jeers, where she used to be escorted by one of the sexiest men in Halesville.

"Jeannie Jonson?" A hand reached out and grabbed her arm. "Haven't seen you since…"A forgotten name from the past stumbled over the fact that Max and she were divorced. Then he leaned closer to whisper, "Honey, you got a nickel note?"

Choking back a clever reply, Jeannie said, "Sorry; you'll have to see Max about that stuff." Jeannie stood in the midst of the crowd feeling torn between two worlds. Last year, she lived on the fringe of the drug world with Max. This year, she was alone, but she was free to choose. She whispered to herself, *Be honest. You know you miss the high of Max.*

Jeannie edged through the crowd and made her way to the bar. The bartender moved up and down behind the counter mixing drinks. College coeds exposed early summer, tanned cleavage as they leaned over the bar. Guys and gals hollered their drink orders at random. "Hey Roscoe, over here. I'll have a…"

Jeannie needed a drink to fit her mood. She eyed the frosty glass the girl next to her was tipping to her lips.

"Mmm!" the girl set her drink down. She acknowledged the question in Jeannie's eyes.

"You're wondering what I'm drinking, right?"

Jeannie nodded.

"Between the Sheets. You should try it. Nothing better." She picked up her glass and gazed at the amber liquid. Then, grinning, she said, "Except maybe the real thing."

Jeannie smiled. She let her gaze wander down the bar, labeling the drinks. Buttery Nipples: not tonight, she decided. Orgasm: definitely not!

Finally, she hollered her order to Roscoe, "Scotch and soda." Taking her drink with her, Jeannie wandered over to check out a comedian clowning it up on the stage. Familiar flashes of light that could only belong to the flashbulbs of Maximum Exposure's cameraman, Shutterbug Max, drew Jeannie's attention to the dance floor. She joined the crowd, watching a petite blonde doing a solo performance, which promised to be a slow striptease.

"Where are you, Max? I'd know your flashbulbs anywhere. They're just as elusive as you," Jeannie murmured. Flashbulbs continued to provide stark drama on the dance floor as the blonde discarded a bit of fluff here and a bit of fluff there.

"Hi, hon. I'm Derek." The guy beside Jeannie edged closer. "Who's the broad?"

Jeannie shrugged.

Another flash outlined the blonde in silhouette as she kicked off stiletto heels. She hunkered to strip off sheer hose.

"Hey, that's Lynn Copper Sherman. She's Richard Copper's daughter, as in President of the Board of Regents, owner of the Copper Chain of Holiday Cruise ships. She's got a snoot full of more than liquor," Derek said.

The crowd gave a collective gasp as the blonde performed a dip and grind to the rhythm of canned music.

"That's Professor Brent Sherman's ex-wife?" Jeannie asked aloud. Privately, she mused, *My English Lit teacher was married to her?*

"Yep. Guess her name's still Sherman. I heard she divorced the guy because her daddy didn't approve," Derek said.

The crowd resumed clapping encouragement for Lynn Copper Sherman, who was down to her Victoria Secrets, which wouldn't cover secrets much longer.

Chapter 3

A blinding flash from across the room assured Jeannie that Shutterbug Max was on the job shooting pictures to be sold to the highest bidder. Jeannie knew how it worked. If the media wanted to bid against the person in the photo, the best man won. She blushed, remembering a short year ago when she followed Max around carrying his equipment.

The crowd parted as three people headed toward the dance floor. A disheveled Brent Sherman strode toward where his ex-wife was almost naked. Bartender Roscoe brought up the rear. And between them was—Jeannie couldn't believe her eyes—Rita Gibson, college glamour gal in line for the title of Miss Hale University, wearing a Hale University jersey."

"What's going on?" Jeannie asked.

"Looks like the rescue squad's arrived." Derek grinned.

A line of college men dressed in tight jeans and Jeers t-shirts hugging their jock muscles closed formation behind the group. Among them was Jeannie's seatmate in Lit class, Bo Hankins, a black football jock. He winked at her as he strode past.

Jeannie's cell phone rang. Damnation. Maybe the cursed thing would stop. She couldn't take her gaze from the action on the dance floor. Professor Sherman grabbed up the nude Ms. Copper Sherman. Their exit route moved close to where Jeannie stood. In passing, Professor Sherman glanced her way, flushed, and looked away quickly.

"Ladies and Gentlemen," Roscoe shouted the message like a barker at a carnival sideshow, "may I introduce Ms. Rita Gibson, Jeers' signature candidate for Miss Hale University."

He leaned toward Rita and whispered something in her ear.

She frowned. Then she nodded and flashed a smile at someone in the crowd.

The jocks jollied up the crowd with a rousing cheer as they lifted Rita to their shoulders.

"For Miss Hale U, may we suggest?

Rita Gibson, yes, yes, yes!

Hale yes!

Rita Gibson's got it in her—to be a red-hot winner.

Hale, yes! Hale U! Hale, yes! Hale U!"

They paraded off the dance floor with Rita waving from her elevated position. The crowd showed their appreciation with foot stomping, wolf whistles, and applause.

Jeannie's cell phone alerted her of a message about the same time Tyler Vaughan, the handsome blonde hunk who managed Jeers, waved at her. Jeannie fumbled her glasses off and stuffed them in the pocket of her denim skirt. Using her fingertips for a brush, she quickly fluffed out her tumbled curls to frame her flushed face.

Tyler pushed his way through the crowd toward Jeannie.

"Hey there!" she said, preparing herself for a get- acquainted-hug. Jeannie's cell phone rang again. Searching her pocket for the confounded distraction, she completely missed Tyler as he sped past.

"What the—" Abashed, Jeannie turned to see Tyler hit on Rita Gibson, who was surrounded by a bunch of Tri-Sig sorority girls. They were toking up in spite of the no smoking signs.

Jeannie pieced together tidbits of conversation as she passed the cozy group. Tresa Vaughan, the owner of Jeers, was in town.

Hmm! That must be Tyler's sister. He didn't seem too happy about it. He was gossiping with Rita about unloading something.

Squeals of laugher mingled with the sweet smell of smoke tantalized Jeannie as she headed for the exit of Jeers. Disappointment was a regretful reminder that she was a twenty-five-year-old divorcee and confirmed the fact that Tyler Vaughan definitely wasn't interested in her. Bummer!

"When people are up against the stem nothing matters but puffing the weed," Jeannie whispered, peevishly. This time last year she was with Max and he had a habit going on. She was glad that was all behind her.

Chapter 4

Pulling out her cell phone, Jeannie checked the caller ID. Great! The call was from her perfect big sister, Renee Day Allen. She returned the call.

"It's about time, Jeannie. I need a favor, desperately," Renee said.

"I can barely hear you, Renee. Give me a minute. I'll find a quiet place."

"What's all that noise? Where are you? I thought you were staying in this evening," Renee said.

Jeannie steeled herself for a reprimand.

Sure enough, Renee let her have it with both barrels. "All I asked you to do was ride to the Parkview graduation with Cloie. But no! You had to stay home and study for your big finals."

Jeannie interrupted, "Renee, you were eleven years old once. Did you want your aunt trailing after you whenever you went somewhere?" Jeannie knew that was the wrong thing to say as soon as the words were out of her mouth. Cloie wasn't like Renee. Her niece was Miss Independence with a capital "I."

"Whatever! We'll discuss it later. I really need your help now," Renee said.

"What's wrong?" Jeannie felt the first stab of fear "Sis…Renee, what is it? Give me thirty minutes and I'll be at your house."

"No, don't come here. Cloie's at the Parkview football stadium. It says on Channel Three a thunderstorm is moving into Halesville—"

Jeannie pocketed her cell phone after assuring Renee that she would drive across town and pick up Cloie, who'd missed her ride home.

Chapter 5

Near the front exit, Jeannie saw Rita and Tyler deep in conversation. Her attention averted, she slammed into someone exiting the men's lavatory.

"Mic Davao!" she exclaimed.

Mic was married to Madam Davao, who owned Davao's Department store in the Mall. Max used to call Madam "old money bags." Jeannie thought the Davaos were a charming couple, so devoted to each other.

Mic's face flushed. "Ms. Jonson, it's so good to see you."

"Good to see you, too. Where's Madam?"

"She's working, as usual. How's that charming husband of yours? Max, isn't it?"

It was Jeannie's turn to flush. "Mic. You do know Max and I aren't together anymore?"

Mic moved closer and gave her a comforting hug. "Sorry, hon. I'd buy you a drink but I was just on my way out."

"Thanks, Mic." Jeannie eased away from the over-long hug. "I was just leaving, too."

Mic's glance darted toward a secluded corner where a flashy redhead stood. "Got to go."

Moving toward the exit, Jeannie turned to glance behind her when she heard a woman's brassy voice raised in anger. "...next time he gets in trouble, I'm through."

"It'll all work out, Tresa," Mic said, as he took the flashy redhead by the elbow and steered her into one of the private party rooms.

"For God's sake, just let me out of here," Jeannie grumbled. Was there no preservation of the illusion of wedded bliss? She struggled against the crowd coming in the entrance to get outside. As she reached the door, Jeannie burst into tears.

Chapter 6

Rita Gibson, sensing Jeannie's distress, broke away from Tyler and hurried out the door after Jeannie. "Wait, Ms. Jonson, please. Can I help you?"

"I'm fine." Jeannie swiped a hand across her eyes. Turning to Rita, she asked, "But how did you know my name?"

Rita shrugged elegantly, "Oh, I've met your husband. Max, isn't it?"

Jeannie nodded. She might have known.

Rita seemed to sense her thoughts. "He's a brilliant photographer. Jeers is sponsoring me in the Miss Hale University contest. They made arrangements with Max to do contestant competition photos."

Rita chatted as she walked with Jeannie.

Jeannie found herself telling about getting caught in the middle of her sister and niece's problems. She babbled on about a storm coming in and how she hoped nothing had happened to her niece.

"Oh, my gosh, I have a niece, too. I know exactly how you feel, Ms. Jonson."

"What's with this 'Ms. Jonson'? I'm not that old. Call me Jeannie."

Rita gossiped about family and college. But she kept glancing around the dark parking lot as she followed Jeannie to her Explorer. "I can't wait to get back home. I've got some studying to do, too."

Distant thunder accompanied flashes of lightning, confirming Rene's weather report.

Rita stayed close as Jeannie unlocked the Explorer. Jeannie climbed into the driver's seat in a hurry to get to her niece. She realized how vulnerable Cloie could be alone at the ballpark as a jagged vein of white lit up the sky. "If anything happened to Cloie I'd just die."

Rita shivered like a cold wind had just blown down her collar.

"Rita, thanks for—for everything. You're not at all like I imagined." Flustered, Jeannie tried to pull her foot out of her mouth. "I mean for a glamour girl you're not phony." Jeannie turned the key and the motor roared to life.

Rita flushed. "Jeannie, there are things I can't—" Rita stopped talking abruptly. She looked around as if she thought someone or something was going to pounce on her. Then she turned back to Jeannie and smiled. "I hope we see each other on campus. Please be careful. Find your niece and return her home safely." She reached her hand out to Jeannie.

Thinking Rita was going to shake hands, Jeannie extended her hand. Rita placed a card in it. Expecting to find a vote-for-me card, Jeannie was surprised to find a professional business card.

"Jeannie, if you need anything please call me. In fact, call me anyway and let me know if everyone arrives safely at home." Rita looked toward Jeers, frowned, and looked back at Jeannie.

"There's another number on the back to call if you can't find me." Rita walked toward the back of Jeers. She turned to wave just as a jagged streak of lightning illuminated the parking lot. The brilliance outlined Rita's figure capturing her with a tin-type-photo-image.

Jeannie pulled out to the highway. She looked toward the entrance of Jeers. She caught a glimpse of Mic Davao and the flashy redhead exiting the building. Rita was nowhere to be seen.

Moving onto Kearney Street, Jeannie headed west. She mused at the happenings of the evening. Lines from Shakespeare's *As You like It* ran through her head:

"All the world's a stage,

And all the men and women merely players:

They have their exits and their entrances;

And one man in his time plays many parts."

You couldn't judge a book by its cover. Rita Gibson, the swankiest gal on campus was just a Plain Jane when it came right down to it.

Lynn Copper Sherman had everything life could offer. But she had nothing to offer to herself. Or to her relationship with Professor Brent Sherman.

Jeannie and the professor were in complete synch quoting the masters. But they were strangers to other parts of each other's lives.

Mic Davao had lowered her estimate of men one more notch.

And Max—"My Lord!" Jeannie slapped the heel of her hand against her forehead. She'd completely forgotten about Max.

Pulling the Explorer out into the passing lane, Jeannie roared past a semi like it was standing still. She hoped there were no patrol cars around because she had to get to her niece. Her family was her life.

She'd once thought Max was her life. Max and Jeannie had wallowed in life. But Max was a stranger to her world of literature. Or maybe not—maybe Max just expressed himself in a different way.

Jeannie grinned, remembering how Max summed up Shakespeare's all the world's a stage quote. "It's simple, Jen. It's kind of like 'another brother by another mother.' People screw up their lives. They leave shit behind. It affects others." He ran his fingertips gently down the side of her cheek bone and said, "Don't give up on me, Jen. Who knows what the future will bring?"

Max, Max. She still couldn't live with him. But she could never live without him. One thing was sure: she'd never forget him. Or the excitement he brought into her life. She breathed a wistful sigh.

The trip across town took twice as long because of holiday traffic. Jeannie's fingernails were down to the quick when she pulled into the parking lot at the Parkview football field. The lot was empty.

Chapter 7

"Cloie, where are you, baby?" Jeannie hollered as loud as possible to the deserted field.

Thunder distorted her words and returned to her. "Where are you, baby?" Oh, my God, how could she screw up everything? If something happened to Cloie, it would be her fault. Jeannie continued yelling Cloie's name as she prowled the empty lot.

Flashes of lightning outlined people of the night scurrying about doing their dastardly deeds. They slunk deeper into the shadows. After each flash, Jeannie's eyes adjusted to the dark. Near the football field, she rousted young lovers who'd snuggled beneath the football bleachers.

"Wait, have you seen my niece, Cloie?" Jeannie yelled after the departing figures.

Headlights cut through the gloom. They spiraled skyward much like the fireworks which had filled the heavens over the football field a short time before. Drivers switched their beams on high, trying to discern if she was the predator or the prey. But none cared enough to become involved.

The shrill ring of a cell phone sounded somewhere in the night.

Jeannie gave her forehead a reminder slap. "Thank God! I'll call Cloie on her cell phone." Then she remembered. Renee told her Cloie called on her friend's phone. Cloie's cell phone battery was down.

Jeannie knew she should call her sister, but she refused to admit defeat. She continued to prowl the area, screaming herself hoarse as desolate and alone as her niece must be.

"Cloie, honey, baby. Oh, Cloie, where are you?"

Chapter 8

"Auk—Jeannie, help!" the shrill, feminine voice screeched.

He grabbed her from behind and began dragging her across the parking lot to the open door of the waiting van. "You should have stayed where you belong, honey. We've got some walking and talking to do. Got to get you in the van before it starts pouring down."

Fighting to free herself, she kicked and bit down hard on his hand. "Help me, please someone!" she screamed.

The man's hand jerked back. "Sons of a bitch!" His voice was filled with enraged hurt. He renewed his efforts to clamp his other hand over the girl's mouth.

For a moment, his hands loosened their grip and the girl kicked backward once more. Her heel found its target.

"Damn you, girl! I'll show you—" His voice took on an urgency as across the way the outline of two people, voices raised in anger, became more visible with each flash of lightning.

Feeling herself being drawn closer to the van, she concentrated her efforts to project a scream that might be heard by whoever was approaching. Twisting her head from side-to-side, she struggled, kicked, struggled, and elbowed.

The man held her in a strangle hold. He was once more moving her closer to the open van door. "Now, now, it won't be long and we'll be alone. Maybe this time you'll answer my question."

Tears flooded her eyes. Dampness slipped from beneath her lids wetting the man's hand clamped over her mouth. What could she do? The things she'd been taught fled her mind as blind panic took hold of sanity.

The voices rose and fell with a pattern of angry discontent as a couple moved more quickly toward the van.

The girl slumped, going limp against the man holding her. Her ploy worked, because taken by surprise, the attacker readjusted his grip to hold her upright. For a brief moment, his hand loosened over her mouth.

"Helllp me!" she screamed.

Her scream was cut off quickly as a strong hand cuffed her across the face, stunning her into submission.

"Au–" She opened her mouth once more to scream as the man launched her head first into the back of the van. Her shoulder rammed one side of the back door of the van with enough force to propel her further into the middle. Horrific agony sliced through her back. Pain pushed its way into her chest. She landed with a jolt and settled against the floor of the van. Blood marked the ragged edges of a jagged piece of wood protruding through her breast, pinning her in place. Her mouth gaped. No sound came but the gurgling of fluids seeking release. Her hands flailed as blood gushed from her breast in torrents, soaking her clothes and pooling on the floor of the van.

Chapter 9

The man quickly slammed the door of the van, not realizing the girl had landed on an old ax handle wedged between the rails of a discarded dolly. Hearing nothing, he assumed she was dazed. He moved to the front of the van intending to exchange greetings with the couple. He hesitated just out of sight. He knew the man, who was married to a prominent business woman. The lady with him obviously wasn't his wife. If he ventured into the light he was sure to be recognized. He remained in the shadows. Very nice. He doubted if they wanted to be seen, any more than he wanted them to see him.

Thunder followed close on the heels of a jagged slice of lightning. They continued on their way engaged in angry conversation, unaware they'd just witnessed a murder in process.

Returning to the back of the van, he opened the door, determined to deliver a blow that would silence the girl if she tried anything. "Hey, you! There's nobody but me and you around now. Might as well get our little talk over."

She lay mute, crumpled in an awkward position in the darkness of the windowless van. Her silence infuriated him. Not knowing she was already dead, his right hand shot forward preparing to grab her by the shoulders and pull her upright. The ragged edge of the wooden stake protruding through her chest gouged a strip of flesh from the top of his hand.

"Sons of a bitch!" Thinking she had attacked him, he jerked his arm back quickly. Searing pain shot through his hand. The dim light of the parking lot took on the brilliance of an operating room with the next flash of lightning. He examined the fresh wound on his arm. The skin gaped open near the place where her teeth marks remained.

"Slut!" He hissed the word through clenched teeth. Angrily he shook his arm, hoping the gesture would diminish his pain. His shirt sleeve was covered with a red stain. His wound must be deep, he thought, as blood splattered his clothing, the van, and the parking lot.

"Bitch, I'll show you who's boss. Yes sir, we're going to have us a nice little talk." Determined to teach her a lesson, he slammed the back doors. Racing to the front of the van, he crawled inside. He hoisted himself over the seats. Gingerly, he reached to switch on the interior lights.

"Damnation!" He glared at the body. Her eyes were open. They stared upward at the ceiling of the van. He knew without checking she was dead. Her hand, which had involuntarily grasped the wooden stake protruding through her chest, was covered with blood. Ironically, he felt a sense of relief, realizing it was the girl's blood, not his, which covered his shirt sleeve, his clothing, the back of the van, and the parking lot.

Sounds of the night closed in on him as he stared at the corpse who had minutes before been so alive, so vibrant, and so full of information.

Realization hit him like the force of a lightning bolt. "Jesus!" He was in big trouble. His stomach heaved, resulting in a spasm of vomiting. He moaned and wiped his mouth with the sleeve of his shirt. Averting his gaze from the lifeless body, he crawled back to the driver's seat. "What are you gonna do now, man? A lot of people are going to be mad."

As if in answer to his question, the sky opened up and rain fell in torrents.

Chapter 10

In the early morning hours, he drove the van slowly along Interstate 44 near Halesville. He pulled off the four-lane to an outer road and turned onto a deserted farm road. The route was familiar. He eased the van into a clump of trees at the edge of a wooded area away from farm houses. Cutting the lights, he grabbed a flashlight. The rain had stopped. The thunder moved on, taking with it the ferocity of the night.

"Oh, yeah," he nodded. He'd picked the perfect place. The growth of trees was thick enough to hide the van from anyone driving along the farm road. Ground cover was a mass of fallen leaves ripened into mulch. Broken limbs and straggling tree roots demanded slow passage. Beer cans littered the ground near trees, as though hunters had stopped to refresh themselves while waiting for their prey.

"Git'er done!" Steeling himself against the metallic smell of blood, bile, and urine, he opened the back door of the van. Heavy rainfall would probably erase traces of blood from the parking lot, but it would take a major scrubbing to wash out the violence wrought this night in the back of this van. Memories of the mind were another matter. They could never be erased.

The sound of an approaching vehicle on the farm road beyond the clump of trees disturbed the morning silence. Easing the van doors shut, he edged closer to the rear of the van.

Chapter 11

Headlights filtered through the trees quickly and flickered downward as a truck sped around the curve and disappeared.

"Bloody damn!" He wasn't aware he'd been holding his breath until it came out in a released rush. Rotating his shoulders quickly to ease tension he prepared himself to reopen the van doors. Without glancing at the covered body, he unloaded a shovel and headed into the woods. Soon the scrape of metal against hard-packed earth echoed throughout the wooded area, causing wildlife to huddle in their dens or take flight.

"Whoooo, whoooo?" an owl questioned curiously as the man returned to the van. He eased the already-stiffening body onto the dolly and wheeled the girl's corpse into the woods.

Wiping sweat from his forehead, he hefted his shovel. Chunks of dirt tumbled over the plastic-covered form at the bottom of the grave. He pounded dirt into a mound with his shovel. Taking a large tree limb, he smoothed dirt over and around the grave. As the first rays of sunlight filtered through the woods, the man surveyed the job. Satisfied, he trailed the limb behind him to cover his return to the van.

Seated in the driver's seat with head bowed over the steering wheel, he massaged the base of his skull and counseled himself. "Got to get going and steam clean this van. If anyone finds out what happened tonight, you're dead. You not only murdered the girl, but you never talked to her first." Slapping the steering wheel, he berated himself. "Stupid! You left a whole lot of loose ends."

What if she told her girlfriend something? Had the other girl seen him? A crafty light lit up his eyes. "Maybe, just maybe, I better find me that other girl."

The van's engine roared to life. Slowly and carefully, the man backed the van out. Just before he moved onto the farm road, he looked once more towards the wooded area where he'd buried the girl.

Satisfied, he nodded. "They'll never find her here."

Wind blew up from nowhere and rustled the soft leaves of spring. Had he imagined it or did it sound like an omen repeating the warning that spawned from his mind? "They'd better never find her. Better that they think she just disappeared."

Slowly, the van made its way back to Halesville.

Chapter 12

"Cloie, honey, baby. Oh, Cloie, where are you?" Jeannie continued to prowl the parking lot screaming herself hoarse, as desolate and alone as her niece must be. "Oh, honey, where are you?" If she didn't find her niece soon, she'd have to call Renee and admit defeat. They'd have to call 911. She raised her eyes to the heavens. "Please, please, let this be a bad dream. Let me wake up and find Cloie is safe at home. I promise, Lord, I'll never—"

As if in answer, Jeannie's cell phone rang. Rain poured down. She ran to her Explorer.

Jeannie missed the allotted rings her cell phone allowed before it reverted to message mode. Accessing voice mail, she waited.

Renee's voice sounded loud and clear in the confined space of the Explorer. "Jeannie, Jeannie, where are you? Why didn't you call me? You and Cloie are both on my black list."

"Oh, my God! Renee–" Being on her sister's blacklist wasn't anything new to Jeannie. But losing Cloie would be more than Jeannie could bear. Her niece's love blasted Jeannie into another dimension. What would she do without her? And it was all Jeannie's fault.

Renee's voice continued, "Thank God for Max! He brought Cloie home safely."

Jeannie sagged against the Explorer, faint with relief.

Then she was filled with a raging vengeance. "Max!" If anyone was on a blacklist, it was Max. He probably knew Jeannie was supposed to pick up Cloie and—Jeannie saw the red light still blinking on her cell phone alerting her of another message. She hadn't heard her phone ring. How could there be another message? Switching on the light in her truck, she checked Renee's message. It was sent thirty minutes ago. She must have been hollering so loud she missed hearing her cell phone ring.

The new message was from the call she'd just missed. "Hello, Aunt Jeannie, I'm home. Thanks to Max. You owe me one. And don't forget our shopping trip tomorrow night at the mall."

Hitting redial on her message, she couldn't wait to hear her niece's voice. "Cloie, Cloie, what would I ever do without you, darling?" Relief washed over Jeannie in waves, and she was giggling hysterically with relief.

Lifting her eyes to the heavens once more, she repeated Cloie's words differently. "Thanks, I owe you one."

A soft summer rain pounded against the top of her Explorer as Jeannie arrived at her apartment exhausted. Parking the truck at the curb, she ran for the front door, unlocked it, and went inside, heading for bed. She had an early morning class. A small card dropped from her pocket as she removed her skirt. Reaching to retrieve it, she remembered the new friend she'd made tonight at Jeers, Rita Gibson.

"And you promised to call and let her know if everyone was safe," Jeannie reminded herself, reaching for the phone. Her bracelet watch read twelve o'clock. It was too late to call anyone tonight. Besides, she'd see Rita on campus tomorrow. Out of habit, Jeannie placed Rita's card on her desk where she kept business cards. Jeannie rediscovered a brochure relating to a trip to Mexico that her Spanish class was going to take this summer. She had asked her dad about the trip. If he'd just come through with some extra cash, she could stay in Halesville this summer and maybe go on that trip to Mexico.

Turning out the lights, she crawled into the middle of her queen-sized bed. One thing about living single: you could hog the whole bed. But as sleep crept in, Jeannie's hand reached toward the far side of the bed where a short year ago Max had slept. Why was she still holding onto that lost dream?

What was it Max told her? *You hang on too tight, Jeannie. Hang on loosely, but don't let go.* Is that what she was doing?

Jeannie sighed, *Girl, you need to get a life.* Tomorrow she'd sign up for that trip to Mexico.

Chapter 13

"Bada bing!"

The mailman handed Jeannie a stack of bills with a letter from home as welcome as a Brad Pitt lookalike on a blind date. Tearing open the flap, she fingered the inside of the envelope, hoping to find dough from her dad. Instead, she pulled out an invoice with scribbles on it from her dad's Bull Creek, Missouri car lot.

"Bummer!" She turned the envelope upside down and shook it. Nothing! "Thanks a lot, Dad." She hadn't felt this deflated since she was chosen third runner-up in the Miss Bull Creek pageant with a field of only four contestants.

She smoothed out her dad's note and began to read. "Jeannie Day Jonson, you can't go to college for the rest of your life. You're twenty-five years old, for God's sake! If you really want to stay in Halesville this summer, hunt a job to help support yourself. Or come home to Bull Creek. I can always use another used car salesman."

"Not on your life, Dad." Spend the last summer before she graduated from Hale University in a one-horse burg like Bull Creek? She thought not!

Jeannie grabbed an armload of books and slammed out of her apartment.

Marching down the sidewalk toward her black Explorer parked at the curb, a trade-in from her dad's car lot, her footsteps beat out a cadence, *get a job, get a job!*

Fumbling for her car keys, Jeannie considered the ludicrous line in Dad's letter. "Get a job?" Was he serious?

"Jeannie," she said to herself, "when your dad uses your first and last name, he's serious. When he tacks on the married name of your ex-husband, he's damn serious!"

She could sense her dad's aura as surely as if it had crawled out of the envelope she'd just received from him in the mail. She knew if she concentrated, she could perceive his thoughts as surely as if he was speaking to her in person. But Jeannie was in no mood for that right now.

Uh-uh, Dad, a summer job, no, way! She'd much rather go on tour with the Spanish club to Mexico. Hmm…the Mexican tour wasn't until the second week in July. Maybe between now and then, she could find a job that paid big bucks.

Grinning at the thought, she dumped her load of books in the passenger seat of the truck and climbed in behind the wheel. A job paying big bucks? Sure! And, maybe her rich uncle would die and leave her a million.

Glancing in the rearview mirror, she was accosted by her mirror image staring back with raised eyebrows. The mirror image smirked, *Sure honey, and maybe our ex- hubby, Shutterbug Max, the picture taking man, will show up on our doorstep with the divorce settlement money the court awarded us!*

Would that be the same money he lost in Vegas as soon as he sold our house?

Right.

Jeannie gave herself a mental nudge, repeating the sage advice she gave to Cloie, *Grow up!*

Then, it hit her. She was grown up! Like her dad said, she was twenty-five years old, for God's sake. She could fill out an application for chaperone on the Mexico tour, a position with expenses plus.

Problem solved, she wadded her dad's letter into a little ball and tossed it into the back seat of the Explorer. Gunning the motor, she headed for Lit class at Craig Hall. She could check out the Mexico tour sign-up sheet at the bulletin board on her way.

Chapter 14

As luck would have it, traffic crawled and parking space was scarce. Spying a vacant place, she aimed the Explorer for it. A silver Porsche did a U-turn in mid-block and prepared to do battle for the same spot.

"No way, Jose!" Jeannie yelled, wheeling into the parking space in one smooth motion.

Grabbing up her backpack, she climbed out, flipping the bird to the yobo hanging out the window of the Porsche. The Porsche burned rubber, leaving her in a fume of exhaust.

Trudging up Sorority Row, Jeannie spied Max's shutter-buggy parked under the side columns of the Tri-Sig house. Thank God her dad had come through with the Explorer. If not, she'd be traveling around campus in that dark room on wheels with a Maximum Exposure logo painted on the side.

"Sell it, Dad!" Jeannie demanded when she drove the shutter-buggy to his car lot last year and told him she and Max were getting a divorce.

"Give it up, Jeannie. No one will buy it." He finally convinced her to return the van to Max, so her philandering ex-husband could make a living and possibly contribute to her support.

Right! Like that was going to happen.

"Honey, be reasonable. Max's family lives in Bull Creek. His mom plays bridge with your mom. We all go to the same county club, the same place you and Max had your wedding reception. It'll be hard enough to weather the local gossip without the shutter-buggy sitting on my car lot to remind the town of your break-up." Bless Dad's heart; he never once reminded her he'd tried to talk her out of the marriage.

So, here she was on campus in her borrowed Explorer. And here was Max on the same campus with the shutter-buggy parked at the side of the Tri-Sig house. She was glad he was out of her life completely.

Sure, you just cut him out of your life completely. If that's true, what in God's name were you doing at Jeers last night? You're just mad because he has an early morning photography shoot at the Tri-Sig House, a little voice in her head reminded her.

An early morning photography shoot? I think not. He must have come directly here after he took Cloie home. The scoundrel! How could he be so nice and naughty at the same time? She glanced once more at the Tri-Sig house, vowing to never see him again. Jeannie shook her head, remembering the times he'd tried to explain his way out of a "Kodak moment" with a co-ed.

Same old Max, flaunting authority with no thought to campus gossip. Then, she saw his dilemma. In spite of herself, she smiled, surveying the array of sports cars blocking his exit. The shutter-buggy was a Tri-Sig captive. Max would have a hard time keeping photo appointments or any other appointments today.

Appointments! Jeannie glanced at her wrist watch and quickened her pace. Brent Sherman, her Lit professor, might be a lot of things but being tolerant of tardiness wasn't one of them. And he might not be in such a good humor today, considering the incident at Jeers last night with his ex-wife. She'd check the information on the Mexican tour on the bulletin board after Lit class.

Chapter 15

At Craig Hall, Roe Winthrop, the Tri-Sig president, and her clique were ahead of Jeannie. They maneuvered their way toward Sherman's room, looking fresh in spite of toking it up at Jeers last night. The thought occurred to her Max might be out and around since the Tri-Sigs had moved their cars. She couldn't imagine them hoofing it to class.

As though sensing her thoughts, Roe turned and let her gaze flicker over Jeannie. She leaned toward her Tri-Sig sisters. Glamour Gussie was a bosomy, copper-toned blonde whose tanning-bed skin was a shade lighter than Charming Cyra, who'd been blessed with naturally dark skin that no amount of sun could duplicate.

Whispering, Roe tilted her head with a slight nod in Jeannie's direction.

Gussie and Cyra stopped, backing up traffic.

Turning to Jeannie, Gussie demanded, "As Max's ex, I bet you'd know where he hides the keys to the shutter-buggy, right?"

As Jeannie considered the question, Cyra took center stage, jiving around Gussie like a contestant auditioning for *Popstar*. "I bet she'd know, I bet she'd know."

Jeannie busied herself admiring the "Vote for Rita—No One Sweeter" poster pictures of Rita Gibson for Hale University Queen hanging like banners from the ceiling down the main hall. She vowed to cast her vote for Rita. She smiled, recalling their brief meeting last night and the card Rita had given her with the number to call reporting on Cloie. She hoped to see Rita around campus today and let her know why she hadn't called last night.

The vivacious Cyra sashayed in Jeannie's direction, eyeing her critically. "Pay attention, woman. Unh-uh, she was his woman. Honey, I said she WAS his woman." The intricate loops of dreadlock curls atop her head rivaled Medusa's serpentine coiffure. Students paused to enjoy the sideshow. Most of them must have viewed the shutter buggy's overnight parking space.

"Were you addressing me?" Jeannie asked,

Gussie smirked, gathering her sorority shroud around her. "How many other of Max's exes do you see standing around?"

Jeannie let her gaze travel lazily over Gussie and her friends. "Oh, I don't know. How many, exactly, are there in your group?" She mimicked Cyra's lead, eyeing the Tri Sig's unmercifully. "Red, or yellow, black or white, they are precious in his sight. My Max loves the little coed's of the world."

Cyra sputtered.

Gussie delivered a most unoriginal line, "Well, I never!"

Never one to pass up playing the straight man, Jeannie countered, "I seriously doubt that."

Even Roe chuckled at that remark. "Come on, Gussie, Cyra. Ms. Jonson may have his name but she's certainly not in the game. As Max says, if he found a pot or bottle, rubbed it, and a real genie came out, she'd probably be colder than a dead mackerel, just like his ex-wife, Jeannie."

The crowd guffawed.

Cyra's voice underlined the laughter like backup for an orchestra, "Uh-huh, uh-huh."

Roe's remark hit home. It was the stock-phrase Max tossed out when asked about their divorce. Jeannie smiled sweetly and tossed them a bone. "Max isn't very knowledgeable about fish, but he would certainly know about pot and bottles."

The smiles on their faces froze colder than the mackerel to which she'd just been compared. Roe turned and moved forward toward the Lit room. With one haughty sweep, her coterie followed.

"Umm, I must have touched a nerve," Jeannie said to no one in particular.

No one in particular giggled and moved on toward Lit class.

Chapter 16

On the edge of Roe Winthrop's sorority crowd, who'd dismissed Jeannie and moved on to better things, Jeannie got a lesson in creativity for Literature class.

Roe complained. "...Smug, arrogant, conceited! I can't take another day of Sherman's course."

Cyra said, "Pompous, vain! Honey, I haven't a clue what's he's saying."

Glamor Gussie smiled. "Go easy on him, sugar. You saw last night what he has to put up with. Besides, underneath he's all male."

In harmony the group gasped. "What?"

Gussie scolded. "Quit trying to understand his quibbling and do what I do."

Right there in the doorway they all stopped, once more, creating havoc. "What do you do?"

Gussie smirked. "The first time I competed in a beauty pageant, I cringed at the thought of parading in front of all those critics in my bathing suit. Aunt Lea told me to look at the judges and imagine them in their underwear. It worked! I tried it in Sherman's class. Like I said...underneath, he's all male! If you squint real hard, he looks like Channing Tatum, all male."

Cyra snickered, "Hush, baby! I love that Channing Tatum."

Roe giggled. Moving forward, she jump-started her entourage. Jeannie trailed in their wake, toying with the possibilities of Gussie's suggestion.

Chapter 17

In her assigned seat in Lit class, Jeannie watched Professor Brent Sherman strut back and forth on the dais spouting poetry, bare as the day he was born, except for the fantasy loin cloth she'd loaned him and a thick bandage on his right hand.

Huh, a thick bandage on his right hand? What kind of an imagination retained trauma? Probably a result of his encounter with sweet Lynn last evening. Or a later date—she stopped not wanting to go there. Quickly her imagination erased the bandage, ignoring the injury, and moved on to more interesting facts. Squinting real hard, she turned her head from side to side but she couldn't find even a hint of Channing Tatum.

"But oh, baby!" She placed a hand over her mouth, holding the laughter inside. Roe Winthrop and her sorority sisters were right! If you used a little imagination, you could get through Professor Sherman's class even if you didn't love Lit like she did.

Jeannie glanced sideways at Roe's clique seated in the next section of theater seats, stifling giggles as they leaned forward to squint. She felt sure they were using their own advice. She hoped they salvaged a little of the professor's dignity by leaving him a fig leaf.

Although Sherman's Lit class was labeled boring, it had few late arrivals. University students learned the penalty of being late early in the semester. Bo Hankins, the football jock who'd transferred from Alabama State University, had unwittingly scheduled Lit class as an easy credit. At the beginning of the semester, he tried to sneak in late and ended up on Sherman's torture rack.

Hearing a soft snore to her left, Jeannie sneaked a peek at Bo taking a snooze. He must have stayed late at Jeers last night. His earlier classroom experience might not have taught him to be alert, but he was always an early arrival. The sleeping giant seated beside her was a far cry from the Bo Jeannie remembered earlier this semester standing alone on Sherman's stage trying to interpret A.E. Housman's, "To an Athlete Dying Young." His attempt to explain iambic tetrameter with four da-dum feet per line had convulsed the class with laughter. Jeannie remembered that day last spring as through it were yesterday.

Chapter 18

Professor Sherman had almost seemed human that day as he claimed Bo's seat beside Jeannie. He laughed along with the rest of the Lit class when Bo hammed up his presentation. Then, Sherman turned in her direction and smiled his lopsided smile displaying teeth worthy of a toothpaste commercial. A strain of dark hair fell across his forehead just above slightly bushy eyebrows.

Jeannie realized she was favoring him with a goofy grin when she saw her image mirrored in the depths of his luminous apple green eyes. Her reflection was so vivid she decided he must wear contacts. Yes, sir! There she was a frumpy, dishwater-blonde in horn-rimmed glasses. Without makeup, she looked every day of her twenty-five years. He must be wondering what she was doing in his Junior Lit class. He wasn't alone, because she was wondering the same thing.

"Da-Dum fits him, don't you think?" he mused, as he critiqued Bo's rhyming.

"Fits a lot of us. Sometimes…," she paused, "more than we know." She could have kicked herself the minute the words were out of her mouth.

Sherman's eyebrows pulled together in concentration. "Astute observation, Miss…?" His eyes seemed to flip like a Rolodex searching. He accessed J: "Row four, seat twelve…Jeannie Jonson, right?" Mentally, he patted himself on the back.

Once more she spoke without thinking. "It's MRS. Jeannie Day Jonson."

The spark of interest which burned briefly, sputtered. "Of course, the admitting office must have made…" he paused, giving the next word a stressed syllable, "another mistake."

Foot in Mouth continued. "Technically, admitting is right. I'm divorced."

The spark flickered briefly. "Divorced? Ah, those of us who have weathered the storm and ended up on the rocks should recognize a kindred spirit." He hesitated.

So, the professor is divorced, too, she mused.

As though reading her thoughts, he shrugged eloquently and glanced toward the stage, assuring himself Bo was still da-dumming. "Might thou be kin to Ben Jonson?" He chuckled at what he probably considered his private joke.

Who, he must have thought, but the gifted Dr. Sherman would know he was referring to Ben Jonson, who was the first poet laureate in the modern sense, although King James the first, had never officially appointed him?

"Since I married into the Jonson family I'm afraid I didn't remain long enough to research their poetic background. But judging by my ex-husband's performance, I'd say he could definitely be a descendant."

Sherman leaned toward her in earnest. "And, how might that be, Miss, er,…," he searched for a title, "MRS. Jonson?"

"My former husband has a poetic way of dilly-dallying with words, which was wonderful when we were dating. After we were married, he continued to share those odes with the fairer sex. I personally decked him with an honorary degree of divorce."

"Exit husband, end of Scene One, right?" Sherman dismissed her marriage.

Briefly, she wondered if he dismissed his marriage as casually. "Oh, he still has his offstage moments," she said ruefully.

A frown creased Sherman's brow as he considered.

"Not with me, of course. But, Max has developed quite a following around town, especially with the photogenic ladies on campus, which have discovered 'Maximum Exposure.'"

Sherman's brow furrowed with concentration as he cataloged this latest bit of information. "Max Jonson? You were married to Max Jonson?" He studied her intently as though he couldn't reconcile the facts.

"Guilty, as charged." She grimaced.

"Ahh!" Sherman began. He hesitated, his attention once more drawn to the stage where Bo preformed.

A wave of laughter swept over the class as Bo reached the final two lines of his poem. "Man and boy stood cheering by, And home we brought you shoulder high."

Sherman, the almost-human, turned back to her. "So much for chit-chat…divorce and all that." He stopped, chagrined, and delivered a slight chuckle to emphasize his delivery. "I can't believe I slipped into a bathos."

Did he believe she hadn't studied the list of definitions he'd given them? *Bathos: Sentimentalism; descent from lofty to commonplace; may move one to laughter.*

She was still gawking at him as thunderous applause announced Bo had finished reducing Housman's poem to commonplace.

Sherman rose, as if acknowledging the acclaim for himself.

He spoke in a loud voice, allaying the room to silence with a single word. "Bravo!"

He motioned for Bo to return to his seat and moved past Jeannie to the aisle. In passing, his knees brushed hers, generating an electric current that shocked her upright. Jeannie found herself standing face-to-face, within kissing distance, of the esteemed professor.

He drank from her soul as he peered deeply into her eyes. Then, as though satisfied she had not been the conduit of electricity, he continued on his way, thundering his deliverance of William Cowper's verse, "I am monarch of all I survey, my right there is none to dispute, from the center all round to the sea."

His performance was flawless. He was standing in front of the podium on stage as he completed the last line. "I am lord of the fowl and the brute."

Sherman's gaze prowled the crowded theater. It came to rest on Bo, who was now seated by Jeannie. "As for you, Bo, my dear brute, you have entertained the class well. That's not to say you haven't murdered poor Housman's work." He bestowed his lopsided smile on two giggling girls in the first row.

"Da-dum!" Jeannie muttered, realizing she'd spoken aloud when Bo looked her way.

"Just a new idiomatic expression I acquired to preface my skepticism, dear Bo!" she assured him, mimicking Sherman's usage of the language.

Bo shrugged and turned his attention back to Sherman.

"Let this be a lesson to you, class! I will not tolerate tardiness. Far be it-that my class is subject to foolishness like we have just witnessed when we can be studying the masters."

And study the masters they did, for the rest of the semester. As the class progressed, Sherman seemed less a man and more a young god, as he postured and preened across the stage, trying to download his love for English Literature into minds intent on experiencing now relationships instead of what they considered a dead poets' society.

Chapter 19

Abruptly, Sherman's assignment voice jarred Jeannie from her reverie. She glanced toward the dais and there he stood, fully clothed, once more. "Your homework for tomorrow is Sonnet CXVI. Might I have a student who is familiar enough with this poem to give me the author's name?"

Jeannie smiled at the pomposity of Sherman, who spoke roman numerals rather than common numbers. Bo sank deeper into his theater seat. He had learned his lesson well.

Silence reigned.

"Come, come! Surely a class of juniors at our esteemed university will have at least one student who can provide me with an answer to this simple request?"

The bell announced the end of the class. The students rose as a group.

"Halt!" Sherman bellowed. "You will not leave my classroom until you are dismissed. And, until someone tells me the author of Sonnet CXVI."

Grumbles of disapproval sounded over the room, but no one volunteered.

"Hee-haw!" Sherman yelled the words like a cattleman stampeding a herd of cattle.

Bo dropped the pile of books he'd grabbed to make a hasty exit from Lit class. He gawked at the stage. "Sherman's finally flipped out," he said.

Jeannie grabbed for the books as they fell. "At least he got the students' attention."

The students reluctantly sat back down. They stared at the stage, dumbfounded.

"Stopped you in your tracks, didn't I?" Sherman pushed the lock of dark hair from his forehead. "Just to prove a point: how many of you can tell me the title of three songs Garth Brooks sang at his Branson opening this weekend?"

Hands shot up all over the classroom, hoping to improve their grades.

A droning of voices became chanting as titles roared forth like thunder, "I know one," "Cowboy Bill," and "Working on a Full House."

Sherman knew most of his class would be late for their next class. Although he demanded punctuality, he obviously didn't care if it hindered others. He stood with head bowed, shaking his head in disgust. "I rest my case. If you retained knowledge of the classics like you horde titles of guitar-thumping, stage-gyrating cowboys bellowing out what they claim is music, I'd have a class of masterminds."

Slowly, Jeannie raised her hand.

"Here, over here!" Voices called attention to the lone raised arm.

Sherman's gaze scanned the classroom. A look of amusement crossed his face. "Why am I not surprised Miss, er, MRS. Jonson? Pray tell me, who is the author of tomorrow's assignment?"

Jeannie hesitated. The class inhaled as a unit. "I believe the answer to your question," she delivered her lines like a dramatic dialogue enunciating the roman numerals as she identified the assignment, "is William Shakespeare. He composed Sonnet CXVI!"

The vacuum remained until Brent Sherman spoke crisply, "Class dismissed."

The gust of exhale might have blown a lesser man from the stage. Sherman merely closed his book, bowed his head, and waited for relief from the ignorance of the masses. The students gave Jeannie a round of applause and rushed out of the theater.

Above the noise, Roe's voice carried, "Dead fish and dead poets. Seems fitting, doesn't it?"

"Sure does," giggled Cyra. "I bet that gal don't even know who Garth Brooks is."

"'Low Places,'" Jeannie said. "One of Garth Brooks' best hits is 'Low Places.'"

Jeannie gathered her books to make a hasty exit. She was stopped in her tracks by the sound of laughter coming from the dais. Certain Sherman had heard Roe's remark, Jeannie turned.

The professor was leaning against the podium, chuckling into his cell phone, unaware of the drama playing out in his theater. Sherman looked almost boyish as he tossed the dark lock of hair from his eyes and turned to find her staring at him.

Startled, Jeannie gave him a feeble salute as she left.

His voice followed her through the door, "I buried her in the woods last night. Tonight we can meet at the same place. Bring a shovel so we can dig a hole and shoot the big one. No one can hear us out there."

Jeannie stopped dead in her tracks, trying to reconcile the conversation she'd just heard with the man who was her professor, Brent Sherman. Retracing her last few steps she peered into the room.

It was empty!

Chapter 20

"I buried her in the woods last night. Tonight we can meet at the same place. Bring a shovel so we can dig a hole and shoot the big one. No one can hear us out there."

What had Professor Brent Sherman's words meant? Jeannie decided she'd probably heard him wrong. She worked her way toward the bulletin board just in time to see her Spanish teacher, Ms. Wingo, taking down the sign-up sheet for the tour of Mexico.

"Wait!"

Ms. Wingo turned with a puzzled expression on her face. She smiled when she saw Jeannie.

"Is the chaperone position still open? I'd like to talk to you about it."

"Too late. Darcie Patterson called earlier. But I can still add your name to the list."

"Can I let you know?"

"Soon?"

"Soon!"

Bull Creek was closing in on her. Jeannie could see herself trying to sell automobiles this one last beautiful summer before she was lost to a bogus world of enterprise.

A group of students were checking out posted information on the bulletin board. Publicity pictures of the candidates for Miss Hale University were displayed prominently near the top of the board.

"Rita is so cool! I know she'll win," one student said.

"I didn't see her in class this morning. I've got some PR for her. If you see her, tell her to get in touch with me, okay?" another student answered.

The reminder of Rita Gibson caused Jeannie to search in her pocket for Rita's card. She was determined to call her. Rita seemed to have a lot of contacts. Maybe she would know someone who needed to hire some help. She gave up when she remembered she'd left the card at her apartment.

Jeannie sighed, "I've got to find a job!" She turned and found herself self-face-to-face with Brent Sherman.

"Ms. Jonson, I'm glad you're still here. I met Ms. Wingo in the hall. She told me you wanted to apply for the chaperone position for the Mexico tour, but it had already been filled. Are you hunting for a summer position?"

"Well, yes, sort of," she stammered, "Actually, I need a high-paying job for a short time that will let me go on tour to Mexico with the Spanish club." She could feel color creep up her neck and cover her face as she realized how ridiculous she must sound.

Sherman gave her an amused smile. "Indeed, I was just starting to post this." He indicated a card in his hand. "It may be just your cup of tea."

"What kind of work?" she inquired, reminding herself beggars can't be choosers.

He smiled. "Actually it's exciting if you don't mind long hours, adventure, and meeting all kinds of people." He hesitated, "You told me earlier in the year you were divorced. Do you have any other relationship that would hinder your working nights?"

"None!" she answered too quickly and blushed again. Surely he was reminding himself he had seen her alone at Jeers last night.

"Fine! I'm in a bit of a rush. Can we talk tomorrow after class? I will need to discuss this with my partner." He folded the card in one quick motion, pocketed it, and strode down the hallway before she could answer.

As Jeannie made her way across campus, she reviewed Sherman's job description. "Exciting!" God knows she could use a little excitement in her life. He'd mentioned long hours, adventure, and meeting all kinds of people. Maybe this job was the answer to her dad's ultimatum!

Her dad's thoughts came through loud and clear: *Is this the same man you heard say, 'I buried her in the woods last night. Tonight we can meet at the same place. Bring a shovel so we can dig a hole and shoot the big one. No one can hear us out there'? What is it about the men in your life, Jeannie? First Max with drugs, no money, and now this—Sherman—promising big bucks for God knows what.*

You promised you wouldn't throw Max in my face anymore, Dad. And, all this is your fault. You're the one who demanded I get a summer job.

Jeannie could imagine her father looking cautiously over his shoulder to see if her mom was listening before he put a finger to his lips. *Shh! Your mom will have my hide! Just forget I ever mentioned a job. Come on home for the summer. Didn't I offer you work already?*

How embarrassing, she thought. *Any self-respecting divorcee wouldn't have to depend on her father's finances.*

You made your bed, Missy. Sleep in it. Or buy one of your own. Money doesn't grow on trees, Jeannie Day Jonson. When are you going to learn that?

Chapter 21

After her last class of the day, Jeannie hefted her backpack and headed to retrieve the Explorer. Surveying the Tri-Sig drive, she saw Max's panel wagon still planted in the circle of sports cars. "Talk about Maximum Exposure!" she sighed, and hurried toward the space where she'd parked.

She stared at her Explorer. It was a perfect example of how not to parallel park. No way! She certainly hadn't parked her truck this way. Someone had moved her vehicle. Then, she saw it, a piece of paper stuck under a wiper on the front windshield.

"Not a ticket, please, not a ticket," she whispered, reaching to snatch the offending piece of paper from the front of her truck.

Scooting in behind the wheel, she discovered two things. The scribbling on the piece of paper looked familiar. And the inside of her Explorer reeked with the odor of weed. She stared at Max's handwriting as scenes from their marriage passed before her eyes, perfumed with odor of marijuana.

She blinked at the paper and read, "Thanks for the wheels, Jen. I had some film-shoots I couldn't afford to miss. The girls had me penned in. I left your spare key where I found it. Take care of the stash in your console, hon. It was a little risky leaving it in the shutter-buggy."

"The nerve of him," Jeannie said.

"I left the last roll of negatives from last night. I didn't have time to develop everything. I'm still using my dark room to develop negatives. Our divorce wiped me out. One day, I'll upgrade, but for now, the gals still think my camera's sexy. Feel free to screen them like you used to do. You should consider changing where you hide your key, hon. No telling who might drive away in your rig. You going to ring me up and thank me for saving Cloie from God knows what last night?—Max."

"Of all the nerve!" Jeannie tried to stir up a world of hate for the inconsiderate lout. But the thought of Max Jonson and his blithe sexuality still turned her insides to jelly. Squeezing her eyes shut, Jeannie gripped the steering wheel, trying to blot out Max's 'Matthew McConaughey' persona. Her fickle fingers caressed the leather wheel cover, drawing from it memories of the virile masculinity that was Max. His bold fingers had moved over this leather like they once played over her body.

"Snap out of it!" she told herself, half-high on the thought of self-denied pleasures.

Jeannie switched on the key and put the Explorer in gear. She felt the need to get out here quickly before Max's stash became her problem with the campus police. And God knows what other incriminating things he stashed in her console.

Jeannie eased the Explorer out and into a line of cars and drove toward the main drag. Lost in thought, she slammed on her brakes as a beat-up, tan Dodge Ram with a tarp stretched over the heavily loaded rear end pulled out and around her. Horns blared and tires squealed as traffic protested.

"All right, already!" she yelled out the window, mentally recalling the face that grinned at her from the passenger side of the pickup. *Brent Sherman?* Could her eyes be playing tricks on her? Jeannie wrestled her truck into an opening in traffic just in time to see the pickup go through a yellow light and continue on down the avenue.

"So much for law and order...let's race for the border." Jeannie stopped, chagrined. "I can't believe I slipped into a *bathos*."

Somewhere deep inside her, a little voice whispered, *I can't believe you forgot the professor's phone conversation.*

Chapter 22

The man who had just offered her a short term, big money job had uttered these words, "I buried her in the woods last night. Tonight we can meet at the same place. Bring a shovel so we can dig a hole and shoot the big one. No one can hear us out there."

Buried who? Shot who? Where in the country could you shoot or bury someone and no one would know? Jeannie had to know. Her foot pressed down on the accelerator. She wove in and out of traffic as she scanned the vehicles ahead. Her efforts were rewarded when she glimpsed a streak of tan moving onto the four lane.

Exceeding the speed limit, Jeannie kept the Dodge in sight. Recalling the demonic grin Sherman cast her way, she reasoned that if a cop was going to stop anyone, it would surely be the fiend in the pickup. God forbid it was her, with stash in her console.

"Thanks for the driving lessons, Dad," she murmured, remembering the many hours they'd spent on the road transporting cars to auctions.

Echoing from the past, Dad's voice reassured, *Jeannie, even though your foot is a little heavy on the gas, you're one of the best drivers I know. But what are you doing racing after a man who's riding in a worthless piece of junk like that when you should be searching for a summer job?*

*Dad, Sherman's not a man, he's my Lit professor, and he just offered me a job…*She must be nuts! Pushing aside that comment, she concentrated on the Dodge. It had just pulled off the four lane to an outer road. She almost lost them when their truck turned onto a farm road.

The route was deserted. It twisted and turned enough for her to stay out of sight. She rounded a curve. Up ahead, the Dodge was parked by the side of a dark green panel wagon near a thicket of trees.

Chapter 23

What now? Jeannie shifted into reverse and backed around the bend. As luck would have it, there was a lane leading into a pasture with a stand of trees just made for her truck. She turned off the motor and settled back to wait. Curiosity soon overcame caution, and she crawled out of the Explorer. She worked her way through the thick stand of wooded area. Rounding the curve, she had an excellent view of the two vehicles. The van was backed up to the Dodge now. It almost hid the tan truck. Three men seemed to be transferring objects from the Dodge to the van.

A gruff masculine voice echoed through the wooded area. "What held you up, Roscoe? We've got people dying for this stuff."

"You're not the only game in town, boss," Roscoe replied.

"You trucking for the competition, too?" This voice had to belong to Sherman.

"Money talks and Roscoe walks," Roscoe said with a hint of laughter in his voice.

"A little less talk and a lot more action and we'll get these punks switched," the gruff voice commanded.

"Yeah, I'd like to get my van unloaded so I can get back to town. Trucking's not my only job, you know," Roscoe complained, rubbing his gloved hands over his arms briskly as though trying to relieve an itch he couldn't seem to scratch.

"Jeers have any problem with you moonlighting?" Sherman asked.

"Jeers?" Jeannie whispered. Of course. Roscoe was the bartender at Jeers. The van must belong to them. What in God's name was going on?

"What the Jeers lady doesn't know won't hurt her. Miss Classy

Cash spends her time in Tulsa with the family trucking company. Her little brother Tyler is my main man. He comes in real handy at times. As long as I keep my end of the job up, my off time is my own business," Roscoe said. "But let Tresa find out different, and I'll be looking for another job."

"Fine, no sense in getting it mixed. But I did appreciate your help last night. Sorry about the disturbance," Sherman said. "Nice idea to distract the crowd with the jocks and Rita Gibson."

"No sweat. But tell your ex, Miss Lynn, to keep her clothes on. One of these nights we're not going to be around to help. And she's going to find herself in trouble," Roscoe said. "She's getting it on heavy lately."

"I warned her. Hey, you're not dealing with her, are you?" Sherman's voice held an edge of anger.

"She's too risky. Her old man put the word out he'll nail anyone he catches messing with her. You should know that better than anyone," Roscoe said.

"Keep your nose out of my private business, Roscoe!" Sherman yelled, as he pushed a dolly loaded with crates to the back of the van.

Gruff spoke harshly to Roscoe in hushed tones Jeannie could barely make out. "We've got too much at stake for you two to—" He broke off as Sherman appeared with the empty dolly.

"You sure you removed evidence of where I buried her last night?" Sherman asked.

"If I told you I did, I did!" Roscoe grunted. "And I started digging the hole for the big one just before you guys showed up." He paused to wipe his gloved hand over his brow. "Think you're man enough to handle the rest of the job?"

"One of these days you're going to find out just how much man I really am, hotshot." Sherman moved toward Roscoe raising his hands in a fighter's stance.

Gruff yelled, "You're going to have all three of us in the clink. You're done here, Roscoe. Get your tail on back to Jeers. Tell your boss lady we'll stop by later to settle up."

"You settle with me. Leave the boss lady out of it. If you stop by the bar, do me and Tyler a favor and don't recognize either of us," Roscoe said with a grunt. "That's the last one. Are you going to chance shooting these big ones out here?"

"That's the plan. Too bad you can't stay for the action." Gruff said.

"Fine with me. I'm going to get the hell out of Dodge. Just give me a head start before you blow them to blazes," Roscoe said as he came around the side of the van.

"You want to be paid?" Gruff yelled.

"Shit!" Roscoe stopped with his hand on the van door.

Instinctively, Jeannie leaned back, although she was completely hidden. She caught a glimpse of a Saint Louis Cardinal t-shirt, red ball cap, and long, jean-clad legs, as Roscoe turned to retrace his steps to the Dodge.

Jeannie figured if the van belonged to Jeers, the truck must belong to Gruff. The name Tyler rang a bell. He had to be the blond hunk from last night who was jumping Rita's bones. So he was the brother of Tresa, the lady who owned Jeers. And their family owned a trucking company in Tulsa? Roscoe returned to the van door minutes later. He rested his lean frame against the side of the van and began leafing through a wad of green bills. Fumbling, he dropped part of the cash. It fluttered to the ground.

"Sons of a bitch!" Roscoe yelled. He stripped off his work gloves carefully and began groping around in the dirt for the bills he dropped. Satisfied he had retrieved all the bills; he stood and continued counting. He rolled the cash into a tight roll. Transferring it to his left hand, he stuck it in his skintight jeans front pocket making a nice round package.

"Big bucks for trucking what?" Jeannie whispered aloud.

The van's motor started. Roscoe's tires caught traction. He roared her way, leaving the Dodge in a cloud of dust. Sure enough, the van had the Jeers logo on the door. When the dust cleared, Jeannie surveyed the scene. The Dodge seemed to be deserted. She listened closely and could barely discern voices in the woods by the pickup.

Hoofing it down the country road, Jeannie was glad her attire matched her personality. Plain old Jeannie blended into the countryside. Cautiously approaching the Dodge, she could see the cab was empty. Where were the passengers? Had they already executed their unfortunate victims?

"Yeah, right!" Jeannie actually giggled.

Chapter 24

It was evident the only place to hide anyone was in the back of the pickup, which still held three shapes under a heavy tarpaulin. Reassuring herself no one was around, Jeannie sneaked closer. She studied the three shapes. Could they be people? Where they dead? Hoisting herself up on the rear bumper, she reached over the tailgate. She started to raise the tarp, "Hey, you in there. Can you hear me?"

Boom-m-m! The noise shook the pickup. It jarred her into motion. Jumping from the bumper, Jeannie fled into a grove of trees just in time to hear another resounding *BOOM!*

Concealed behind the trunk of a tree, she pushed the green vine that encircled it aside and peered at the pickup. Jeannie's bracelet wristwatch showed six o'clock. *Where are you, Sherman?*

She heard their voices before she saw the two men emerge from the woods shouting excitedly.

Had she followed the wrong people? The first guy's bleached-out jeans moved with his body like a second skin. His faded t-shirt outlined a divine Channing Tatum torso. It was only when he tossed the lock of hair from his eyes that he resembled Brent Sherman.

"What did you think of that one?" he asked in a voice that was without a doubt her Lit professor. Glamour Gussie was right: underneath, Brent Sherman was all male.

The older man's camouflage sweats made him an extension of the woods. He remarked in a gruff voice, "Impressive! But do it right the first time, Sherman. It's the mark of an amateur to have to shoot twice." He reached over the side of the pickup. "Give me a hand moving these punks. We'll carry the big one out to the woods."

"Da-dum!" Jeannie disappeared behind the tree trunk.

Grunts of effort narrated their dirty deed as they prepared to move another punk into the woods. Curiosity outweighed caution and she peered through the tangle of vine hugging the tree.

Sherman's voice was filled with excitement. "This next one is supposed to be the hottest thing in town, right?"

Camouflage groaned with the effort of the load he carried. "That's what the big boys say!"

Could it be a woman? The hottest thing in town? The big boys would know! She had to get out of here. Right now!

Chapter 25

The men were moving back into the grove of trees where they had shot the last poor soul. No way could they see her. But Jeannie couldn't leave until she knew what was really happening. Lulled by their distant voices, she moved deeper into the trees on a line parallel with them. The late afternoon sunshine filtering through the tree leaves suddenly became brighter. She realized there was a clearing ahead. She hesitated in a thicket near the edge.

Sherman stood, foot planted on the blade of a shovel. As Jeannie watched, he bounced and brought his weight down.

"Oomph! Roscoe barely made a dent in this ground. It's like concrete. Are you sure we need to dig a trench?"

Camouflage materialized dragging a box big enough for a casket. "If you want to shoot this one you've got to put her in the ground."

She cringed. Put her in the ground! They were digging a grave!

"Better hurry! All this shooting is enough to invite noisy neighbors." Camouflage planted his boot on the lid of the casket and surveyed the area. His glance seemed to stop as it came to rest on the trees near where Jeannie stood. "Dig it deep. If the marshal gets wind of this—" He broke off as a crackling noise sounded nearby, "What the…"

Paralyzed, Jeannie waited. What other evil lurked within these woods?

Crump, Crunch—suddenly a flock of birds took flight, causing Sherman to drop his shovel. Then a doe and her fawn appeared in the clearing.

"Man! It's only a deer." Camouflage emitted a sigh of relief.

"Hey, there are two of them." Admiration softened Sherman's voice. The doe's head went up and a silent message passed between mother and child.

"Run!" Jeannie whispered, knowing if these two men could kill humans so casually they would surely shoot two beautiful deer.

As if heeding her warning, with heads erect, the doe and her fawn bounded across the meadow and disappeared into a stand of trees.

Despite the coolness of the approaching evening, Jeannie's body was covered with a thin sheen of perspiration. Strands of hair hung in limp disarray around her face. Moisture steamed her glasses. Her body was on fire with an itch that demanded scratching. Jeannie carefully prepared to edge back to her truck, keeping her sight trained on the two men who had returned to their task. Her heel caught on a tree root. Arms flailing, Jeannie did a reverse-to-stomach in midair, executing a perfect belly buster atop a mound of soft earth.

"Oomph!" Jeannie waited, expecting any moment for the two men to come tearing through the trees.

Nothing! Her hands kneaded loose dirt, trying to gain traction for a silent pull-up. Attaining an upright position, Jeannie surveyed the mound of dirt, wondering if Brent Sherman and his partner might have already buried someone beneath the spot. Nonsense! It was probably a coyote's hole. Jeannie prepared for flight. It mattered not if the coyote had two or four legs, she was ready to run.

Camouflage's voice stopped Jeannie in her tracks, "Competition is hitting heavy on me. There's a new punk on every corner. We've got to get some more help. Have you found anyone yet?"

Jeannie's blood turned to ice as Sherman replied, "Matter of fact, I just talked to a girl in one of my Lit classes who needs a job that pays good money for short-time work. She wants to go to Mexico."

"Has she got any experience?"

"I don't think so, but she's a quick study. I may have to up the ante to interest her, but there's not too many places around here you can make this kind of quick money and walk away."

Chapter 26

And Jeannie thought Bo was dense.

Brushing debris from her blouse, Jeannie picked her way carefully through the woods and returned to the gravel road. Shadows lurked behind every tree moving with the jerky rhythm of a silent movie as shifting sunlight played tricks with the mind. Hesitating, she considered checking the pickup again. Maybe she was jumping to conclusions.

Her dad's voice echoed in Jeannie's head. *Sure! You must want that high paying, short term job really bad if you're trying to sugarcoat this one, Missy!*

An explosion echoed through the woods. Was it a gunshot? Jeannie raced for the security of her tree.

What should she do now? A frenzy of itching caused her to forget caution. She dug her nails into an area near her collar and scratched furiously. Relieved, Jeannie decided to dash for her truck. She stepped cautiously over the ditch and onto the gravel road. Immediately, she jumped back and returned to the safety of her tree when she heard voices in the woods near the pickup.

"What's your problem, Brent? Look at your arms! You've scratched the hide off." Camouflage trailed Sherman, who was rubbing his arm in a manner Jeannie could appreciate.

"You think it's too early for poison ivy?" Sherman's words gave a name to the dainty green vine that covered the trunk of her tree.

Jeannie's fingers were caught in the act of pushing aside a portion of bright green, triangle shaped leaves. She quickly snatched them away, too late!

As the men made their way back into the woods, Jeannie moved onto the road and raced for her truck. What was it her mom used for rashes? She could picture herself covered with a layer of pink stuff tomorrow that would surely match the esteemed professor's.

Between scratching and driving, Jeannie wondered what she should do. Alert the authorities that her college Literature professor and his partner were lugging punks to the woods, shooting them, and burying them in shallow graves? How would she explain her presence at the murder scene?

By the time Jeannie pulled onto the four-lane and headed back into town, she was halfway hoping a highway patrolman would stop her. It would save hunting for…for whom? The authorities! Having always been a second-rate, law-abiding citizen, she didn't have a clue where the authorities were located, thank God! The campus police, maybe, but the authorities?

Some of Jeannie's favorite movies were mysteries. Mental flashes of people on the witness stand giving evidence against criminals in a court of law gave her pause.

Would they laugh at her? Had she actually seen the bodies? What was she doing at the scene of the crime? Could she be arrested as a co-conspirator? *Jeannie Day Jonson, for one time in your life keeps your wits about you. If you don't say anything, who will ever know you were there?*

As Jeannie reached the city limits, she wondered where the closest pharmacy was. Calamine lotion! That was what she needed!

The crowd waiting in line at the pharmacy assured her poison ivy could infect every part of your body from the top of your head to your toes. It could even invade your mouth! Disgusting!

Chapter 27

In the privacy of her small apartment, Jeannie stripped off garments polluted with poison ivy. As her fingers moved gingerly over her body, she wondered briefly about Sherman's rash behavior. A play on words: he would appreciate the thought.

Jeannie called up his professor image and compared it to the confirmed shooter in the woods, who was possibly a cold-blooded murderer, she reminded herself. A chill ran up her spine, lifting the hair on the back of her neck.

"Possibly," she said, hugging her naked body to ward off the chill. "Possibly" was the key word: she had no proof. All she had from that soldier of fortune was the offer of a dubious, short term, good paying job.

"And, a fine dose of poison ivy, which is my own fault for being a snoop," Jeannie reminded herself, reaching for a robe. "If I'd minded my own business, my English Lit assignment for the next day would be my greatest worry."

Jeannie reached for her book. Life must go on. She was exhausted. She had a nagging thought she was forgetting something important. Leafing through the book, she reassured herself school was a necessary part of life, poison ivy or no poison ivy. Jeannie pushed aside the little voice that whispered, *Murderer or no murderer?*

Jeannie re-read her Lit assignment, savoring every word of the Shakespeare sonnet. Being the youngest in her family, books had been her solace, and this particular Sonnet was a favorite. Preparing for bed, she foolishly wondered if that first brief conversation between her and Professor Sherman had birthed this assignment.

"Don't be absurd," Jeannie scolded herself. "He's got his hands full with his ex-wife. Besides, he probably doesn't even remember his little chat with you."

Jeannie's eyelids drooped. What was it with her and men? Did she have a fetish for losers? Jeannie had been wooed by fickle words and betrayed before. *There's no such thing as true love. Men are just bushwhackers lying in wait for easy prey.*

This time it was her mother's soft whisper that cradled her over the edge of sleep: *Don't doubt true love, baby girl; just look at your dad and me.*

Chapter 28

Jeannie woke to a new day in a tangle of pink sheets scented with Eau de Calamine. The landline phone was ringing. She groped for it with a rash-covered hand. Squinting at her bare pink wrist to check the time, she mumbled, "Hell-ooo?"

"Jeannie? Is that you?"

And who else would it be? Her mom's cheery voice caused the retort to die an early death.

"Hi, Mom. You got a pre-dawn appointment somewhere?" She glanced at the bedside digital clock as the numbers did a slow shift and became a new hour, eight o'clock.

"Eight o'clock!" Jeannie breathed heavily into the phone as she pulled her stiff body into a sitting position, ready for a hasty conversation, a quick shower, and an attempt at covering the pink flush that appeared to spread over her hands, arms, and neck.

"Yes, dear, it's eight o'clock! I know you have a class at eight-thirty, but I thought I'd chance catching you." Jeannie imagined her mom sitting in their family kitchen, cozy in her bathrobe, sipping a cup of coffee. The scene lulled Jeannie into slow motion as she pulled the long cord of the phone into her small bath.

"So, what did you need?" Jeannie reached for her toothbrush. She layered on neon blue paste and stuck it in the side of her mouth to soak.

Seating herself, Jeannie began her daily ritual as she listened to her mom try to smooth over Dad's ultimatum. "And...I told your dad he was wrong to make you find a job. You need to spend your time studying. You'll be cast into the work world all too soon...Why did that line sound familiar?

Rising to stand before the cracked enamel basin with no vanity space, Jeannie cradled the phone between her shoulder and face as she brushed up a lather with her free hand. She emptied her mouth of toothpaste and rinsed. Finally, Jeannie raised her eyes to examine how much damage the ivy had wrought.

"Da-dum!"

Her mom's voice stilled for the first time in five minutes.

Jeannie waited, then cleared her throat.

"Did you say something, Jeannie?"

As if I could break into your marathon of chatter, she thought. Aloud, Jeannie answered, "Just brushing my teeth, Mom. Was there anything else? I'm in a rash, er, rush."

"Jeannie, I distinctly imagined I heard you call me dumb. Please tell me those weren't your words. I only called to try to help you with your trip to Mexico, you know..." As she rushed on non-stop, Mexico caught Jeannie's attention.

"Mom...Mom...MOM!"

Silence.

"Mom?"

Silence, the kind Jeannie remembered from childhood, cast a feeling of uneasy guilt.

"Mom, are you still there?" Dragging the phone cord into her tiny bedroom, Jeannie flung clothes from the closet, looking for a not-too-warm, long sleeve, turtleneck t-shirt to cover the itchy blush of summer.

Jeannie decided she'd try one of her mom's methods. "Mom, I'm waiting."

Was that a sniffle? "Jeannie...," her mom began, "if you don't want to use the money I saved for new bedroom furniture, just tell me."

What? "Mom, I'm sorry I must have missed something. You're buying new bedroom furniture?"

"Was, darling. I decided to let you use the money for your Mexico tour. I can just hear the mother of your ex-husband when I mention at the club my Jeannie is not only going to graduate from college next year but is touring Mexico this summer..."

"Mom …mom …MOM! Stop it! Right now! Mexico is not that important …," Jeannie lied. Visions of Zelda Jonson, Max's society mom, and Marie comparing notes in front of the whole country club set put Jeannie's just brushed teeth on edge. "Besides, I already have a job. A big-buck job with short hours that I can walk away from in time to go to Mexico." What had she said?

"Jeannie, I knew you could do it! I told your dad you'd find a job! Well, I'll tell them to go ahead and deliver my new furniture."

Jeannie could hear a sigh of satisfaction as her mom murmured, "Goodbye, darling," She actually giggled, "Don't work too hard."

Jeannie knew her mom couldn't wait to get to the club and chance a meeting with Zelda Jonson.

"Digging your own grave, aren't you, Jeannie?" she asked the slightly flushed face that glared at her from the mirror.

"Actually, darling, pink is your color!" Jeannie complimented her image, as she reached for the jingling phone again. It could only be her mom. Maybe she could amend her last statement, change it, and retract it completely. "Mom …remember what I just said…?"

Giggles erupted. No way could this be her mom.

Cloie, her niece, who switched emotions quicker than a mood ring, demanded, "Aunt Jeannie? Where were you last night?"

Slamming a sticky, pink palm to her forehead, she finally remembered what she forgot last night. Mentally, Jeannie scolded herself for standing her niece up. "What can I say? Gosh, kid, I'm so sorry I missed out on the mall shopping trip!"

Jeannie could sense her niece's pretty pout.

"You promised, you know! What earthly excuse could you possibly have…?"

Having recently watched *The Godfather* with her niece on DISH, Jeannie tried to mimic her way out. "Look, kid…I got an offer I couldn't refuse." She lied, sort of.

"You mean you had an actual date?" Why was it even an eleven-year-old had a hard time believing she might attract a man? Or was that accusation in her voice? In her own way, Cloie was in love with Shutter-Bug Max, who wooed her like every other woman in his life. Doggedly, she believed one day Max and Jeannie would get back together and live happily ever after, and he would be her Romeo uncle again.

Cool!" The pout had evaporated, replaced by genuine astonishment. "So, what's his name? When do we get to meet him? Where'd you go?"

"Cloie, Cloie, CLOIE!" Jeez! It was her mom in a different form: her granddaughter. "No, no, it wasn't a date. I was following up on a job offer for the summer."

Cloie's disappointment was audible. "Sorry, Aunt Jeannieeee!" Her voice rebounded as she dribbled into the next phase of the conversation, "But never mind! Renee filled in. Good thing, too. We found it! Dreamyyyyyy! And it emptied your big sister's purse completely." Her reasoning was, of course, Aunt Jeannie's billfold would have been too slim, skimpy, and completely defunct.

Cloie called her mom "Renee," and Renee seemed perfectly comfortable with the idea. Marie thought it wasn't ladylike, but she'd given up saying anything to her granddaughter.

"Can't wait for you to model for me, Cloie."

Once more, Cloie's mood switched. "Aunt Jeannie, I modeled for Max. He actually took a picture of me in the on-fleek outfit!"

Jeannie could feel Cloie, the matchmaker, closing in, again. "Hey! What was Max doing at the mall? You didn't actually ask him to go shopping with you? Cloie, I'm still upset with him for picking you up the other night and not calling me. Do you know how scared I was that something had happened to you?"

Cloie completely blew off the remark about the other night. "Aunt Jeannie, give me some credit! I didn't ask him to go shopping. Max had a photo shoot at Davao's Department Store. He told me he had an appointment with the husband of the woman who owns the place. He'd just given him a packet of pictures when he saw me trying on clothes. He came over and shot some film." Her voice dropped to a secretive whisper. "They may use me in their layout! That would be totally lit!"

Remembering her chance meeting with Mic Davao at Jeers Monday night, Jeannie didn't have to wonder what kind of pictures

Max had taken of Madam Davao's husband that might make Max some extra money.

"Yes, I can imagine. You'd made a great model, sweetie."

Cloie mood switch, "Are you and Max tight again?"

"No! What makes you ask that?"

"He said you let him use your truck, and he left you a present. What did he leave you?"

The rat! Setting her up with Cloie like this. She would definitely get rid of his stash. "Nothing important. Listen, kid, I've got to run. You should be hitting the pavement for school, too! And I won't forget your summer basketball league tonight at the Courts. Love you."

"Waiiiit…don't hang up! I want to know about you and Max." Sensing a quick hang-up, she rushed on, "Remember, you promised I could borrow your dangle watch. It'll go perfect with the straight-fire outfit I'm wearing this weekend." Cloie paused. "Aunt Jeannie? You still there?"

Jeannie rummaged through the mess atop her dresser in search of her dangle watch. In a weak moment, she had promised Cloie she could wear it. Jeannie planned to drop it off at the jeweler and have the clasp fixed first. She couldn't chance her losing her graduation watch. Marie had spent far too much for the one-of-a-kind bauble with an inscription, "JD, you made our Day!"

Where did I put that watch? Jeannie sighed. Vowing to do a thorough search tonight, she strapped on her generic watch.

"What! You didn't lose it, did you?" Cloie's voice took on an accusing tone, "Is our deal dead?"

"No way, José. You'll get it as soon as it comes back from the jeweler. Later." Jeannie hung up to kissing sounds from the other end. Her niece! If she drove Jeannie wild, what would she do to the male population at her middle school? And with that new, hot outfit, too! What was it Max said? "YOLO!" Yeah, you only live once.

Scribbling a reminder of Cloie's league game that night, Jeannie posted it on the fridge. If she missed two nights in a row with Miss Cloie, she'd be moving in with her. Jeannie's niece was the love of her life, and the feeling was mutual. Recalling Cloie's surprise at the thought of her old aunt bagging a date, Jeannie vowed to shape up her act.

Sure! Guys will be falling over themselves to fill your date book when they see this outfit. She tugged on the too-tight capri pants that matched her only turtleneck t-shirt which promised to halfway cover her pink plight. She grabbed an armload of books and hurried from the apartment.

Jeannie adjusted the volume on the radio with one hand while she wheeled the Explorer away from the curb.

Easy listening music stopped abruptly. The announcer's voice said, "Police are asking for your help in finding a missing woman. Rita Lee Gibson, twenty-four, was last seen Monday evening at ten p.m. in the vicinity of Jeers Nightclub on East Kearney in Halesville, Missouri. Ms. Gibson's car was found in the back parking lot. Her purse and identification were locked inside."

Jeannie slammed on the brakes. "Oh, my God!" Easing her truck to the curb again, she turned the volume up further. "Rita Gibson is described as 5 feet 8 inches tall, with blonde hair and green eyes. Police said Ms. Gibson is a student at Hale University. She is active in student affairs and is a candidate for Miss Hale University. Anyone with information on her whereabouts is asked to call the state police."

"Jeers parking lot? Ten p.m....Oh, my God! That's about the time Rita walked me to my truck!" Jeannie exclaimed. She remembered how Rita started up the walk and turned to wave. Something was wrong with this picture. Then it struck her: Rita hadn't been heading for the entrance where they came out. She had been heading for the back parking lot. No wonder Jeannie didn't see Rita as she left. Then she remembered. She had seen Madam Davao's husband and his lady friend standing near the front entrance of Jeers. Max would have left Jeers about that time to have picked up Cloie before Jeannie got there. Was that when he took the pictures of Mic and his lady that he was obviously showing to Mic last night?

A honking horn interrupted Jeannie's thinking. She realized she was parked in front of the driveway of the apartment house next door. Waving an "I'm sorry," she gunned the motor and headed for the college. She'd find out more about Rita's disappearance there.

Lunch in the cafeteria was almost as depressing as her morning classes. Topic of the day was Rita and her disappearance. Jeannie munched her tuna sandwich. She tried to bury her head in a discarded newspaper in hopes she might tune out the next table where Roe and her friends were reliving their bar-hopping night on the town.

"You were simply first rate, Gussie! You were sooooo much better than that stupid, joke-telling moron." Roe's voice rose in pitch, pronouncing the word MOOOOR-ON.

Whatever could they be talking about? Jeannie pulled the newspaper closer and started at a headline which read, "Coed Rita Gibson Still Missing...Drugs May Be Involved..." Jeannie shook her head thinking, *No way would Rita Gibson be involved in drugs.* Jeannie stared at Rita's picture. She was a beautiful girl, great figure, in a great picture. Jeannie was surprised that Rita was twenty-four. She seemed younger.

Mmm—I bet this is one of Max's pictures.

A shriek of delight from the sorority table caused all heads to turn, "Ah declare, Roe, honey. I bet you'd win that big prize if you'd do your striptease!" sorority sister number one giggled. "If you don't walk away with the First Place portion of that five thousand dollars, at least you'll have your garter belt full of cash!"

Jeannie frowned, trying to shut out the confusion behind her as she continued scanning the news. "Area farmers filed complaints with the sheriff's office, claiming hunters poaching on their land are leaving unusual rubble littering the countryside."

Gussie pushed her chair back and stood in one motion, banging into Jeannie's table. The collision upset Jeannie's drink, soaking her second-hand newspaper, and spilling onto her second-skin capris.

Scooting her chair back, Jeannie turned to glare at Gussie as she applied napkins to her lap and folded the ruined newspaper.

Hands on hips, Gussie confronted the Judas at her table. "You wouldn't dare, Roe! You all wouldn't even know about the Jeers talent contest if I hadn't invited you to come with me Monday night."

Silence descended at the adjoining table just as Jeannie murmured, "Da-dum broads!"

Gussie turned her fury on Jeannie. "Dumb broads? Did you call us dumb broads? Miss hoity-toity, smarty pants, poetry know-it-all." Trying to regain her sorority status, Gussie smirked. "I guess you think your dull-witted knowledge of poets would do better than my singing." Gussie favored her friend with a conspiratorial smile. "Or Roe's stripper act?"

Jeannie's face flushed as she stared at Gussie. "What, what..."

The lunch crowd was enjoying Jeannie's discomfort. It was a diversion from the disturbing news of Rita Gibson. She noticed Bo Hankins seated across the room with his football jocks. Hoping for a friendly soulmate, Jeannie shrugged her shoulders, raised her eyebrows, and held her hands palm up in a what-can-a-lady-do gesture.

Bo huddled with his friends. Suddenly, the jocks started stomping their feet, pounding their tables, and urging, "Jean-nie, Jean-nie, Jean-nie!"

Thanks, Bo. Now, Jeannie felt like an on-stage personality for a late night reveal-it-all talk show.

The room suddenly became silent. Professor Brent Sherman stood framed in the doorway with a what's-going-on expression.

Bo walked over to Sherman. Gesturing toward the sorority table and Gussie, Bo mimicked a soloist with hands stretched wide, palms up. Then, glancing toward Roe, he held both hands shoulder high, extended apart, and caressed the outline of an imaginary feminine form. The table of jocks stomped and whistled.

Sherman silenced them with upraised eyebrows and an icy countenance.

Bo shrugged and indicated Jeannie with a thumbs up sign as the jocks threatened to erupt again. Bo held out his hands in a crosswalk patrolman stance. He pulled a chair from a nearby table and offered it to Sherman almost as a challenge.

Professor Sherman nimbly stepped atop the chair and held up his hands for silence. In a sing-song, barker-style voice, he announced, "Ladies and Gentleman. Come one, come all! You're invited to Jeers this weekend to witness college finesse. Who will win? Gussie of the melodious voice, Roe's bare facts, or Jeannie and her copper kettle of poetry? For Lit students, this will amount to extra credit. Just bring me proof you were there."

Bo gestured at Sherman and said something that made students at nearby tables snort with laughter and break into applause.

Sherman held up his hand, "All right! By popular demand, I'll be there, too. With a little persuasion, I might do a verse or two."

Picking up her tray, Jeannie laid the napkins and soggy newspaper over the ruins of her lunch. Trying to avoid the disapproving glares of the sorority sisters, she scurried for the door only to be accosted by Sherman.

"Well, well, Mrs. Jonson. It seems we meet again. I hope you don't take that challenge lightly. I'd hate to see my prize Literature student lose out to a song-and-dance act. Bonus points might help raise a few of your fellow students' low grades up to passing. Once more, your knowledge of the masters can save the common man."

Staring down at her tray, Jeannie rediscovered the newspaper and locked eyes with Rita Gibson, the missing coed. Flustered, Jeannie stammered, "I never. I can't…I won't…" trying to imagine herself competing onstage at Jeers.

Sherman leaned close and whispered, "Wimping out, Jeannie? Surely you've heard what happens to losers?"

Jeannie looked up to find herself face-to-face with the soldier of fortune she remembered from yesterday and hissed, "Don't mistake me for one of your punks…" She slapped a hand over her runaway mouth.

He shrugged, tossed the black lock of hair from his eyes, and chuckled evilly. "Whatever! This has nothing to do with the job offer. We can discuss your potential employment after class as decided."

Chapter 29

They say there's a fine line between love and hate. Tone the word LOVE down to LIKE and Jeannie was walking that tightrope. She listened to Brent Sherman quote Shakespeare as he paced the dais dressed in a turtleneck with a slight edge of pink at the neck. Curious, she mentally undressed him again and searched for tell-tale signs of rash covered in pink.

"Let me not to the marriage of true minds
admit impediments. Love is not love
Which alters when it alteration finds,
Or bends with the remover to remove."

Were his eyes searching her out? If so, they moved on quickly as he prowled the confines of the stage. Jeannie drooled over his delivery of the sonnet. Even as she questioned how this man could be the same man she'd seen in the woods yesterday, she was once more convinced this recitation had spawned from their first brief encounter in this very room.

"Oh, no! It is an ever-fixed mark
That looks on tempests and is never shaken;
It is the star to every wandering bark,
Whose worth's unknown, although his height is taken."

Bo nudged her, and she realized she was reciting the words aloud. Jeannie compressed her lips into a thank-you smile. Her attention returned to the stage. She had missed the middle of the sonnet. Sherman was quoting the last line and his gaze was resting on her. Or was it Bo and her?

The slight frown disappeared. His gaze locked with hers and held as he delivered the last two lines:

"If this be error and upon me proved,

I never writ, nor no man ever loved."

Her lifeline was cut. Jeannie was adrift on a sea of idolization as he slowly lowered his head in an actor's bow. She contemplated early signs of baldness for a moment before his glance once more sought hers. Jeannie felt color flood her cheeks. Had he discovered her thoughts?

"They say kindred souls are those who have experienced the same grief and survived. I'm sure there are those among us," he continued.

Don't even go there, Jeannie warned herself, as his glance rested briefly on hers. Then, his gaze moved on to converse silently with other damsels who might believe they were his sole concern.

"Oh, you fickle cad!" Jeannie was trying to separate the man from the muse. "What a piece of work is man! How noble in reason! How infinite in faculties!" Bo nudged her again, and she realized she had spoken aloud from Hamlet.

Loud enough, it seemed, for Sherman to have noticed, "Mrs.... Jonson? Did you have something to contribute to the class?"

Without thinking, as usual, Jeannie summarized her feelings of disillusionment at how evil man can be with the same words Hamlet had expressed himself, "I have lost all my mirth…the earth…seems …sterile."

Puzzled, Sherman nonetheless mused, "Methinks you bounce back and forth between admiration at the nobility and beauty of man and his own disillusionment at how evil man can be. I sense a kindred spirit!"

He had completely misjudged her remark, thinking she was referring to her ex-husband, Max. The professor was delighted to have sparked an emotion.

"Egoistical" came to mind, along with a few other words she wisely kept to herself.

Murderer? Her dad's voice sounded inside her head. *Would "murderer" be the word you're trying so hard not to say, Jeannie?*

Jeannie squeezed her eyes shut and closed her ears. On her mind's backdrop of black appeared a picture of Rita Gibson. Jeannie gasped! She'd been so involved with Literature class, she'd forgotten about Rita's disappearance.

Why, indeed, Jeannie? her dad's voice asked.

A series of remembered words and phrases surfaced. "If we shoot this one, we're going to have to bury her. She's the hottest thing in town."

Murderer. Rita Gibson.

Bo nudged her. "Wake up, Jeannie."

Jeannie's eyelids sprang open. She was surprised to find herself in the tranquil classroom surrounded by complacent students who had nothing on their minds but an assignment and a passing grade. And an occasional thought about a coed's disappearance. But Jeannie—she was convicting their professor of murdering a coed. She looked down at her notebook where she had written:

"Life is but an empty dream!"

For the soul is dead that slumbers,

And things are not what they seem.

~Henry Wadsworth Longfellow (1807-1882)

Sherman summarized the work he expected the class to cover in the brief week before school would be out for the summer. "We have studied the masters. I'd like to find out what poetic talents masquerade in the guise of students. Tomorrow, I'll expect an original poem from each of you."

Groans of protest resounded around the theater.

Sherman held up his hands as if to ward off an attack.

Bo startled her as he rose from his seat, cleared his throat, and asked, "Mr. Sherman, what about finals? Did you mean what you said in the cafeteria?"

"Ah! There's the rub. I'd say answers lie with the fair damsels of our class. What say ye, Roe? Gussie? Jeannie?"

Bo looked down at Jeannie with pleading eyes. She knew he was hoping for an easy boost to his almost-passing grade by spending the evening in a local bar like Jeers.

The thought of Jeers brought back memories of last year when Jeers was a hangout for Max and her. Those thoughts faded and were replaced with events from Monday night, the drug scene, Lynn Copper Sherman's disrobing, the parade of the jocks, and Rita Gibson.

Jeannie paused, trying to remember any detail that might help the police find the missing woman. She reviewed her time with the coed as Rita lent comfort by listening to Jeannie's problem. Rita had walked Jeannie to her truck. Jeannie left, and something—what was it—had happened to Rita?

"Jeannie?" Bo's voice interrupted her thoughts.

Jeannie looked up at Bo. He was her friend, but she hated being put between a rock and a hard place. What kind of a lesson was Sherman hoping to teach by encouraging jocks to watch her and the sorority girls toss out their favors for the crowd to choose? Would the jocks blurt sexist remarks back and forth on their JeersBerrys? Would they text on the JeersBerrys with the girls as the brunt of their humor?

"Alas, poor Yorick! I fear you are a fellow of infinite jest, of most excellent fancy," Jeannie taunted Bo, deliberately misquoting Hamlet.

"Huh?" The big ox didn't have a clue.

In the next section of seats, Roe and Gussie had been whispering. Roe stood, assuming a provocative pose. "Professor Sherman, it is our understanding that any English Lit student who visits Jeers for their talent showcase this weekend will receive credit for this class. Is that correct?"

Questions abounded from classmates who had not been in the cafeteria.

"Quiet!" Sherman waited. "How poor are they that have not patience!" His quote from *Othello* went unnoticed except for but a gifted few. Yet, he continued, "What wound did ever heal but by degrees? Thou know'st we work by wit, and not by witchcraft..." He left the quote unfinished. "I would consider this year not a total loss if someone," he glanced toward Jeannie, "with the exception of Mrs. Jonson, could finish that verse."

The room was closing in on Jeannie. Ivy was screaming for another coat of calamine. Every word Sherman uttered brought back memories of the scene in the woods where he and his partner were committing unspeakable crimes. Quickly, Jeannie turned the page of her notebook and scribbled a few lines. She kicked Bo's shin as Sherman's glance prowled the room of silent students.

"Huh?" Bo responded.

Frowning, Jeannie indicated the scrawl on her notepad with the answer Sherman had requested. Six short words. Could Bo manage that?

Standing tall, Bo uttered the words he'd committed to memory. "And wit depends on dilatory time."

The classroom erupted with cheers! Laughter! Celebration of "Not a total waste"!

Sherman grew in stature at least three inches; his chest expanded. He raised his hands over his head locked in a champion's stance. The flesh-colored gauze of bandage on his right hand blended with pink expanses of what could only be calamine-coated poison ivy as his long sleeves slipped over his wrist.

Jeannie tugged at her sleeves, trying to cover the tell-tale pink.

Always the skeptic, Sherman pushed his luck too far. "Bo, you just went up in my grade book. Would you like to try for A plus?"

Jeannie saw Bo's Adam's apple shift rapidly. Without seeming to budge, his eyes moved sideways to glance at her.

Sherman didn't wait for Bo's answer. "What, my dear Bo, does dilatory mean?"

Sweet Bo drawled, "I guess it would be tardy, kind of like me, before I learned my lesson."

Sherman beamed, "Excellent!"

Bo whispered, "I owe you one."

You had to hand it to Bo. He had picked the right definition that completely won Sherman's heart from the four (late, lazy, remiss, and tardy) Jeannie had hastily scribbled on her notebook.

Roe repeated her question.

"Let's mull the question overnight, dear Roe. We'll broach it again tomorrow when each of you prime the pump with original poetry. Why then, tonight, let us assay our plot." Sherman's reference to a bedroom caper escaped them all.

Jeannie recognized Sherman's reference to how Helena embarked on a plot to pave her way to true happiness by employing what came to be known as the Bed Trick.

"Class, this has been a most enjoyable experience. I trust our young ladies will think over the situation that can help you all and let us know their decision in class tomorrow. Remember, tomorrow, original poetry. For today, class is dismissed." He moved to close the text that lay open on his stand.

The Lit class didn't need to be told twice. As they moved up the stairs of the lecture theater toward the door, Bo placed a hand on Jeannie's shoulder. "Jeannie, I meant what I said. I owe you big time!"

"Thanks, Bo. Just don't expect me to make a fool out of myself on stage at Jeers."

"Mrs. Jonson!" Sherman's voice stopped them. "I'd like to see you after class. I believe we have something we need to discuss."

Startled, Bo peered at Jeannie, as she automatically retreated a step and stood beside him. "You think he knows you called the play on my definition touchdown?"

Jeannie shook her head. "Bo, you do have a way with words."

"Don't worry." He moved up to the step she'd just vacated preparing to follow his classmates. Reconsidering, he turned, "I'll be right outside if you need me. Just whistle!"

Jeannie believed she knew what Sherman wanted to discuss. And Jeannie knew just what her answer would be. "Bo, I don't think I can."

Bo's eyes widened, "You don't think you can wait after class with Sherman?"

Deadpan, Jeannie quipped, "No, I don't think I can whistle."

"Sure, you can." Bo put his two pointer fingers in opposite sides of his mouth, grinned, and assured her, "Just blow!" A deafening screech, which most certainly registered ten on the Richter scale, caused Jeannie to move quickly back from Bo. She lost her balance and rolled down several stairs. Her glasses stayed in place long enough to sight her books flying in all directions; then they slipped from her nose and followed.

Footsteps beat a staccato from below and blended with the heavy tread of Bo's size twelves descending from above to the place where Jeannie lay sprawled in a heap. Pushing a mass of unruly curls from her eyes, Jeannie tucked thick strands of hair behind her ear, and stared at an expanse of pink calves poking from beneath her capris.

"Jeannie!" two male voices replied.

"Are you okay?" Bo's hands slipped beneath Jeannie's armpits and hoisted her upward with one mighty heave.

"Lummox!" Sherman's voice roared. He mounted the final step and reached toward Jeannie's flailing calamine fingers. "Be careful. She may have broken something."

Bo jerked his hands from beneath Jeannie's arms, leaving her suspended in mid-air and backed up a step. "I didn't think…"

Jeannie could almost hear the announcer's voice shouting, "Bo Hankins fumbled the ball on the thirty-yard line. Sherman moves to recover it."

"Jocks…never think!" Sherman fingers slid over her skintight capris searching for leverage as Jeannie pirouetted like a second-rate ballerina on the step above him doing the pigskin polka. *MMM-mmm. If I die, I hope I come back as a football,* Jeannie thought as she swayed toward Sherman.

Bo snatched the neck of Jeannie's t-shirt and hauled her backwards. "You okay, Jeannie?"

Regaining her footing on the step above Sherman and below Bo, Jeannie fought to regain a portion of her dignity. Instead, Jeannie's fingers raced over her body in a scratching frenzy as ivy once more surfaced. "Sure, I think…" Jeannie faltered, watching Sherman dig at his body in a similar state of violent physical agitation.

"Okay, just wanted to be sure." Bo released her t-shirt. Jeannie shot forward like a paper wad from a rubber band headed for the esteemed professor.

They collided with enough force to take them down two stairs. Over, under, and together, they rolled to a stop entwined in a calamine heap. Her fingers itched to scratch. His fingers must have felt the same urge as they rested on Jeannie's bare midriff where her t-shirt had slipped up from her capris.

"Mmmm-mmm, a little higher and to the right," Jeannie urged his fingertips as they eased the itch.

"Sure, and dig in a little more to the left," Sherman directed as her fingers moved beneath his collar.

"Bo, are you coming?" a voice hollered from the top of the stairs.

Bo stood above them, staring at the tangled mess of twitching limbs that was Jeannie and Professor Brent Sherman. Blinking, he turned to find the hallway door packed with students gaping down at a most remarkable sight.

"Hey, man! What's going on?" one of Bo's teammates hollered.

"Uh…Professor Sherman asked Jeannie to stay after class because he wanted to…" Bo hesitated, looking to Sherman for confirmation. "What was it, exactly, you wanted with Jeannie?"

Sherman's fingers kept moving over her pink rash as Jeannie emitted moans of delightful pleasure while returning the favor.

"I was going to offer Mrs. Jonson a job."

Sherman's words jerked Jeannie back to reality. Quickly, she untangled herself and returned her fingers to the rightful body. She tried to straighten her nerdy outfit.

"Mrs. Jonson!" Professor Sherman's voice returned their situation to student-teacher status as surely as if he were standing on the dais delivering a lecture.

"Yes, sir?" Jeannie lay there a moment trying to assess the situation. Should she have Bo summon the authorities while she had the professor pinned on the stairs? Jeannie envisioned tomorrow's headlines—"Calamine Coed Tangles with Ivy-Covered Campus Murderer." Her lips twitched with suppressed laughter at the absurdity of the situation. Testing the stretch of her capris, Jeannie heaved herself off Sherman. She began picking up her textbooks while searching in vain for her glasses.

Sherman continued as though stressing a point in a teaching assignment. "Were you not interviewing for a position with me for the summer?"

Considering the position they'd just been discovered in, Jeannie found it hard to deny. "Yes, sir," she replied, as she continued to hunt for her elusive glasses.

The crowd at the hall doors had doubled. More students were pushing in to see what was causing such a commotion.

Sherman stood, straightened his trousers, tucked in his shirt, and assumed his lecture stance. "Mrs. Jonson needs a high-paying job for a short time that will let her go on tour to Mexico with the Spanish club. Isn't that right, Ms. Jonson?"

Jeannie nodded trying to keep the corners of her mouth from creeping up. The crowd of students chanted backup like jubilant gospel singers. "Yes, sir! Oh, yeah! Uh-huh!"

Sherman was becoming visibly agitated, yet, he plunged ahead. "I told her I had a job that might be just right for her—exciting, long hours, adventure, and meeting all kinds of people." He hesitated. "She told me earlier she was divorced and didn't have any other relationship that would hinder her working nights." Pausing, he reflected on how the last statement replayed, and asked, "Isn't that right, Mrs. Jonson?"

Before Jeannie could answer, the students' gospel choir chorused, "Oh, yes! Uh-huh!" So, she just smiled at Sherman and nodded in unison as she listened to Sherman dig himself a deeper grave.

The thought of a grave was sobering. How many witnesses would it take to hang an innocent divorcee, college junior underclassman? Sherman was weaving a web of circumstantial evidence around her as tightly as if she'd held the gun that shot those punks in the woods. Jeannie raised her hand, waving it like a student with all the answers on test day.

But, before she could interrupt, Sherman continued, "Before Bo emitted his shrill whistle which started all this…" Sherman looked around at the disruption of his classroom. For once, he was at a loss for words.

Jeannie lowered her hand, deciding she could wait no longer to disassociate herself from this murderer. In her best Scarlett O'Hara voice, Jeannie vowed, "As God is my witness, I have not and never will work for this…" Before she could say "murderer," Sherman frowned and broke in.

"Mrs. Jonson, are you sure you don't want to run a fireworks tent for me and my partner this summer? It's perfect for you! Short time, high pay, and it'll let you be finished in time to take the tour to Mexico."

"Uh-huh! Oh, yeah!" The students were shouting it out.

"Fireworks? You didn't say anything about Fourth-of-July fireworks! A tent?" Jeannie stammered. "You didn't shoot someone? You were shooting off fireworks?"

Sherman strained to hear her above the chanting of the backup choir. "Yes, fireworks. I'm offering you the job as manager of one of our fireworks tents. Do you want to discuss it?"

Realization slowly began to creep into reality. Professor Brent Sherman was not a murderer. He was in the fireworks business. Even Sherman's telephone conversation made sense. "I buried her in the woods last night. Tonight we can meet at the same place. Bring a shovel so we can dig a hole and shoot the big one. No one can hear us out there."

Jeannie stared at the floor hard, trying to concentrate, and saw her glasses. Picking them up, she placed them back on her nose, adjusted them and looked directly into the face of who she hoped would be her new boss, and said, "Da-dum!"

"Dum! Dum! Dum!" Titters of laughter echoed around the almost-empty theater as Jeannie's words became a chant. Roe and her friends had returned to Lit class in force. They were perched in the doors at the top of the theater stairs like vultures waiting to pick the bones of their prey.

A brilliant flash of light appeared in their midst, outlining the group in a ghostly black-and-white-tintype fashion.

"Max, Max, Max!" they shrieked as Shutterbug Max flashed another round of what would surely become front-page graphics for the *College Review*.

Chapter 30

"We have studied the masters. I'd like to find out what poetic talents masquerade in the guise of students. Tomorrow, I'll expect an original poem from each of you." Professor Brent Sherman's assignment flashed through Jeannie's mind, blotting out all thoughts of the slapstick comedy scene on the stairs of his Lit classroom earlier in the day.

Poetic talents, Jeannie pondered, digging her nails into the calamine-covered, poison-ivy skin on her bare midriff where the skimpy top of her PJs had slipped up. Thoughts of Sherman's fingers caressing or scratching this very spot earlier did little to help her mind form poetic lines, at least poetic lines she could use for Professor Sherman's Lit assignment.

Brash words bounced across the screen of Jeannie's mind forming limericks. She felt the need to sing aloud as she'd seen audiences do in old-time movies as they watched a bouncing ball point out the words.

"There once was a young lady name Jeannie—" *What rhymes with Jeannie? Houdini? Weenie? Queenie? NOPE! That would never do.*

What about another name? Roe? Let see, what was her major—math? What was her talent for the Jeers talent contest? Stripping? Heh, heh.

There was a math major named Roe
Who figured to win best of show.
Her costume was slim, and
When she raised the hem
It allowed her assets to show.

"Not bad. Let's seeee: what about Gussie?" Jeannie giggled. "See, she already rhymed."

There was a Tri Sig named Guss–ie.

Whose gifted voice could reach high C.
She imagined the judges bare
Or in their underwear
And performed her talent perfectly.

"Gussie, the troublemaker," Jeannie whispered. If she'd kept her mouth shut, their Lit class wouldn't be involved in Jeers' talent contest. And one-half of the female students in Professor Sherman's Lit class wouldn't be imagining him in his underwear, or worse.

Underneath, he's all male. Remembering Gussie's words switched her limericks to Sherman.

Our Lit professor, Dr. Sherman, I declare,
Tumbled his prize student, Jeannie, on the stair.
He obviously didn't know
That Bo would let go.
So he gave her a job as they lay tangled there.

Jeannie read the verse again and burst into laughter. She'd need to change the last line. But why? No one would ever see or hear it.

Bo, she thought. *What could I write about dear Bo?*

There once was an obtuse jock named Bo
Who was late wherever he'd go.
His professor gave him a fright
When he made him recite.
Now, Bo's not late any mo.

Any mo? You're reaching, Jeannie, she told herself. *What about a limerick about you? Yeah, what about me?* she wondered. Why did she always put herself last?

There was a divorcee named Jen
Who'd like to find true love again.
But no one would choose her.
Was she really a loser?
Or did she just pick the wrong men?

Limericks were fun, but they weren't getting her Lit assignment for tomorrow done. Grabbing up the stack of nonsensical verses, she stuffed them into a folder. *Concentrate,* Jeannie told herself as she stared at a clean sheet of notebook paper. Fixating her gaze to paper didn't write poetry. Five minutes later, the page was still blank.

"Blank verse!" Jeannie giggled.

Her verse was not only blank, but it stank. "At least that rhymes." She giggled again.

What was the matter with her? Was she high on sniffing calamine lotion? Or hysterical from relief that her Lit professor wasn't a murderer? The word "murder" brought to mind Rita Gibson. But she hadn't been murdered. She was only missing, wasn't she? Thoughts of where Rita Gibson might be still tugged at the edges of her mind, surfacing at the most unexpected times.

Jeannie's cell phone rang, interrupting her reverie. Sighing, she answered without bothering to look at the caller ID. "Hullo."

"Hey, Jen, you can take your coat of anonymity to the flea market and sell it. Your old man just elevated you and your Lit professor to stardom," Max said.

At the sound of his voice, her pen moved over the blank page, scrawling MAX. "You're not any man of mine. I still have a bone to pick with you over picking up Cloie the other night. How'd you even know she was there?"

"I got my sources. And I got her home safely, didn't I?" Max said.

Leave it to Max. Of course he'd never think to call Jeannie and let her know he'd picked up Cloie. Jeannie's feelings didn't matter. So what if she thought something had happened to her niece? So what if she hunted for hours, thinking it was her fault.

"Hey, you still there? Well, thanks to me, you and the professor's photo made front page of the *College Review*," Max bragged.

"Scumbag!" She tapped the phone icon, breaking the connection.

The phone jingled again. Jeannie answered. "Max, you idiot!"

"Hey, Jen, don't hang up! Just listen, I'm giving you a head start on the Jeers talent contest with a little PR. Dress up your body and do that little bump and grind routine you did in the Miss Bull Creek Pageant, remember?" Max's voice reeked of smirk.

Jeannie rattled off a few choice words that convulsed him to laughter.

"Sorry, babe. I'll make it up to you. I'm sending you a present."

Remembering the stash and negatives he'd left in her console, Jeannie screamed into the phone, "You bring any more of your pot around and I'll turn you over to the campus police. And I haven't looked at your negatives yet, but I bet one of them has to do with Madam Davao's husband."

"Hey, hey, my present is nothing like that. It's just a little something to perk you up. Maximum Exposure can't have its main associate looking less than sexy when she appears on stage in a nightclub." He snorted, "Wait till my mom tells your mom and the ladies at the country club about this."

Jeannie didn't stop to wonder how Max knew about the contest. He always had known and always would know everything and didn't hesitate to broadcast it. She dropped her voice to wheedle mode. "What goes on in Halesville stays in Halesville, remember?" That had been their bargain when they went their separate ways on the same campus.

"Tell your mom that, Jen."

Their conversation had always been barbed with parry and thrusts like sword fighters waiting to deliver the fatal stab. "You breathe a word about this contest, and I'll deliver a certain package you left in my console to your house in Bull Creek."

His silence lasted long enough to let her know her sword had struck a nerve.

"Babeee, how about a truce? Just be on the watch for a delivery."

Jeannie started to protest, but he broke in, "No, no, it's not weed unless you call clothes divorce weeds. Whatever, this vest is STYLE in capital letters! I bought it off eBay, and it's being delivered to your apartment. And that was a very good guess about Madam Davao's husband, or did you see the odd couple Monday night, too?"

"Max, no presents, please! And be careful what you tell Cloie. She circulates information indiscreetly." Jeannie had gone shopping with Max before. One time he steered her into Victoria's Secret and tried to get her to charge lingerie to her dad's credit card.

"Let your hair down, Jen. Live a little. Yolo. Buy some skintight black jeans that fit like your awful capris in the picture."

His words formed graphics in her mind. "My capris showed up skintight in the picture?"

He emitted an evil chuckle, "Sure did, front and center wrapped around Sherman's thighs."

"Max, we were standing when you flashed that picture."

"Not the first one! It turned out perfect without a flash. Man, you were really groping each other."

Jeannie screamed, "Get the picture back! Don't do this to me and Professor Sherman."

"Too late. Hey, you got the hots for Sherman?"

"The hots? I think not!" And yet her face flushed more red than pink thinking about "the hots" even as she denied it. "He's not only my Lit professor, but he's going to be my boss, shortly."

"What was I thinking? Iceberg Jeannie with the hots. You going to type for him or transcribe his notes on Shakespeare?" His belittling tones irritated almost as much as rash from ivy.

"Nope," Jeannie was the one smirking now. Maybe Max didn't know everything. "I've been offered a short-term job that pays big bucks which will allow me to go on tour to Mexico this summer."

"Doing what?" His voice suggested a few things that Jeannie dismissed indignantly.

"I'm going to manage a pyrotechnic business."

"You're going to sell nudie films?"

"Fireworks, Max, I'm going to run a fireworks tent for Sherman and his partner."

"Listen, Jen. Maybe you should rethink this job. I only know one guy that has anything to do with fireworks. His name is Roscoe, and he's a dealer and a real loser."

"What do you mean?" Jeannie tried to match the world of fireworks, which she knew nothing about and the world of drugs, as in dealer, which Max surely knew everything about, and came up without a clue.

Max's voice was grim. "Don't play Miss Innocent with me."

Jeannie lashed out. "Max, you and Roscoe can just mind your own business. Keep away from my fireworks tent. It has nothing to do with drugs." Yet, as Jeannie spoke, her mind raced back to the woods where she thought Professor Sherman and Camouflage had murdered some punks. She remembered Roscoe had been a part of their fireworks world. So, Roscoe was a part of the drug world, too? How involved was he in the world of drugs? For that matter, how deeply involved in the world of drugs was Max? Or Mr. Straight, Brent Sherman? And then there was Ms. Lynn Copper Sherman and the missing Rita Gibson? There was an answer to this puzzle, and one day soon all the pieces would fit together.

"Whatever." Max dismissed her warning. "Anyway, you don't need to work. Your parents will pay for your trip. Or you can use the divorce settlement money." His voice belied the fact that he knew he'd gambled her trip money away before she ever got her hands on it.

"We won't even go there, Max." Jeannie said. "I'll work and I will go to Mexico. But, first, I've got to live down your blasted photo in the *College Review*." And, she told herself, *think of something clever to do for the talent contest at Jeers. And write something besides limericks for Lit class tomorrow.*

The doorbell to her apartment rang. "Got to go. Someone is at my door."

"It's probably my present. Get Cloie to go shopping with you. Wear the vest bare, with a bustier under it."

"A what? Oh, never mind." Jeannie hung up on him, ending his rambling critique of her talent costume. Opening the door, Jeannie found Cloie and Renee standing on her doorstep dressed for a basketball game, with Phantoms emblazoned across their t-shirts.

Oh, no. Jeannie was supposed to go to the Courts and watch Cloie's game today.

Cloie stared at Jeannie in disbelief. "Did you draw a blank? Again?"

"What makes you think that, baby girl? I was just getting ready to walk out the door."

"In that?" Cloie and her mom said together.

Jeannie's fingers moved to scratch and discovered her bare midriff and skimpy pajamas.

"Well, I must say, you look awesome in the pink!" Renee smirked. Her gaze traveled over Jeannie's exposed expanse of calamine.

"I had a bout with ivy." Jeannie hurried to grab her discarded capris and turtleneck top.

Cloie giggled. "Yep, that's the outfit all right." She handed Jeannie a copy of the *College Review*.

There they were, Jeannie and Professor Sherman, sprawled on the stairs of his classroom gawking up at the camera like they'd been caught doing—what?

"Max!" Jeannie screamed. She could kill him! He'd called the gift he promised to send her divorcee weeds. Jeannie might just make that gift of his widow's weeds.

"Where'd you get this?" Jeannie shook the newspaper at Cloie.

"It was on your doorstep along with a delivery man. He said he had a COD package for you. We paid. You owe." Cloie handed Jeannie a brown bag eBay special.

"I paid that man a hundred and fifty dollars, Jeannie." Renee extended her hand.

Jeannie stared at her sister in disbelief, knowing Max was up to his old tricks.

"Sis, can I pay you later?"

Renee glanced at Cloie and shrugged Jeannie we'll-talk-about-this-later.

Cloie gave Jeannie a quick hug. "I'd loan you the money if I had it." She gave her mother a pleading look.

Renee shook her head slowly. "Cloie, you're too much like your aunt. You think money grows on trees."

Cloie patted Jeannie's shoulder.

God, she hated this pity party. Everyone knew she was broke. Surely they were wondering why she was ordering expensive things from eBay. Jeannie wasn't about to tell them it was from Max. Nope, she wasn't going to open that can of worms.

"Well, you going to open it?" they asked.

"Whatever!" This day couldn't get any worse, Jeannie thought. That was before she tore open the package and shook out the contents. A black leather piece of material studded with rhinestones and edged with fringe tumbled out.

Jeannie held up what looked to be a biker-babe short vest. She hoped a whatever-the-word-Max-had-said she should wear with this was a long-sleeved, turtlenecked sweater.

"Wow!" Cloie and her mom said in admiration.

As they walked toward the car, Jeannie asked. "What's a bustier?" Cloie grinned up at her mom.

Renee shook her head and rolled her eyes.

Cloie grabbed Jeannie's arm and moved her forward. "You're getting it, Aunt Jen. A bustier is a sexy bra top. A bustier is exactly what that vests needs. And a totally hot pair of tight, black jeans with rhinestones down the side to match the rhinestones around the front and armpits of the black leather vest with fringe."

"It sounds like all that outfit would need is the black boots with the rhinestones up the sides we saw at the mall," Renee said in disgust.

"Super-A, Mom!"

The crowd at Cloie's basketball game was a world away from the college scene. It took Jeannie back to her comfortable family days in Bull Creek. At halftime, Jeannie perched on the top row, munching popcorn as she glanced around the gym. Children of varied ages and color vied for attention as their parents tried to focus on the game. Kids squirmed over people, spilling refreshments and paying no attention when told to sit down

The referee blew his whistle, and the game started again.

Jeannie glanced at the scoreboard, reassuring herself the Phantoms were two points up on their opponents, the Rockets.

"Watch it, Sis!" Renee nudged Jeannie to stand as people swarmed in front of them to the other side of the bleachers.

Jeannie glimpsed a disheveled blonde seated at the end of the bleachers in jeans with a Rocket logo on the back of her red and gold t-shirt. Over the logo was printed "Annie's Mom." The blonde's Kate Hudson-pallor was in direct contrast to the ebony tones that outlined the chiseled profile of her companion's silhouette. She was carrying on a spirited conversation with the baldpated man garbed in Rocket gear with the name "Leblanc" emblazoned on the back of his shirt.

"Renee, are they–?"

Renee silenced Jeannie with the kind of frown she used to give her when she asked about sex or a subject Renee considered not suitable for a lady.

Renee caught Jeannie staring again and elbowed her as she hissed in her ear, "Quit staring and pay attention to the game. We're behind!" Aside, she whispered, "That's Annie's parents. They're a biracial couple who live single."

As if to prove Renee's point, the couple jumped to their feet, cheering. "Way to go, Annie!"

Jeannie's attention was drawn to the court where a girl-child whose skin was the color of burnt honey had just put the ball through the hoop to put the Rockets ahead of the Phantoms by two points. The name "Leblanc" curved over the number 10 on the back of Annie's jersey.

Annie turned to flash a smile at the couple and missed seeing Cloie as she dribbled the ball past her, went the whole way, and made a layup for two points. The score was tied.

Renee and Jeannie were on their feet shouting, "You go, girl!"

"Pay attention, Annie!" The man barked like a staff Sergeant issuing orders.

The woman tossed her blonde mane out of her eyes and yelled something at Leblanc.

He gave her a disgusted sneer and moved the whole six-foot-plus length of himself down a row.

"Cloie! Don't foul!" Renee hollered.

"Shoot the ball, Annie!" Leblanc urged, and the girl threw the ball in what would have been a perfect touchdown pass if she were on the football field.

The ball bounced off the backboard hard enough to rebound almost to half court, where Cloie was standing open-mouthed. With only a few seconds left on the clock and the score tied, Cloie grabbed the ball and dribbled to the edge of the circle. She let fly a perfect three-point shot that ripped the net with a swish. The Phantoms won!

Renee and Jeannie ran onto the court to hug Cloie. She grinned and joined the line of players who were smacking hands with the Rockets as each team did at the end of the game.

"Annie!" Leblanc called arrogantly.

Annie motioned to the line and started toward it. Leblanc grabbed her arm and pulled her over to the bleachers where he proceeded to berate her for shooting the ball. She sat looking straight ahead, never reminding Leblanc that he was the one who'd told her to shoot the ball.

"Chill, Aunt Jeannie." Cloie grabbed Jeannie's arm and dragged her along with her. "Annie's pops is basketball radical. She's my BFF. We overnight with each other."

Jeannie couldn't help looking over her shoulder to watch as Leblanc delivered the last of his sermon. He patted Annie on the shoulder. Slinging an arm around her, he pulled her toward the concession room. The blonde gathered up their belongings. Annie broke away to join her team for a coach's meeting. The couple continued on to the concession room.

"Jeez!" Jeannie muttered.

Renee stopped to chat with Cloie's teammates' parents while Jeannie started to the little girls' room. Passing through the concession room, Jeannie glimpsed people waiting at the counters to order food. Annie's parents were seated at a small table in the corner.

A huge television screen at the front of the room was filled with pictures of local sports figures in action. The announcer said, "We interrupt this program to bring you a special bulletin."

Suddenly, Rita Gibson's picture flashed across the screen and stopped Jeannie in her tracks.

The announcer continued, "The police are following up on clues discovered near Halesville where the body of a young woman was found in a shallow grave. The body is believed to be that of the missing coed Rita Lee Gibson, twenty-four, a student at Hale University."

Jeannie's legs refused to hold her. She sank onto one of the stools at the counter. Her gaze was glued to the television screen.

The newscaster chattered nonstop. "The body of the missing coed was discovered by drug dogs on maneuvers near Halesville. Authorities were following up on a report from a farmer who had discovered unusual paraphernalia on his property where the dogs discovered the body."

As the photographer's camera panned the scene of the murder, a feeling of déjà vu engulfed Jeannie. Why was the scenery so familiar? Annie and a group of her teammates clamored into the room. Annie headed toward her parents' table.

Annie's dad, who had been watching the TV screen intently, stood, leaned over to say something to Annie's mom and bolted for the exit.

Jeannie swallowed the lump in her throat and escaped into the bathroom. Inside the privacy of her stall, she cried for Rita Gibson. *Why would anyone want to kill her?*

The door outside the bathroom opened. Jeannie could hear two people's voices as they came into the bathroom.

"Annie, you know your dad loves you. He just doesn't know how to show it."

"Sure, Mom, but it's so embarrassing. Pops is totally boot at round ball. He's radical. He needs to get lost."

"Honey, you don't mean that. Be glad he takes time from his busy schedule to come to the games."

"Well, the only thing I care about right now is that we lost to Cloie's team."

"I thought you liked Cloie. Aren't you planning to spend the night at her house later this week?" Annie's mom asked.

"Yes, Cloie's cool. But that don't mean I like losing to her team," Annie said. "That's what Pops said, too."

"Excuse me. I thought you didn't care what your basketball dad said." Annie's mom's voice held humor.

"Well, that's different. Some things we agree on. One of them is the Rockets are going to beat the Phantoms next time," Annie said with conviction.

Someone else came in, and Jeannie lost the rest of the conversation. When she came out, Annie and her mom were gone. As Jeannie stood at the wash basin, she glanced in the mirror, watching kids and their moms. The lines from Shakespeare's *As You like it* ran through her head, as they had the night of Rita Gibson's disappearance.

All the world's a stage,

And all the men and women merely players:

They have their exits and their entrances;

And one man in his time plays many parts.

How many parts was one person required to play? Jeannie reminded herself if she and Max had made a go of their marriage, she might be lugging a Jonson baby along with her right now. The Jeannie in the mirror was staring longingly at a little girl who'd gone to sleep cuddled against her mom's shoulder.

Jeannie shook her head. *Dingy, you got to have romance in your life to own one of those.* And yet she could almost imagine a dimpled darling balanced on her hip.

Watch this. The Jeannie in the mirror focused on the mom and daughter. *There!* Jeannie said, as she mentally copied the images of the girl and her mother onto the computer screen of her mind. She did a quick paste job and they had them a Jonson babe on their hip.

Wow! Jeannie exclaimed as she leaned closer to the mirror trying to make out if the Jonson babe looked like her side of the family or Max's. God help the poor child if she had Zelda Jonson's nose.

The bathroom door flew open. Cloie and Renee barged inside. Renee went inside a stall. Cloie came to stand beside Jeannie and began to wash her hands. "So, are you ready?"

The reflection in the mirror stared wide-eyed at the little girl in the background. She'd been sleeping against her mom's shoulder and had awakened with the slam of the bathroom door. The kid was bawling her head off.

And so was the Jonson babe on Jeannie's hip. Jeannie knew she wasn't ready for this yet. *Get rid of the kid!*

The fantasy Jeannie pouted but mentally pushed Save as she stored their babe in the archives of their computer mind. She left Jeannie with this thought, *Your biological clock is ticking, girl. What you need is a little romance. Even your buddy Shakespeare knew that.*

Jeannie glared at her.

The Jeannie image shrugged and receded into the depths of the mirror, quoting,

"When birds do sing, hey ding a ding, ding:
Sweet lovers love the spring."

Her image was replaced by Cloie peering at Jeannie intently. Jeannie replayed Cloie's last bit of dialog, "So, are you ready?"

Jeannie asked, "Ready for what, Cloie?"

"What else? To go to the mall and find those black rhinestone boots."

Conversation stopped to listen. In the mirror, Jeannie saw the mother with the bawling baby look wistfully at two lucky people anticipating a trip to the mall.

Jeannie smiled at her and mentally apologized for borrowing her babe.

The woman patted the little girl, cradled her back in the nook of her shoulder, and headed out of the bathroom. Her body language spoke louder than words: "I have more important things to do than go shopping. But once upon a time I was a fashion queen and strolled through the mall."

With the image of the Jonson child gone, Jeannie's hip felt decidedly lighter. The world of family was a good one to visit, but she had a lot of living to do before she was ready to settle into that world. Jeannie hugged her niece, and they headed for the door. "Sure, let's go find those boots. I might even get a bustier." Bold words for someone with an empty wallet and a debt of $150 hanging over her head.

The Wednesday evening crowd at the mall was picking over sale items. Memorial Day weekend depleted their funds, but the first of the month was in sight.

"Where did you see the black jeans with rhinestones?" Jeannie was tired of window shopping.

"The specialty shop near Davao's," Renee said.

"The boots were at Davao's. Madam has them on special." Cloie headed in the direction of Davao's.

Jeannie purchased the jeans, boots, and some hoop earrings.

Cloie yelled at her aunt from across the aisle. "Come here. I've found you a bustier." She was holding up a fancy top that wasn't much more than a bra."

"In a minute." Jeannie started toward the lingerie section when she saw Mic Davao and Madam speaking to some customers. She tried to redirect her route but Madam spied her and Renee and waved them over.

"Jeannie, Renee, where is that delightful Cloie? We have a surprise for her." Madam smiled at Mic. "Honey, go get the photos Max brought you.

Mic's face paled at the mention of photos.

"Hurry, darling. The ones of Cloie for the layout, remember?" Madam reached and touched his cheek lovingly.

Jeannie hung back, recalling the Monday night scene with Mic at Jeers. Disappointment still lingered in her feelings for him.

"Jeannie, why don't you walk over with me? We can catch up on gossip." Mic took her arm and steered her toward a small office. By the time they were inside the office, Jeannie had convinced herself to mind her own business.

"Mic, Cloie told me Madam might use her in your store layout. I think that's great!" Jeannie watched as Mic unlocked a filing cabinet and pulled out a folder.

"Ms. Jonson, you told me you and Max weren't together. I know you saw me with Tresa Vaughan Monday evening, but I would never have thought you would alert Max to do something like this." Mic held out a folder with Maximum Exposure's initials ME at the top.

"Mic, I have nothing to do with Max's business." Jeannie tried to hand the folder back to Mic, but he was busy getting another folder from Madam's desk drawer.

"I find that hard to believe due to the circumstances." Mic had tears in his eyes. "If Madam saw these pictures, she'd be very hurt."

Jeannie started to protest, but Mic stopped her. "I know, I know, it's my fault. But I never meant to hurt my wife. She's married to the store and has no time for me. A man gets lonely." Mic swiped at his eyes with his shirt sleeve. "Tresa is a memory from another time. It was my misfortune to meet her again when I was vulnerable, and she was troubled."

The word "lonely" pushed a button with Jeannie. She felt anger at Max that he would put her in this position. "Fine, Mic, I'll take care of this problem with Max." She turned to leave but turned back. "Let me tell you a secret, Mic. Seeing you and Madam together and the love you share is like an advertisement for marriage. My mom and dad share the same kind of love. If you have a love like that, don't mess around with it. It can go sour. Believe me, I know."

Jeannie turned back to the door. Standing in the doorway was Madam, Renee, and Cloie. Jeannie flushed, wondering how much they'd heard.

Madam was beaming. She walked the short distance to Mic and leaned up to kiss him on the lips. "I'm not sure what you and Jeannie were discussing, darling. But hearing a compliment like she just gave us about our love makes me wonder why I spend so many nights at the store."

"So, what about the surprise, Madam?" Cloie was at the 'it's all about me' stage.

Madam reached to take the folder from Jeannie.

Mic reached to put the one he'd taken from her drawer in her hand. "Here, love; these are the ones you need."

"Yes, Madam, these are some films Max left by mistake. Mic asked me to take care of them." Jeannie winked at Mic. "I'll take care of them, Mic, you take care of Madam."

Cloie let out a squeal as she surveyed her photo in the layout for the store. Everyone agreed a delightful young girl was a welcome addition to the brochure.

Renee never asked, nor did Cloie, about the other folder of pictures. Jeannie was glad because she was suppressing a fury that kept building inside her. When Renee dropped Jeannie off at her place, she took her purchases inside and dumped them on her bed. Pulling out her cell phone, she dialed Max's number.

"Shutterbug is busy. Leave a message after the tone. I'll get back to you in a snap." Max's cell phone message came up three times before Jeannie stopped calling.

Finally, she took the film Max had left with Mic and laid the pictures out on her bed. Sure, enough, there was Mic and the flashily-dressed woman he'd said was Tresa Vaughan. She peered closer. Yes, it was the same lady she'd seen him with inside Jeers. Max was good at shooting intimate poses. There were some outside shots of the couple near the entrance of Jeers taken from a distance. In one picture Mic leaned close listening attentively. Another shot caught the couple huddled together with the brilliance of the storm in the background. The twosome was pictured at an angle with a vehicle in the background. Two other people embraced near the back of the vehicle. Another film showed Mic kissing the woman as he stood near a Hummer.

Her cell phone rang. It was Max.

"You should be ashamed of yourself." Jeannie tore into Max for what seemed an hour. She ended by telling him what had happened in Madam's office. "I promised Mic I'd take care of the pictures. I have them here. Please don't contact him again about them. I was so embarrassed that he'd think I encouraged you to do what you did."

Max was still on the line but didn't say anything right away when she finished. Finally, he said, "Fine! Do what you want to with the film. I can feel for the guy. I know what it's like to want something from your woman, and she's not in the mood." Click. He hung up.

Jeannie wanted to destroy something. She headed out to her Explorer. She'd hit Max where it hurt. She'd destroy the stash he left in her console and the roll of negatives. She lifted the lid on the console. It was empty.

Chapter 31

"Did William Shakespeare indulge in a good deal more than a pinch of tobacco while penning his sonnets?" Max asked.

Jeannie's ex-husband stood on the dais behind Professor Brent Sherman's lectern. Max's lazy grin belied the assumed posture of a professor as he gleefully besmirched Shakespeare's good name. His gaze prowled the classroom as though searching for a rebuttal.

"This has not been proven!" Professor Sherman's indignant voice sounded from beside Jeannie, where he sat in the chair usually reserved for Bo. He glanced at her and hissed the words, "You always have an opinion, Mrs. Jonson. Speak up!"

"Excuse me," Jeannie babbled, ever the arbitrator, "there is no proof the bard delved into narcotics. However, clay pipe fragments excavated from Shakespeare's Stratford-upon-Avon   home in the seventeenth century period show conclusively that cocaine and myristic acid were smoked in Shakespeare's England."

"Thank you, Mrs. Jonson." Max mimicked Professor Sherman's usage of her name. Then, he threw up his arms in a couldn't-care-less surrender. Max's smile encompassed the whole of the classroom as he stepped from behind the podium. He paraded across the stage naked as the day he was born except for the bandage on his right hand.

Roe and her sorority sisters were out of their seats flashing pictures as Max positioned his lithe body in provocative poses.

"Max!" Jeannie gasped. Horrified, she jumped from her seat and started down the stairs only to be tackled by Bo, who appeared from nowhere. They tumbled over and over toward the dais, causing her rash-covered body to burn and her ears to ring and ring.

Jeannie woke with a start and sat up in her bed. Shaking her head to clear fragments of the dream from her mind, she reached for her cell phone that rang and rang. Her fingernails teased the rash still covering her body. "Hullo?"

"Jeannie, do you have your graduation present? Remember the one-of-a-kind watch that I had engraved with JD, 'You Made Our Day'? The one that the jeweler promised me would be the only one in the world?"

"Mom, Mom, Mommmm! Why do you ask? Of course I have your present. Why are you calling in the middle of the night to ask a question like that?" Jeannie glanced at the digital clock as the numbers changed from 7:51 am to 7:52 am.

Her dad's voice replaced the hysteria of her mom. "You've got a lot of questions to answer, Missy."

"What's going on, Dad? I was going to call you this morning to explain that picture in the *College Review*. It was all Max's fault. He took it, and it wasn't what it looks like," Jeannie rambled on.

"Jeannie, Jeannie, Jeannie! Quit babbling. You're as bad as your mom. I don't know anything about a picture, but I'm sure I will sooner or later."

"Dad, that's the bad news; here's the good news: I got a job that pays big bucks, and I can pay my way to Mexico."

"Fine! With the trouble you're in, you better head for the border right now."

"What are you talking about, Dad?"

"We were rousted out of bed this morning by a call from the jeweler who your mom paid a fortune to for your graduation watch. You know, the one that--?"

"I know, Dad, the watch that I was going to take to the jeweler to have the clasp fixed. The one that I promised Cloie she could wear with her fleeky outfit this weekend. It's here somewhere; I just can't seem to put my fingers on it."

"Jeannie, the watch is not there. The police have it! Your graduation watch was found at the site of a murder. They're going to pick you up for questioning. What in the world are you doing? Are you mixed up in drugs with Max?"

"Dad, we must have a bad connection. Drugs! Murder! Max! I

don't have a clue what you're talking about." But even as Jeannie spoke, her mind was remembering the stash and negatives Max left in her console. And the pictures she had confiscated from Mic Davao. And her empty console.

"Jeannie? Jeannie?" Her dad's voice jerked Jeannie back to reality. "Missy, we sent you to college for an education, not to get mixed up in drugs and some coed's murder."

Her half-on, half-off slipper impelled her across the room. Arms flailing, she fell atop a mound of soft laundry piled in the corner of the room.

Déjà vu! Jeannie's ears rang, her head spun. Her mind filled with flashes of scenes from the woods where she'd executed a perfect belly flop onto a mound of soft dirt and wondered if a body might be buried there. Those memories spliced with the news bulletin pictures on the big screen television she'd seen at the Courts. Echoes of an announcer's voice saying Rita Gibson's name reiterated over and over in her head. The photograph Max had taken of Rita for Miss Hale University competition moved against the black screen of her mind.

Still clutching the phone, Jeannie mumbled into the receiver, "Oh—my God!"

"Jeannie? Are you all right? What's happening?" her dad yelled.

Jeannie screamed.

Dropping the phone, Jeannie grabbed her head in both of her hands. She rocked back and forth as tears streamed down her face. With certainty, Jeannie knew the pictures on the newscast of the murder scene and the spot in the woods where she had stumbled were one and the same.

Jeannie screamed again.

A doe and her fawn sprinted across the screen of Jeannie's mind. A shot rang out. Rockets burst into the sky, swerved, and flew toward the animals. A shot pierced the side of the doe and continued on through her fawn. They fell slowly, gracefully. The mound of soft earth on which Jeannie had fallen shifted as the earth fell away. Jeannie stared into the sightless eyes of Rita Gibson.

"Oh, my God!" Jeannie had been lying on top of the murdered coed, and she knew her name, Rita Gibson. And lying beside Rita's grave was Jeannie's graduation watch bracelet with the inscription, "JD, you made our day."

Slowly Jeannie reached for the phone. She raised it to her face and whispered, "Dad, I know where I lost my bracelet watch."

The doorbell rang.

Jeannie climbed from the pile of discarded clothes, shrinking away as if they were a mound of soft dirt. "I've got to go, Dad. Someone's at the door."

"Don't answer it, Jeannie. It's probably the cops." Was this her law-abiding, straight-shooting dad advising her to avoid the authorities? What a mess she had wrought.

"Dad, did you hear me? I know where I lost my bracelet watch."

"Don't tell them anything. I've called Renee. She's on her way to your apartment with an attorney. Your mom and I are on our way. Just be brave, Missy." He hung up.

"Dad, I'm innocent! You know I'm innocent." Jeannie spoke into a dead phone. *Sure, Missy,* her little voice reminded her. *You're innocent of spying on the professor who offered you a job. You're innocent of lying atop a dead coed's grave and leaving unmistakable evidence linking you to her. You're innocent of sugar coating almost anything to get a high paying, short term job, so you can go on tour to Mexico.*

Oh, my God! Brent Sherman! Should I call him? A Max voice inside her head kicked in. *And tell him what, Jeannie? Interesting that you thought of him, of all people, to call first.*

The doorbell rang again, more insistently.

Damn you, Max! You're the guilty one. I'm innocent.

A loud knock rattled Jeannie's front door demanding attention.

The knocking became a pounding. *Maybe it's Renee and the lawyer.* Even her sister's disapproving look would be better than cops on her doorstep. Whoever was on her doorstep were definitely not her sister, Renee, and the lawyer. Renee had a key for emergencies.

Jeannie pulled on her robe and walked to the door. She opened the door, and on her step stood two police officers, just like in the movies. A tall, blond guy and a shorter ebony-skinned officer, who seemed vaguely familiar in an out-of-place sort of way. Where had she seen this man before?

"Ms. Jeannie Jonson?" the blond officer asked.

"Yes, sir."

"Can we come in? We have some questions to ask you," the blond officer continued.

Deciding to play dumb, Jeannie asked, "Is this about a parking ticket?"

"No, Ms. Jonson. We need to ask you some questions—" The shorter officer moved forward as though to enter.

Jeannie remained planted with the door between her and the cops.

"Ms. Jonson, we can do this here. Or we can take you downtown. Either way, we need some answers to a few questions," the shorter officer said.

Opening the door wider, Jeannie revealed her state of dress. "Can I put on some clothes?" she asked.

They nodded. Jeannie sighed with reprieve and invited the officers inside. No sense in giving the neighbors a free show. As the two officers moved inside, Jeannie suddenly realized where she'd seen the officer with the polished skull before. He was Annie's father, whom she'd seen at the Courts last night. Jeannie didn't know whether to be embarrassed or relieved.

Clutching her rumpled robe closer, Jeannie motioned to her sparsely furnished living room. "Officers, I'm afraid you have the advantage on me. You seem to know my name, but I don't have a clue as to yours. In fact, isn't there some kind of law that you need to show me some identification?"

Annie's father reached into his pocket and produced a billfold, which he flipped open to reveal a police ID. Jeannie studied it carefully. The picture matched the man whose name was Leland Leblanc.

Leblanc's partner's papers identified him as Clint Anderson.

"Can I ask what exactly you're here to question me about?" Jeannie stammered.

"Why don't you get changed, Ms. Jonson? Then we'll talk about why we're here," Leblanc said.

Leblanc showed no sign of recognition toward her, so she assumed he hadn't noticed her at the game last night. Should she mention that she was Cloie's aunt? And that she'd seen him at the Courts last night and knew he was Annie's father?

Her dad's voice in Jeannie's head counseled, *When in doubt, Jeannie, keep your mouth shut.*

As Jeannie hurried to dress, she reminded herself she was in big trouble. Thanks to the phone call from her dad, she knew why the officers were there. What should she tell them? Of course, she'd have to admit she'd lost her bracelet watch. Should she say she knew where she lost it? Would they believe someone found the bracelet? And lost it in the woods?

Oh, my God! They will want to know why I was in the woods and what I was doing there. She could tell them she was spying on Professor Sherman and Camouflage. But she'd have to mention the men were shooting off, what she'd come to learn was fireworks on property where they were trespassing. Would the police, too, think the men might have been there for other purposes? If Jeannie ratted out her teacher and future boss, would she lose the job that she'd just got?

Jeannie, Jeannie. Her father's voice sounded weary. *Get your priorities straight.*

Sure, Dad, but what should I say?

Just answer their question with a yes or no. Remember KISS.

Jeannie smiled in spite of herself, remembering Dad's meaning behind KISS: *Keep it simple, stupid.* Maybe Jeannie wouldn't have to involve Professor Brent Sherman after all.

Jeannie walked back into the living room full of confidence and stopped abruptly. Leland Leblanc was reading the copy of the *College Review*, which Cloie and Renee had brought to her last night. The copy that she'd tossed on her coffee table when she came in from shopping. The *College Review* with the picture of Jeannie and Professor Sherman entwined on the stairs of the professor's theater classroom stairs.

"Da Dum!"

The two officers stood as Jeannie entered the room. Lebanc extended his hand that held the *College Review.* "Interesting newspaper the college puts out. Nice picture of you and—" he looked once more at the paper as though to verify—"a Professor Brent Sherman, right?"

Jeannie swallowed hard and nodded. *Nice going, Jeannie. You ratted out the professor without even saying a word.*

Officer Anderson cleared his throat, "Even more interesting is the name of the person who took the picture—Jonson. Jonson is a common name, but the way you spell your last name is different—J-O-N-S-O-N—isn't it?"

Jeannie nodded.

"So are you acquainted with this—" he checked the paper again, "Max Jonson—Maximum Exposure, who took this picture?"

Jeannie nodded.

"And what relation might he be to you, Ms. Jonson?" Leblanc asked.

"He's my husband, er, I mean my ex-husband," Jeannie stammered.

"And, what about this Sherman? What's your relationship to him?"

"He's the professor of my Lit class."

"Mmm, so your ex-husband, Max Jonson, took this picture of you and your professor while you were engaged in," he paused, "studying Lit?"

Jeannie nodded.

"If he's your professor and you're studying Lit at the college, that would make you a coed, right?"

Jeannie nodded.

"Does your husband, er, ex-husband, take a lot of pictures of coeds around campus?" Anderson asked.

Jeannie nodded.

"You are a woman of few words, Ms. Jonson. Are you always this silent?" Leblanc said.

Oh, jeez! Did she ever have the right to remain silent! Jeannie nodded.

Anderson held a copy of the *Halesville News and Leader* out to Jeannie. On the front page was a picture of Rita Gibson. "Do you recognize this coed, Ms. Jonson?"

Jeannie nodded.

"And you know her as—?" Leblanc asked.

"Rita Gibson. Everyone knows Rita. She was a candidate for campus queen."

"That's right. What a nice picture. And who does it say took the picture?" Anderson held the picture out for Jeannie to read the photographer's name.

"Maximum Exposure," Jeannie mumbled.

"And that would be Max Jonson, your husband, er, ex-husband, right?" Leblanc asked.

Jeannie nodded.

"Max is a big man about campus. Always Johnny on the spot with his camera, right?" Leblanc said.

Jeannie nodded.

"I bet he's real popular with the coeds, right?" Leblanc asked.

Jeannie nodded.

"Maybe that's why he's your ex, right?" Leblanc chuckled.

Jeannie stared straight ahead.

"Well, Ms. Jonson? Is that why he's your ex? Max must be really cozy with the coeds, taking pictures, maybe giving gifts?" Leblanc asked.

Jeannie continued to stare straight ahead.

"What about you, Ms. Jonson? Did Max give you presents?" Leblanc's voice dropped to a more intimate tone.

Jeannie nodded.

Anderson reached into his pocket and brought out a photo. He held it out to her. "Would this be one of the presents he gave you?" Leblanc asked.

Jeannie stared at a picture of her bracelet watch lying on the ground. The picture had been cropped and enlarged so the bracelet was easily recognized. It didn't show Rita's grave, but Jeannie knew it was there.

The doorbell rang.

Both men turned toward the sound.

Jeannie started forward as if to open the door, but Anderson stepped between her and the door. "Let's answer officer Leblanc's question before we answer the door, Ms. Jonson."

"No, Max didn't give me that gift." Jeannie reached for the door knob.

Leblanc pushed forward and placed his hand on the door knob.

Anderson persisted. "Ms. Jonson. We know this bracelet watch is yours. It's been identified by a local jeweler as yours. The inscription reads, 'JD, You made our day.' Do you mean to tell me that you deny the bracelet is yours?"

"No, the bracelet is mine, but Max didn't give it to me."

"And who did, Ms. Jonson? Would that be your other friend, Professor Sherman?"

Suddenly a key turned in the lock and the door was pushed open. Jeannie looked toward the door and there stood Renee and a man Jeannie had never seen before. And the look on Renee's face was one of concern, not I-knew-this-would-happen-to-Jeannie-sooner-or-later.

"Renee!" Jeannie had never been so glad to see anyone in her whole life.

Renee rushed forward and embraced her. "Jeannie, Jeannie, are you all right?"

Jeannie nodded and leaned into her sister's hug. Suddenly, she burst into tears.

Renee patted her sister's shoulders. Then she pulled away enough to say, "Officers, this is our attorney, L.D. Stone."

L.D. Stone said, "Jeannie, your father retained me to counsel you. I'm advising you to not answer any questions."

"Too late," Jeannie sobbed.

Stone turned to the officers, "Gentlemen, I'd like to confer with my client."

Renee gave Jeannie another quick hug. Then she stepped back to look at Jeannie as she rubbed a residue of pink from Jeannie's blouse off the sleeve of her own blouse.

Officers Anderson and Leblanc looked at each other. Their fingers moved over their forearms in a motion Jeannie was starting to find familiar.

Looking closer, Jeannie did a little police work of her own. She saw traces of pink extending from beneath Officer Leblanc's uniform sleeve. Jeannie was not naive enough to believe that poison ivy only grew in the woods where Rita Gibson's body was found and which she believed to be the very same woods where Professor Sherman and his associates were shooting fireworks. It seemed more than coincidence that they all had contacted poison ivy, and they all seem to have been in those particular woods.

Officer Anderson took out his notepad and jotted something down. He glanced at Leblanc, who was staring at Renee in a puzzled way. "Leblanc? Anything else we need from Ms. Jonson?"

Leblanc's attention jerked back to Jeannie. "We may have some more questions for you later, Ms. Jonson." He looked at L.D. Stone. "With your attorney present, if you wish."

Stone nodded. "So Ms. Jonson is not being charged with anything?"

Officer Anderson shook his head. "Not at this time. Your client can resume her normal schedule as long as she's available for further questioning."

Officer Leblanc turned to Jeannie. "If you think of anything you might want to tell us, here's my card. Feel free to call me at any time." Leblanc moved toward the door with Anderson close on his heels. Suddenly, he turned and said, "Ms. Jonson, there's one more thing. You and your sister seem very familiar. I'm trying to remember where I've seen you before, in case it's related to this case."

Renee's head was bobbing up and down as though she suddenly had a brainstorm. "Officer Leland Leblanc! You're Annie's father! I'm Cloie's mother! The Phantoms played the Rockets last night at the Courts."

Jeannie put in her two cents worth. "Actually the Phantoms beat the Rockets last night at the Courts. My niece, Cloie, made the winning basket."

A scowl replaced the grin of recognition, which had begun when Renee spoke, on Leblanc's face. "Ms. Jonson, you're dead right."

Jeannie's front door closed with a resounding bang.

Chapter 32

"Dead right!" Leblanc's words pounded inside Jeannie's head like the thud of a judge's gavel.

Officer Leblanc does have a way with words, Jeannie thought, placing his card where she placed all her business cards—on top of her desk.

Renee sank down on Jeannie's small couch and motioned to the attorney to sit beside her.

"Before we get started, do you mind if I use your facilities?" Stone asked.

Jeannie showed the attorney to the small bathroom off her bedroom. "Excuse the mess. I wasn't expecting a gentleman caller in my bedchamber," she stammered, "especially not an attorney." Red-faced, she gave up explaining. As soon as the bathroom door shut, she pulled a hasty spread over her rumpled bed and kicked some of the disarray into the small closet. Returning to the living room, Jeannie seated herself on the inquisition chair across from the couch.

Renee was looking at the *College Review*, which lay open to the picture of Professor Brent Sherman and Jeannie entwined on the stairs of his Lit room. Renee's polished fingernails beat out a staccato on the coffee table that echoed Leblanc's last words, "Dead right, dead right."

"Strange that Officer Leblanc turns out to be Annie's father," Renee said.

"I recognized him when he removed his cap earlier. I wanted to avoid any conflict, so I didn't draw attention to the fact."

"Avoid any conflict?" Renee smiled wryly. "You mean like pointing out the fact that your niece made the winning basket that beat his daughter's basketball team last night?"

"He knew I was right," Jeannie said.

"Yeah, dead right. Leblanc may have a way with words, but he also seems to have something else in common with you, Jeannie."

"What?" Jeannie asked.

"Calamine lotion."

"You noticed that, too!" Jeannie said. "I bet he got it in the woods where they discovered Rita Gibson's grave. It's full of the little green vine."

Renee gasped. "Jeannie! You mean you really were in the woods where they found the coed's body? And that's where you got poison ivy?"

Jeannie nodded.

"Dad told me on the phone earlier your bracelet was found at the scene of the girl's murder. What on earth were you doing at the scene of a murder?"

"Yes, I'd like to hear the answer to that question too, Ms. Jonson," L.D. Stone said as he crossed the room and sank to the couch beside Renee. Pulling out a notepad, he scribbled on it. "It seems we have a lot of unanswered questions to pursue."

Jeannie's cell phone sounded. She glanced at the caller ID and saw Brent Sherman's name. She ached to answer his call. If she could hear his voice, she knew everything would be okay. Somehow she'd draw comfort…no, that wasn't the word. Confidence? No. Then what was it? What was he in her life besides her Lit professor, future boss, and—? Jeannie licked her lips trying to moisten the dryness of them. As Jeannie's tongue traced the outline of her mouth she could almost imagine the firmness of Brent's mouth pressed against hers. A delicious shudder rippled across her shoulders as realization dawned on her. Thoughts of her Literature professor were as sweet as a favorite piece of clandestine candy that one sucked on in private moments and gained satisfaction. Brent Sherman was an elusive sweetness in her life.

Da-dum! Jeannie said to herself.

"Jeannie, Jeannie, Jeannnnnie!" Renee's voice cut through the imagined moment, paring Sherman from Jeannie's mind, lips, and mouth, as surely as if she'd had her mouth washed out with soap.

Jeannie jerked to attention, trying to erase the silly, satisfied, grin from her mouth. "What?"

"Turn off your cell phone and keep your mind on the business at hand. You're in a lot of trouble, and we're trying to help you. Pay attention!" The big sister voice of remembered childhood snapped Jeannie back to the problem at hand. She turned her cell phone to vibrate/silent mode. Then she took a deep breath and tried to explain to Stone and Renee how she'd been in the woods checking out her future employers, Brent Sherman and his partner, Camouflage.

"You actually believed they were shooting people and burying their bodies there?" Stone asked.

Jeannie nodded. "They said they were moving punks into the woods to shoot them where no one would hear them. What would you have thought?"

"How did you discover the grave?" Renee asked.

"I didn't know it was a grave. I stumbled over a mound of fresh dirt which turned out to be Rita Gibson's grave. That's where I presumably lost my bracelet watch," Jeannie said.

"And you think that's where you and Sherman got poison ivy?" Stone asked.

Jeannie nodded, repeating the story of fingering the green vine and discovering Sherman must have come in contact with a vine, too. "Camouflage asked Sherman why he was scratching his skin raw. I realized I was doing the same thing. When I glanced down and saw the green vine, I realized we'd both probably got poison ivy. Sure enough, the next day he was covered with calamine lotion, just like me."

"When Officers Anderson and LeBlanc showed you a picture of the bracelet watch, you identified it as yours?" L.D. Stone asked, trying to piece together Jeannie's rambling.

"They knew the watch bracelet is mine. It's been identified by the local jeweler where Mom bought it. And the inscription reads, 'JD, you made our day.' At least that's what my dad told me on the phone earlier."

"But you admitted it was yours?" Stone persisted.

"Yes, I said the bracelet is mine, but Max didn't give it to me."

"Why would you say that?"

"They asked me if Max made a habit of giving coeds presents." Jeannie paused. "They asked if he gave me presents."

Stone scribbled furiously on his pad. "So, when the officers asked you if the bracelet was yours, you admitted it was, but that Max didn't give it to you?"

Jeannie nodded. "For some reason the jeweler must not have told them who bought the bracelet. They also asked me if Brent Sherman gave it to me."

"And, you said?"

"That's when you and Renee walked in. I didn't get a chance to answer," Jeannie said.

"Thank God for little favors," Renee said, shaking her head wearily.

Jeannie's cell phone vibrated.

"Are you sure you've told me everything?" Stone asked, checking his legal pad of notes. "You didn't actually tell the officers you were in the woods?"

"No, but if they noticed my calamine lotion-covered poison ivy, I'd say that was a pretty good clue. Especially since I noticed they'd scratched up a pretty good dose of ivy themselves."

"How's that?" Stone asked.

"Leblanc had pink calamine lotion showing from beneath his uniform sleeves. Renee noticed it, too." Jeannie glanced at Renee for confirmation.

Renee nodded.

"And they both were giving their arms a pretty good ivy scratch. Remember, I told you Brent Sherman was covered with it. The woods are alive with that little green vine," Jeannie said, glancing at the clock on the wall of her living room.

"Interesting!" Stone said. He checked his note pad. "You mentioned several people who have poison ivy. They all seem to have been in the vicinity where the body of Rita Gibson was found."

Jeannie nodded.

"Professor Brent Sherman, Officer Leland Leblanc, Officer Clint Anderson, and yourself all seem to have poison ivy." He checked off his pad as he pronounced each name.

Jeannie reflected. "Wonder if Camouflage got poison ivy?"

"Camouflage?" Stone scribbled on his pad.

"Remember, I told you he was Sherman's fireworks partner. They were shooting fireworks in the woods the day I was there."

Stone nodded. "Anyone else?"

Jeannie closed her eyes. "Just Roscoe. But I'm not sure if he was in the woods."

Stone checked his notes. "Is that the bartender from Jeers who was delivering the fireworks?"

Jeannie nodded.

"Didn't you say he told Sherman and Camouflage he had started digging a hole to bury the big one?" Stone asked.

Jeannie slapped the heel of her palm against her forehead. "Sure! Wonder if he's got it, too?"

"It'll be easy enough to check," Stone said. "Anything else you can tell me about these people?"

Jeannie barked a short laugh. "I was just thinking the pharmacies probably made a killing on calamine lotion and bandages."

"Why bandages?" Stone asked.

Jeannie frowned. Bandages? Why had she said bandages? "Sherman's right hand was bandaged and so was Max's hand."

"When was this?" Stone asked.

Jeannie flushed. "It's probably not important. I mean, I'm not sure about it." Fantasy and dreams were a mixture in her mind. "I'm not sure about the bandages. I may have dreamed it."

Stone shook his head, raised his eyebrows, and said, "Well, let me know if you remember." He looked at his watch.

Oh, my God! It was almost noon. Jeannie realized she'd missed her Thursday morning classes. What was happening in Lit class? Today was when they were supposed to read original poetry. Today was when Gussie, Roe, and Jeannie were supposed to decide about competing in the talent show at Jeers.

Oh, my God! Jeannie didn't have her poetry assignment or even a clue what she'd do for talent at Jeers. All she had was a bustier, covered by a totally rad leather jacket. And she still owed her sister $150 for that piece of leather, thanks to Max.

Jeannie sighed. Her new black jeans and leather boots with rhinestone studs were charged to her dad's credit card. The one he gave her for emergencies. Her presence in class probably wouldn't raise her grade one iota. That was, if she still had a grade to get raised in Sherman's Lit class. All in all she probably didn't have much to contribute to Lit class today, except for an exciting story about almost getting arrested.

Renee was gazing at Jeannie, dumfounded.. "Jeannie, I can't believe you would follow two men into the woods when you thought they were murderers. For goodness sake, if you thought they were actually shooting off weapons and killing people, you'd have to be crazy to still want to work for them. And, falling on the grave of that coed, Nita Gibson—"

"Rita," Jeannie corrected.

"What?" Renee asked.

"Rita Gibson. You called the dead coed Nita. If you're going to discuss the dead, at least call them by their right name."

"Jeannie!" her sister reprimanded. "I can't believe you don't realize the seriousness of your situation. I'm sure the first thing I would have done was alert the authorities."

Stone nodded, as though adding a second to Renee's remark. Jeannie knew by the look he gave her sister, he couldn't imagine Renee in the woods in a situation similar to Jeannie's.

Jeannie glanced at the clock again. "Renee, I thought about going to the authorities, but what would I have told them? If I'd told them my professor and his friend were shooting people, they would have found out they were shooting fireworks."

"Would they? Or might they have found they were shooting fireworks and coeds?" Renee said. "I can't believe you didn't tell someone."

"I can't believe what's happened to me in the last few days. I've told you and Mr. Stone everything I can remember. It's not going to help to keep hashing it over. I've already missed half a day of classes. Don't you think when the officer said, 'Go about your regular schedule, but keep your eye out for anything suspicious,' he meant for me to go back to college and my regular schedule?"

Renee shook her head. "Mr. Stone, can you talk some sense into her?"

"I understand your frustration, Ms. Jonson. Bear with me. I just want to be clear on a few more points. Technically, you didn't tell the officers you were in the woods. So they are assuming you were there. I don't think they're giving out the information about your bracelet watch being found at the scene of Rita Gibson's murder, so don't say anything about it," Stone cautioned.

"Do you think they'll question Professor Sherman? And Max?" Jeannie asked.

"I'm sure they'll be all over the campus." Stone looked once more at his notes. "Who, besides us, actually knows you were in the woods that day?"

"Brent might suspect because he knows we both have poison ivy." Jeannie paused to think. "But he wouldn't know I followed them to the woods that day. As far as he knows, I could have got poison ivy any number of places."

Stone nodded. "Officers Leblanc and Anderson might come to the same conclusion."

"But when I told him I didn't want his job, I implied I believed he shot someone," Jeannie said.

"And who was there when this conversation was going on?" Stone asked.

Jeannie slapped a hand over her mouth. "Oh, my God! Most of the Lit class and the students who were watching us when we fell on the stairs." Jeannie felt color rise to her face. "That's when Max snapped the picture that made front page of the *College Review*."

"So, a lot of people heard you accuse Professor Brent Sherman of murdering Rita Gibson?" Stone said, shaking his head.

"Yes, but when I realized the job he was offering me was selling fireworks, all the fireworks language made sense. I realized it was fireworks they were shooting that day, not people," Jeannie stammered. "I even accepted the job."

"Did you really? And how many of the people actually heard that?" Renee asked.

Jeannie shook her head. She didn't know.

"Then we'll assume most of your Lit class overheard?" Stone asked.

Jeannie's cell phone was vibrating up a storm, so she knew she must have a lot of messages. Now the text message ring sounded. Cloie and Max were the only ones who ever texted her. Jeannie pulled her cell phone from her pocket, opened it, glanced over the text. "Oh, my God! The police questioned Max after they left here."

"And?" Stone asked.

"Well, er, he's afraid I might have mentioned something that might have incriminated him." Quickly, Jeannie deleted Max's text which read, "Good thing I got rid of the stash in your console. Did you destroy the Davago pictures yet?"

Jeannie typed in, "No."

Immediately the text ring sounded. "Be careful!"

Stone and Renee were both staring at Jeannie inquisitively. "What?" they asked.

"Just something Max wanted me to take care of," Jeannie said. She had omitted telling them about the stash and the negatives, which might embarrass a lot of people.

"Jeannie, is there something you're not telling us?" Renee demanded.

"It's a personal matter. It has nothing to do with the Rita Gibson case," Jeannie sighed.

Jeannie rose as if to put an end to this session and get back to her real world. Since her fall down the stairs yesterday in Sherman's class, things had all pretty much gone downhill.

"Thanks, Renee, for bringing Mr. Stone over." Jeannie held out her hand to Stone, who returned her handshake.

"If you think of anything else, Ms. Jonson, just call me." Stone turned toward the door just as the doorbell sounded.

Immediately, a key turned in the lock and the door opened.

"This is my daughter's home. I don't care who's here, I'm going in," Marie said over her shoulder to Serle as she barged into Jeannie's living room.

"Jeannie, Jeannie, Jeannieeeeee!" Her mother ran across the room and crushed Jeannie to her with a bear hug.

Her dad's arms encircled Jeannie and Marie. He caught Renee's hand with a squeeze. "Thanks, Sis, for running interference for us. We got here as fast as possible."

"Faster." Marie released Jeannie. She patted her perfectly coiffured hair in place. "Your father drives like a wild man."

As though just noticing L.D. Stone, Serle and Marie turned to greet the lawyer. Jeannie gave up any hope of returning to college that day as her dad settled in to discuss her predicament with the lawyer.

Marie pulled Jeannie and Renee into the kitchen. She sent Renee to pick up food, while she bustled around, turning Jeannie's small kitchen into a place where people eat.

"I can't believe you don't have anything in your refrigerator but beer, cream cheese, and more beer. What on earth do you eat, Jeannie?"

"Beer and bagels with cream cheese," Jeannie mumbled.

"Don't just stand there, Jeannie. Help me get things ready so we can eat when Renee gets back with the food." Her mom's way of coping with a situation had always been to busy herself and everyone around her with work.

Jeannie could still feel her cell phone vibrate with unending phone calls. The landline phone on her bedroom table continued to ring. Occasionally, she'd catch a snatch of the caller's voice as the machine recorded the message. Several times she'd heard Max's voice. Jeannie recognized voices of friends from school. Marie frowned as the phone continued to ring and messages kept pouring in. Jeannie tried to ignore the phone, hoping the machine would fill up and shut up.

"Mrs. Jonson? Jeannie?" The male voice taking on the phone could belong to none other but Brent Sherman.

"Excuse me, Mom, that's my Lit professor. I really need to take this call." Jeannie snatched up her notebook pages of limericks she'd written instead of poetry for Lit class and shuffled off to the bedroom, pulling the door closed behind her.

Before the door could close, she heard her mom's voice, "Lit professor? Brent Sherman? Would that be the one you're hugging on the stairs in the picture on the front page of your college newspaper?"

"Hello," Jeannie said balancing the phone on her lap as she sank onto her disheveled bedspread. She delighted in the thought that she'd never been to bed with the professor before.

"Jeannie? Is that you?" Not pausing for her answer, Sherman continued, "I've been trying to get in touch with you all day."

"Well, you've got me now. What can I do for you?" Jeannie's voice sounded cold and indifferent. What she really wanted to say was, "I need you, help me, tell me what to say so I won't get you in trouble. And, reassure me that you didn't have anything to do with the body in the woods."

Jeannie could almost sense Sherman shifting into another gear. "Mrs. Jonson, a lot of things have been happening at college this morning. Things I'd really like to discuss with you."

"Professor Sherman, I'm really sorry about the photo that Max took. The one that ended up on the front page of the *College Review*," Jeannie said, wanting to get that out of the way.

Sherman cleared his throat, "Well, that, too!" He continued, "However, this has to do with the missing coed, Rita Gibson. Technically, she's not missing anymore since they found her body in the woods."

Noise in the background alerted Jeannie Brent was not alone. Who would be with him when he was calling her? Jeannie felt a pang of unwarranted jealousy and pushed it away.

"I saw the place where they found the body on the news last night," Jeannie said, trying to be vague but needing assurance that Brent recognized the area where the body was discovered.

"Well, the class was all abuzz about it this morning. And," he hesitated "well, we missed your input."

He paused. The whispered voice near Sherman's phone mouthpiece hummed. Jeannie strained to put words to the muffled conversation. Was it a feminine voice? Was it Roe or one of the other students?

"Sorry I missed class, but I was, detained," Jeannie said. Hoping to change the subject she hurried on, "How did the original poetry go? Did Roe and her friends decide to do the Jeers competition?"

"Only a few of the class had their assignments ready. One or two tried to plagiarize verse which earned them a failing grade. And Roe and her friends gave a green light to Jeers, if you decided to give it a go, too. Excuse me, Mrs. Jonson."

In a voice aside, he continued, "Will you quit crowding me? I'll ask her—" The rest of his word were muffled.

Then, he spoke again to Jeannie, " But what I actually called about—what?"

He spoke aside once more and returned to the phone.

"I'm sorry, Mrs. Jonson. My wife, er ex-wife, is visiting my classroom on an errand. I've been trying to explain how we became involved, I mean, how we got hooked up. How I came to offer you a job," he finished.

Jeannie could hear muffled conversation in the background. She jumped off the unkempt bed in one guilty motion. Her voice was that of a woman scorned, "Well, that shouldn't be so hard to explain. I need a temporary job that pays well, so I can go on tour this summer and you graciously offered it to me."

"Actually," the soft edge had disappeared from his voice and he was all professor, "the authorities were in my office today asking questions about my association with coeds. Your name was mentioned. An Officer Leblanc, I think it was, commented on the fact that we, that is you, me, and the officers, all shared the same affliction. And, they wondered where we might have contacted our rash," he said.

Jeannie's fingers moved over the lingering signs of poison ivy on her arm where pink stains of calamine remained. "Beg your pardon?"

A flurry of muffled conversation and then Sherman continued, "To get right to the heart of the matter, Mrs. Jonson, we all have poison ivy. They were wondering where we were exposed to the vine. I explained I was in the woods with a friend of mine trying out some new fireworks shells and must have contracted it there."

Jeannie's throat was suddenly dry. She tried to recall their conversation in his classroom when she learned Professor Brent Sherman was in the fireworks business. At that point, even Sherman's earlier telephone conversation made sense. Had she actually said she was in the woods? Did she accuse him of shooting someone? Jeannie's tongue licked the dryness of her lips. Had she actually imagined his lips on hers a short time before?

"Mrs. Jonson, er, Jeannie, are you still there?" Sherman's voice sounded as distant as a fading dream. Then the professor gave Jeannie her next assignment. "If I introduce my ex-wife to you on the phone, will you reassure Lynn that we didn't give—get--the poison ivy from each other through our rash behavior?"

"Oh, my God! You've reduced our relationship—no, friendship—into a bathos." Jeannie spoke without thinking.

The bedroom door burst open and Jeannie's mom stood framed in the doorway. "Jeannie, are you going to stay on that phone all day? Renee is back with the food and we're ready to eat."

"Sure, Mom. Sorry, Professor Sherman, I've got to run. My folks are here, along with my sister and lawyer, Mr. Stone. We're fixing to eat. Maybe I can catch you later." Jeannie started to hang up. Instead she said into the receiver, "Tell your wife—ex-wife, Lynn—if I was in any way responsible for you having the rash, the pleasure was all mine." Jeannie placed the phone back in its receiver, fell on the bed, and burst into tears.

"What is it about me, Mom? Or is it just men in general? Are they all just—" Jeannie sobbed as her mom cradled her like a child.

Marie listened to Jeannie's version of being the wronged woman in a triangle that didn't even exist with her Lit professor, his ex-wife, and herself.

"Honey…Jeannie," Her mom shushed. "Who is this man? What is it about him that would make you even think of following him into the woods and watching him shoot—God knows what? I thought he was your teacher. Is this how teachers act these days?" Marie asked.

Jeannie knew her mom was tuning up for her parent speech.

"Mom," Jeannie sobbed. "When I followed Professor Sherman into the woods, I didn't feel this way about him. I was trying to justify taking a job with him that would earn me enough money to go on the Mexican tour. And then, we both got poison ivy. Our minds seemed in synch." Jeannie paused to blow her nose into the tissue her mom pressed into her hand. "And, I told him I was divorced, and he told me he was divorced. And then we fell on the stairs and scratched each other's itch—"

"Jeannie Day Jonson!" Her mom stood abruptly, assuming her hands-on-hips posture.

Oh, my God! It was like she was back in grade school. She had just admitted she'd skipped school to go on a picnic with a group that included the opposite sex, boys. "Mom, I didn't mean—"

"Jeannie. When are you going to learn that life isn't a game. It's for real. There's rules that most people follow. When I was your age, twenty-five, I was settled into married life and had two babies."

"Mom, Mom!" Mom, it's just that I can't seem to find a man like Dad. I thought Max was the one—"

Mom guffawed. "We tried to tell you, honey. Max is a—a lady's man, among other things."

"I know, I know, Mom. I found that out—the hard way." Jeannie stood and dried her eyes.

"So, what about this professor? Is there something between you?" Mom asked.

"No, not really. Except the offer of a job and…well, I can't put my finger on it," Jeannie sighed.

"Jeannie, Jeannie, I've seen that look on your face before. Honey, remember when you and Max came to the house to tell us you were dating? It was right after that beauty pageant." Mom smiled, "Well, that look, it's that same gratified look you had then. Are you and that professor involved? Did he drag you into this murder mess?"

Jeannie's head was shaking in denial before Mom's words were finished. "It's not like that, Mom. We've never even been alone together. It's just kinda like—we're kindred spirits—and—"

"And when you lick your lips you imagine his mouth on yours?" Her mom grinned.

"Mom!" Jeannie jerked with a guilty start, wondering if she was licking her lips again.

"I've seen that dreamy look in your eyes when you moisten your lips, daughter. Don't forget your old mom was a girl once, too."

Oh my God! I knew my dad could invade my mind but Mom, too? Jeannie shook off girlie feelings and returned to the world of reality, the world of "this murder mess."

"Well, I'm through with any thoughts like that ever again. I'm never, ever, going to think about a man again. Never!" Jeannie said, cradling her face in her hands.

Her mom put her arm around Jeannie's shoulder and gave her a hug. "Honey, let me tell you what my mother told me once. See if it helps."

Knowing this could take a while, Jeannie sank back onto the bed, pulling her mom with her. What could her mom possibly tell her that would make this sick-to-the-gut feeling go away?

Marie began, "As we grow up, we learn sometimes even the one individual that wasn't supposed to ever let us down probably will. Isn't that right?"

Jeannie nodded.

"Your heart may be broken more than once. It doesn't get any easier each time." Her mom tilted her head at Jeannie, waiting for acknowledgment. Then she smiled. "But Jeannie, you'll break hearts, too. Baby girl, remember how it felt when yours was broken."

Jeannie shrugged, guilty as charged.

"You'll blame a new love for things an old one did." Her mom gave Jeannie's shoulders a reassuring hug. "You'll cry because time is moving too fast. It may seem those around you are living the perfect life and your dreams are falling apart."

Jeannie and her mom sat in the small bedroom on Jeannie's untidy bed with people waiting in the next room to discuss "this murder mess." And even though Jeannie's life was in shambles, suddenly her shoulders felt lighter, knowing that life dealt everyone the same hand. You just had to learn how to play the cards you drew, hoping to win the game.

"Why did Grandma tell you that?" Jeannie asked. "Did you and Dad have a fight?"

"No, darling. It wasn't Serle. It was the boy I was engaged to before I met your dad." Her mom had a dreamy, faraway look in her eyes, like she had clandestine candy, too.

"Mom! You never told me you were engaged before you met Dad!" Jeannie cried. Her mom not only understood how to be a player, she was a hottie!

"Jeannie! Keep your voice down. Your dad doesn't like for me to talk about that time in my life. I told you this so you'd find out what I found out."

"And what was that, Mom?"

"Don't be afraid to live life. Fantasize, laugh too much, and love like you've never been hurt. Every sixty minutes you spend irritated is an hour of happiness you'll never get back."

Marie drew Jeannie to her. They embraced.

"Okay, you ready to face the firing squad?" Marie asked as she headed toward the door.

"I'd face any firing squad with you by my side, Mom!" Jeannie grinned.

"Thanks a lot, girl!" Marie said.

"Mom, I didn't mean—well, you know what I meant," Jeannie said.

Her mom smiled back at Jeannie as she walked ahead of her into the small kitchen where the others were waiting. "I always do, Jeannie. I always do."

Chapter 33

"Murder in the first degree is a class A felony. The punishment can be either death or imprisonment for life without eligibility for probation or parole." L.D. Stone was speaking in a conversational tone to Jeannie's dad, who sat across from him at her kitchen table.

The lawyer's words stopped Marie in her tracks, where she stood in the middle of the kitchen. "Oh, my Lord!"

Following close on Marie's heels, Jeannie bumped into her mom's back, sending Marie careening into Renee, who was clearing the table where Serle and Stone had finished their portion of the Kentucky Fried Chicken.

"Mom!" Renee squealed, dropping a paper plate filled with chicken carcass and catching Marie on the rebound, pushing her away from the table. Jeannie often wondered where Cloie got her athletic ability. Probably not from their side of the family, she guessed.

"Jeannie, Jeannie, oh Jeannie!" Marie regained her balance and covered the short distance between them, crunching chicken bones under foot as she came. Marie caught Jeannie in a protective embrace, not unlike that of an angry mother bear protecting her cub.

"Mom, Mom," Renee cried, trying to get Marie's attention while gathering up as much of the chicken debris as possible. "If you and Jeannie hadn't spent the last hour in her bedroom, you'd know L.D. is talking about Jeannie's professor or Max." Seeing Jeannie's wide-eyed expression, Renee added, "Or whoever the heck murdered Rita Gibson and buried her in the woods."

Jeannie gasped. "You don't really think Brent or Max had something to do with the murder?"

Renee shrugged. "Who knows? You told us you were only snooping. Too bad you had the misfortune to sprawl over the girl's grave and lose your bracelet watch in the process. That seems to be the only clue tying you to the murder."

Jeannie dismissed the Max part of her sister's accusation as improbable. He was a lady killer, but not in the literal sense. And Sherman had a reason for being in the woods, however lame his reason might sound in a court of law. He and his partner, Camouflage, were shooting off fireworks. And that would make Camouflage Sherman's witness. Unless, Jeannie's little voice reminded her, the two of them were in this murder mess together.

As if in answer to Jeannie's thoughts, Stone continued, "If a person aids and abets another person by willfully joining together with that person in the commission of a crime, then the law holds the person responsible for the conduct of that other person just as though the person had engaged in such conduct himself."

Jeannie's dad seemed to think of Jeannie as the aiding and abetting person. He jumped immediately to her defense. "But Jeannie claims she was only following her professor—" He turned to Jeannie. "Why was it you were following this Sherman man into the woods, for God's sake, Jeannie?"

Marie, Renee, and Jeannie chorused, "To be sure he wasn't a murderer, so she could get a short-term job that paid big bucks—"

Jeannie soloed the last part of the sentence, "—so I could go on a tour of Mexico with my Spanish class this summer."

Marie glared at Serle, who sank further into his chair. Jeannie knew her mom's stare laid a guilt trip on her dad. He was berating himself for not shelling out the money for the trip. It was unreasonable, but somehow Jeannie felt justified.

Stone said, "Before any person can be held criminally responsible for the conduct of others, it is necessary that the person willfully associate himself in some way with the crime, and willfully participate in it. Mere presence at the scene of a crime and even knowledge that a crime is being committed are not sufficient to establish that a person either directed or aided and abetted the crime."

Somehow, what he said made sense. It was like a weight lifted off Jeannie's shoulders. Yet her thoughts lingered on "aided and abetted the crime" as Jeannie's mind shifted to the stash and negatives left in the console of her Explorer by Max. Jeannie moved out of Marie's reach, hoping her mom's antenna didn't pick up on her Max thoughts.

"What kind of a jail sentence does aiding and abetting carry?" Dad asked.

"The sentence depends on the jury's interpretation of the degree of the crime committed. It could be a matter of months or years," Stone said.

Although the evidence of her mom having finished off a chicken breast was lying on a paper plate on Jeannie's kitchen counter, Marie said, "Renee, help me put this food away. I've lost my appetite." Marie glanced at Jeannie. "And, I'm sure your sister has, too."

Jeannie felt a hungry growl begin in the pit of her stomach, but she put the kibosh on it and nodded agreement with her mom's words.

Renee grabbed up a succulent chicken breast. "In that case, I'll finish this piece of chicken. I'll join you all at the table as soon as I've finished clearing up."

For the next hour, they discussed Jeannie's predicament, while her cell phone vibrations vied with her empty stomach's vibrations. When Jeannie thought she was brain dead, Stone finally pushed back from the table, glanced at his watch, and said, "I think I have a working knowledge of Jeannie's involvement."

He turned his gaze on Jeannie. "If you think of anything else or hear of anything else that might help you disassociate yourself from this matter, call me."

Jeannie nodded. *Just let this day be over. Let me go to sleep and wake up tomorrow, and find this has all been a bad dream.* The faces of her family looked strained and seemed to mirror her thoughts exactly.

"Did I give you one of my cards?" L.D. Stone handed out cards to Serle and Marie, Renee, and Jeannie.

Jeannie reached to lay his card on her desk with her other cards. She knocked the whole stack of cards onto the floor. Stone leaned over to pick up the cards. The card on the top of the pile read "Rita Gibson."

Stone picked up the card. "Is there a reason you have this card, Ms. Jonson? One you didn't tell me about?"

"Rita Gibson gave it to me the other night at Jeers." Jeannie looked at Renee. "The same night you called for me to pick up Cloie at the fireworks shoot at Parkview."

"What night was that, Ms. Jonson?" Stone persisted.

"Monday night."

"That would be the same night she disappeared, right?" Stone said. Jeannie nodded.

Stone sat back down at the table. Jeannie's parents returned to their seats. Renee just stood there looking at Jeannie with reproach as Jeannie repeated the story of her Monday night adventure.

"Do your realize you might be the last person to see Rita Gibson alive, Ms. Jonson?" Stone asked.

"That couldn't be possible, Mr. Stone," Jeannie said.

"And why not, Ms. Jonson?" Stone said.

"Because the last person to see her alive would have to be her killer," Jeannie said.

Marie gasped.

Serle moaned.

Renee shook her head.

L.D. Stone said, "Ms. Jonson, perhaps now you'll realize what a vulnerable position you are in. I'm going to take this card in case we need to enter it into evidence." As he started to pocket the card, he noticed writing on the back. "This looks like a series of numbers with some letters."

"That's the number Rita said to call if I couldn't find her at the other number."

He held the card out to Jeannie.

She squinted at the writing. "Looks like 800.447.8277 or maybe 8477. The script looks like PL or BL…no; BT, maybe."

"Did you try to call her?" Stone asked.

"No, I thought it was too late that night. I believed I'd see her on campus the next day. I put the card with my other cards. I guess I just forgot about it. And then everything got crazy."

"We'll check this out. Hopefully, I can give it back to you soon." And having said that, he finally left.

Renee lured everyone to her house with the promise of a home-cooked meal for supper. She urged Jeannie to pack a bag and stay overnight at her house.

"Jeannie, your dad and I will drive home tonight knowing you're safe at Renee's. But if you insist on staying at your apartment tonight, your dad and I will stay with you," Mom promised. "I know your space is limited, but I can sleep with you. Serle will be perfectly comfortable on your couch."

The pained expression on her dad's face told Jeannie he remembered the last time he'd spent the night on her couch. She quickly packed an overnight bag.

Renee's husband, Ramie Allen, and Cloie were putting the finishing touches on the table setting when everyone arrived. The tantalizing aroma of lasagna drifted from the kitchen. Renee kept her freezer well-stocked with meals that were easy fixings. Jeannie wandered into the kitchen and found Cloie slicing french bread, hot out of the oven and oozing with butter.

"Can I help?" Jeannie offered. Her stomach turned over, trying to remember the last time it had been fed.

Ramie nodded to the salad bowl. Jeannie set to work, more comfortable in Renee's kitchen with her husband and daughter than she'd ever been in her and Max's home. If Jeannie couldn't marry her dad, she guessed Ramie would be a close second.

"Aunt Jeannie, are you okay?" Cloie asked cautiously.

"Sure," Jeannie answered, knowing she was clearing the way for other questions of a more inquisitive nature. Jeannie knew her niece was bursting to quiz her about the "murder mess." And Cloie had probably been warned to not broach the subject.

"Great job!" Ramie praised her salad fixings.

"Thank you, kind sir." Jeannie moved to the side bar for a towel. Her hand brushed a polished piece of wood lying on the kitchen shelf. It looked familiar. She pulled it toward her and was surprised to find her guitar she'd loaned Cloie. Jeannie smiled as she ran her fingertips over the strings.

Cloie cleared her throat when Ramie stepped into the dining room. Then she began whispering a fast inquisition, "Mom told Dad the policeman who came to arrest you was Annie's dad. You know Annie, the girl who plays with the Rockets at the Courts."

"Cloie, he didn't come to arrest me—" Jeannie began. Her fingertips moved over the strings of the guitar, picking out a melody.

"Whatever. You know the guy with the shaved head who yells at his daughter—" Annie broke off as Ramie came back into the room.

"Cloie! I thought we decided not to quiz Aunt Jeannie about her—" he turned to smile at Jeannie" —her adventures." Ramie tilted his head to a listening angle. "You strum a pretty good rendition of Garth Brooks' 'Low Places.'"

"Thanks. I used to play a lot in my other lifetime." Jeannie smiled a woeful smile. "And I don't mind Cloie's questions. She's just curious."

"Sure, Dad. I was just wondering about Annie's dad. I can't believe he'd think my Aunt Jeannie—" Cloie stammered to a stop as Ramie leveled a stern look at her.

"Honey, if Annie's dad was the cop who came to question Jeannie, you've got to understand that's his job. It has nothing to do with his family. He probably didn't even realize Jeannie was your aunt. Her last name is different—"

Ramie was cut off by Cloie's protest. "He knew when he saw my mom that Jeannie was my aunt," Cloie said.

Jeannie did a dramatic strum, strum, strum on the guitar. "It's okay, Cloie. Your dad is right. Officer Leblanc was only doing his job." Jeannie glanced at Ramie. "Thanks for your support, Ramie." Jeannie picked up the salad bowl and started to the dining room. She turned and winked at her niece. "We'll talk later."

After Serle and Marie were on their way back to Bull Creek and Renee and Ramie had retired, Cloie and Jeannie snuggled into Cloie's twin beds and turned out the lights.

"Thanks for sharing your room, Cloie. I know I'll be asleep before my head hits the pillow," Jeannie said.

Cloie had other ideas. She snapped the lamp back on and crawled under the covers with Jeannie. Quickly, Cloie unfolded a newspaper that Jeannie recognized as the *College Review*. Cloie creased it so the professor and Jeannie were front and center. "Okay, let's hear about this guy. He looks dope, but with you on top of him it's hard to tell."

"Cloie!" Jeannie protested.

For what seemed like the millionth time that day, Jeannie tried to explain the photo Max took of Professor Brent Sherman and her.

"Max was there! He took this picture of you and this professor?" Cloie's incredulous expression told Jeannie Max was still Cloie's hero.

Jeannie reiterated the tale of her trek into the woods. By the time she finished with Sherman's offer of big bucks to manage a fireworks tent for him, Cloie was ready to be her assistant in the fireworks business.

"So this Sherman is just your teacher and your boss? Nothing else?" Cloie cut to the chase.

Jeannie raised her hand in a gesture of denial. "Swear to God!" She said. The little voice in her head finished–*At least not yet!* "Now, you get back in your bed and turn off the light so we can get some sleep."

Jeannie was just drifting off to sleep when Cloie said, "What did you decide to do for the talent show? I can't wait to see you in those black rhinestone-studded jeans, bustier, and the black leather vest, not to mention your new boots. Hey, do you think I can borrow that outfit sometime?"

Jeannie blinked against the glare of the lamp as she switched it back on.

"My gosh! Sherman told me earlier Roe and the girls decided to do the show at Jeers—get this—if I did it. I hate it when people put me on the spot! It makes me look like the bad guy in Lit class," Jeannie said.

"What do you mean the bad guy?" Cloie asked. She was propped back up on her pillow again looking at Jeannie with renewed interest. "Why the bad guy, Aunt Jeannie?"

Jeannie explained about Bo and the other students who needed a boost for their almost-passing grades. She explained how Sherman offered credit to the students who attended the show.

"Gee! I wish we had teachers like that. I wonder if I tell my teacher my aunt is going to do a striptease at Jeers, if she'd give us extra credit when I go to see it?" Cloie wondered aloud.

"Cloie! I'm not going to do a striptease. In the first place, that's Roe's talent and she'd have my G-string if I even acted like I was going to strip," Jeannie protested.

Cloie rolled on her bed convulsed with laughter.

"What?" Jeannie asked.

"I'm imagining you with a G-string." She broke into laugher again. The image broke Jeannie up, too.

"Hey, in there! You two get to sleep. Some of us have to go to work tomorrow," Ramie shouted from their bedroom down the hall.

"So what are you going to do for a talent, Aunt Jeannie?" Cloie persisted.

"Nothing. There's no way I can get a talent ready for Saturday night." Jeannie was so tired her words slurred.

"Why not, Aunt Jeannie? It's only Thursday. Well, technically, Thursday is over, so I guess it's Friday," Cloie said matter of factly.

"Friday! Where did this week go? What could I possibly put together for a talent in a day?" Jeannie wondered aloud.

"Don't worry about it. We'll think of something," Cloie assured her. Switching moods, Cloie suddenly let out a squeal. "I still can't believe Annie's dad was the policeman who came to arrest you. She didn't even know about it yet when I called her. She's staying over tomorrow night. Maybe she'll know something."

Jeannie burrowed her head deeper into her pillow. For the first time that day, she was completely relaxed. Jeannie felt safe, loved, and confident that tomorrow held affirmative answers for that murder mess.

Her little voice whispered, *I hope you feel that confident about tomorrow's assignment in English Lit. Jeannie, Jeannie, if you'd just reassess your talents and exert yourself to higher limits.* The words sounded a lot like the advice her mom had given her before she entered her first (and only) beauty contest.

Jeannie closed her eyes and tried to shut off her mind. But thinking of English Lit brought to mind Professor Brent Sherman, original poetry, and a nagging panic of being on stage at Jeers, with about as much talent as she'd displayed in the Miss Bull Creek Pageant.

As her eyelids grew heavier and heavier, Jeannie was lulled to sleep by the music of a guitar.

In her dreams, Garth Brooks sat on a tall stool with his hat tipped down over his face as he strummed his guitar and sang a strange rendition of "Low Places."

Blame it all on true loves.

Handle them with kid gloves.

A one-night stand or a long-term affair.

He'll be the first one to go.

You'll be the last one to know

you two, are no longer a pair.

So don't be surprised

if he has roving eyes

After he's drunk too much champagne.

And when he starts telling you

"It's just a stage I'm going through"

You can bet he's mixed up with some dame.

And she'll have curves in all the

Right places.

She'll be an easy score when she freebases

She's fine stuff and chases

his blues away.

Then, he'll be okay.

Cause he's a womanizer without social graces.

He's an easy mark for pretty faces.

Oh, I lost him to low-ho places."

Then, Garth raised his head and winked at Jeannie.

Chapter 34

A group of coeds huddled outside Professor Sherman's Literature classroom door. Their conversation became more animated as Jeannie maneuvered her way toward Lit class.

"Lookit! There's Max Jonson's ex. The gal in the *College Review* picture," a female voice trilled.

"You mean the one jumping Prof Sherman's bones?" a male voice chimed in, causing an eruption of laughter.

Jeannie hastened her pace and hugged her books tighter to her chest. She had always wondered what it felt like to be famous.

"I guess infamous would be a close second, " she said under her breath.

As Jeannie pulled abreast of the group, it parted and she found herself face-to-face with her worst nightmare—Roe, Gussie, and Cyra.

"There she is, in person, why not ask her?" Cyra said.

Always the spokesperson, Roe plunged right in. "Word's going 'round you're mixed up with the coed murder." She leaned toward Jeannie as though expecting a full confession.

"Good day to you, too, Roe," Jeannie said, "and here I was thinking you were going to ask me about being a contestant in the Jeers talent contest."

Cyra's smile widened. "I told you Jeannie wouldn't let a little thing like being a suspect in a murder get in her way of helping Bo and the jocks." Cyra opened the Lit door and shouted, "Jeannie's here and she's an affirmative on Jeers!"

The sound of feet shuffling and a roar of approval almost swept Jeannie off her feet. "I didn't...I won't...I wasn't..." Jeannie protested as she was pushed forward by the mob of students into the theater.

A sea of faces stared up at Jeannie. Mouths formed words lost in the classroom noise. Hands reached to pluck at her. Jeannie's books were torn from her grasp. Her notebook fell, with sheets of paper drifting in disarray.

"Silence!" Professor Sherman's voice thundered from the dais. "I demand silence!"

The Lit room became deadly silent.

"Brent," Jeannie whispered. She looked toward the podium.

Their gazes locked. Jeannie was back in the forest observing this man watch a deer and her fawn as they leapt gracefully across a field, fleeing from danger. She remembered the tenderness in his voice as he spoke of the two of them, mother and child. God help her, Jeannie wanted Brent to speak to her in those same tones.

"Is there something I can do for you?" Sherman's voice held a semblance of lost tenderness.

Jeannie searched for an answer to his question. She could find none that she could say aloud in a classroom.

"Yes, you can introduce me." The voice was soft but determined. It came from directly behind Jeannie.

Jeannie turned awkwardly, almost losing her balance on the stairs. Thank God, she hadn't opened her mouth! He was speaking to the petite blonde who'd performed a striptease at Jeers Monday night.

"Steady!" The voice came from directly below Jeannie. An arm reached to balance her. Looking over her shoulder she saw her seat mate, Bo Hankins.

"Excuse us, Ms. Sherman," Bo addressed the woman behind Jeannie. "I think the professor wants us to be seated." Bo took command of the situation as surely as if he were on the football field running an offense.

"Professor Sherman's ex-wife?" Jeannie whispered.

A wide grin flashed across Bo's face as he guided Jeannie to her seat. "You got that right, Jeannie."

"Brent, I asked you–" Lynn Copper Sherman began.

"Lynn, I don't think this is the place. We'll discuss this later," Sherman began.

"You asked me to bring your keys to you, Brent, darling. I made a special trip to the campus to do as you requested. The least you can do is introduce me to the notorious Mrs. Jonson." Venom seeped from the honey-coated voice of Lynn Sherman.

Jeannie's heart did a flip-flop. Brent Sherman might be divorced, but he was definitely not unattached. Bummer! Jeannie turned to face the petite, stylishly-dressed young lady standing on the top stair by the door, staring in her direction. This was decidedly a different Lynn Copper Sherman than the one Jeannie had seen at Jeers Monday night. At least she still had her clothes on.

"Ms. Sherman." Without hesitation, Jeannie rose from her seat and retraced her steps. She stood, actually towered over, Lynn Sherman. Jeannie extended a hand and said, "I'm glad to meet you, Ms. Sherman."

Brent must have vaulted up the stairs because his voice came from directly behind Jeannie. "Lynn, Jeannie. Let's move into the hall." He pushed Jeannie and Lynn forward through the door, with Jeannie still holding onto Lynn's petite fingers.

Babbling like an idiot, Jeannie tried to reassure Lynn Sherman that she had no interest in her husband, ex-husband, whatever. "So, you're divorced? I'm divorced, too, you know."

"Really?" Lynn asked, smugly. "From whom?"

"Max Jonson. He's the owner of Maximum Exposure. He does a lot of business on campus and around town. Perhaps you've heard of him?" Of course, she'd heard of him. She'd probably paid him money for indiscreet pictures. Jeannie rattled on as Brent ushered their party of three into an empty classroom across the hall.

Inside the classroom, Lynn stopped abruptly and turned to ask Brent an obvious question. "Isn't that the same name that was on the picture of you and Mrs. Jonson in the *College Review*?"

Without letting Sherman answer, Jeannie continued, "Yes, that's my Max. He's famous for action photos."

"Yes, I know." Lynn flushed.

Jeannie wondered if Max had already closed a deal with Ms. Sherman for the pictures he took of her stripping at Jeers Monday night. For God's sake, had she carried negatives of those pictures in her console? What a farce.

Lynn sneered, "And does Max follow you around flashing pictures of every man you have a little action with?"

"No, just Brent." Jeannie paused to glance at Brent, who had his eyes half closed and was shaking his head as though she had utterly failed the question.

"What?" Jeannie demanded, glowering at Brent.

"What indeed!" Lynn flashed Brent a look that was half amused, half anger.

"Ladies!" Brent silenced them with one word. "I suggest you both sit down and try to regain a little of your dignity."

"Assuming Mrs. Jonson knows the meaning of the word." Lynn sat primly on the edge of a chair. She crossed her shapely legs and smiled up at them.

Jeannie had no idea where this conversation was headed. But she knew where she was headed—back to class. "I'm sorry, Mr. and Ms. Sherman. I feel I've overstayed my welcome. If you'll forgive me, I'll be getting back to Lit class. If I've done anything to offend either of you, I'm terribly sorry." Jeannie turned and started for the door.

"Hmph!" Lynn grunted ungraciously.

"Wait—" Brent began.

"Just leave her alone, Brent," Lynn said. "After all she's just a—"

Jeannie felt rather than saw Brent turn on Lynn. "She's a little more than a student to me, Lynn. I expect that is what you were going to say?"

"And just what does that remark mean?" Lynn demanded.

Jeannie turned the doorknob, not daring to breathe. What was she to him?

"Mrs. Jonson is a brilliant English student, a lovely young lady, and is also my employee for the summer," he announced with a flourish.

Jeannie turned around to look at her teacher, not wanting to read more into his words than he meant. "Thank you for the compliment, Professor Sherman. I look forward to doing a good job for you in the fireworks tent this summer." Then she turned back and walked out the door.

"I just bet you do!" Lynn said to Jeannie's retreating figure.

"Lynn, I warned you—" Sherman said.

Jeannie heard a noise that sounded like a chair overturning. She whirled around and saw a chair on the floor. Sherman was holding Lynn in an awkward embrace. His back was toward Jeannie. Lynn's head seemed cradled in the nook of his arm. Lynn's lips curved into an evil smile as her gaze locked with Jeannie's.

"Thanks, love," Lynn gushed, clinging to Brent.

"Lynn, 'love' is not a word lightly spoken. Your intoxicated condition is unacceptable and is what caused my love for you to die. You're in no shape to be on campus."

The rest of his words were lost to Jeannie as she crossed the hall and entered the Lit room to a different kind of hell—a recitation of limericks.

Cyra stood behind Professor Sherman's podium reading Jeannie's work. Everyone was so engrossed in Cyra's recitation they failed to notice Jeannie come into the room.

"There was a math major named Roe

Who figured to win best of show.

Her costume was slim, and

when she raised the hem

It allowed her assets to show."

Cheers and hoots resounded as students stomped their feet.

Roe stood at her seat and raised her voice above the din. "Listen!" she yelled. "If you liked that one, you're sure to like Ms. Jonson's rendition of 'Gussie.'

"There was a Tri-Sig named Guss-ie.

Whose gifted voice could reach high C

She imagined the judges bare

Or in their underwear

And performed her talent perfectly."

"Oh, yeah! She's got Gussie down. What else was in Jeannie's notes that you guys picked up? This is better than any old Shakespeare stuff," one of Bo's friends yelled.

Gussie took her place on the dais and began,

"Our Lit professor, Dr. Sherman, I declare,
Tumbled his prize student, Jeannie, on the stair.
He obviously didn't know
That Bo would let go.
So, he gave her a job as they lay tangled there."
Oh, my God! That was the line Jeannie never got around to changing. And the whole class would think—what would they think? It didn't matter, they would never know Jeannie had heard them if she just slipped out the door. Jeannie turned, and bumped into Professor Sherman.

"Jeannie," Brent said, catching her arms to help them regain their balance.

Jeannie saw him through a film of tears that suddenly filled her eyes. As Jeannie looked up at Brent, thinking nothing else could possibly be worse than this, a male voice began to read:

"There was a divorcee named Jen
Who'd like to find true love, again.
But no one would choose her
Was she really a loser?
Or did she just pick the wrong men?"

"No!" Jeannie yelped.

Brent released her abruptly. Jeannie stepped back, realizing the whole class had turned to see her and Professor Sherman in what appeared to be an embrace.

"What else can happen to me?" Jeannie asked.

Brent's face seemed to register her thoughts.

This had to be the worst! Jeannie pushed past Brent, determined to flee this hell, only to find Lynn Sherman standing behind her husband, ex-husband, whatever.

"Da Dum!" Jeannie said.

Lynn glared at Jeannie, misunderstanding her words. And Jeannie felt she knew the true meaning of the phrase, "Hell hath no fury to a woman scorned."

Jeannie looked at Brent, who shrugged, and was for once wordless.

The words popped into Jeannie's mouth and out before she realized she was speaking.

"By eavesdropping of my ears
Something wicked did appear
wickeder than serpent's tongue
crawling upward to seek the light.
Who doth draw nigh?"

It was like Jeannie had pushed a button and Professor Sherman was back in his teaching role again. He grabbed Jeannie's arm and Lynn's arm and directed them down the stairs to the dais, talking all the way. "The verse Jeannie just recited is from the first half of Shakespeare's *Macbeth,* Act Four, Scene One, containing the classic witches', 'Double, double toil and trouble.' The incantation up to the timeless, 'By the pricking of my thumbs, Something wicked this way comes' is portent."

Lynn and Jeannie stood dumbfounded as Sherman turned what might have been a catastrophe into a lesson. "With the help of my former wife, Lynn, and your classmate Jeannie, we've brought to life a scene from Shakespeare. Can anyone tell me what happens when this scene opens?"

The class sat with mouths wide open, gaping at the stage, trying to comprehend what had just happened.

When no one volunteered an answer to his question, Jeannie raised her hand.

A smile crossed Professor Sherman's face at the absurdity of the situation. He acknowledged Jeannie. "Why am I not surprised, Mrs. Jonson?"

"The scene opens in a cavern with a bubbling cauldron. There is a mighty clap of thunder, then the three witch sisters enter..." Jeannie began.

As Jeannie continued to recite, she realized Lynn had slipped from the stage and was making an exit up the stairs and out the door to the hallway. As the words kept flowing from Jeannie's mouth, she glanced at Sherman and saw his gaze had followed Lynn, too.

"Ta, ta, parting is such sweet sorrow. I hope you come up with something better than those awful limericks for the talent show," Lynn yelled and slammed the door.

Jeannie flushed but didn't miss a beat. She continued to the end of her explanation. When she finished, Sherman began to clap. He nodded to his students and they began to clap. Everyone rose and gave Jeannie a standing ovation. Tears streamed down Jeannie's face, unashamed. And then, Jeannie too, left the stage and moved to take her seat beside Bo.

"Way to go, Jeannie! You're my hero," Bo said.

Class resumed. Jeannie relaxed, and was enjoying the class after order was restored until she realized Sherman's words were directed to her. "What is your opinion, Mrs. Jonson?"

Bo nudged Jeannie when she didn't reply.

"Huh?" Jeannie grunted.

"I was just commenting on the way you handled the material on stage which was from the written assignment for today. Your knowledge of literature is excellent, but your doggerel poetry leaves much to be desired. I was disappointed that you didn't respond with a rebuttal, as usual. Were you daydreaming?"

Laughter rippled around the room as the students recalled Jeannie's limericks.

"That doggerel poetry was never meant to be heard in this classroom," Jeannie protested. "Much less criticized by you and your ex-wife."

The professor blushed but smiled a superior smile that seem to belittle Jeannie's words.

He was testing her knowledge of words again. Jeannie rushed to reassure the professor she knew fully well what his remark meant. "Surely, you can't mean my poetry was crudely written. Do you consider humor with comic qualities irregular? I'm sure there are those of us who enjoy something other than blank verse, didactic, epics, or free verse."

A low hum began in the back of the classroom and whispers grew in volume as students conversed among themselves.

Normally, Sherman would have demanded silence, but he just stood there with an arrogant smile as he studied Jeannie like a lesser rodent under a microscope.

What did he think she was, a doormat for anyone and everyone to walk on? Well, maybe she had been, but no more! Jeannie blasted Professor Brent Sherman with both barrels. "You take the freedom of words and bind them up with rules. Are rules made to be broken or is that hyperbole? As for daydreaming, there will be time for that in the summer that awaits. Then we can store up joys that can fuel our imagination when we must return to the boredom of courses, where fantasizing is the only diversion that can get one through some classes."

A patter of clapping hands became resounding applause as the class stood as a group and turned toward Jeannie. What had she done? Surely, they would all fail and have to repeat this punishment next year.

But Sherman bowed to the majority. "I'm sorry, Mrs. Jonson. Your jingles and humorous rhymes are surely a source of enjoyment to some."

"Evidently not to you and your ex." Jeannie knew she shouldn't pursue this, yet the words flowed unbidden. "Who is she to judge what I, or any of us, do for the talent show?" Lynn's parting words still stung even more than Brent's.

"That's true, Mrs. Jonson. Lynn and I shouldn't sit ourselves up as a judge for all people." He paused. "But Lynn has a vested interest in the talent show. Her father is funding the prize money. And Roscoe Rayl asked her to help with it."

A collective groan sounded from the class as Jeannie slumped in her seat.

"One last comment before you're dismissed. Mrs. Jonson, you should write like you speak. You just spoke a poem into existence. Don't you think so, Bo? You seem to be a champion of Mrs. Jonson."

Bo rose to the occasion. "I need the credit for this class, Mr. Sherman. But frankly, it bores the pants off me. And if imagination is what it takes to get some of us through this course, the naked truth may be our redemption."

Roe and her sorority sisters stared at Bo in wonder. Did they think Jeannie was the only one who overheard their conversations? Had Bo imagined the professor in his underwear, too?

"Bo, I pride myself on the fact that you just expressed yourself in a very poetic way. I hope I can claim some of the credit for your remarks," Sherman gushed.

"Believe me, and I think I speak for the whole class, " Bo paused to stare meaningfully at Roe's group, "you have revealed more than the bare facts to us this year."

"Bravo!" Sherman continued to lay out the lesson plan. "For those of you who plan on appearing in the talent show at Jeers, there will be no assignment. For those attending, you know the drill. Otherwise, study for finals. Class, you're dismissed."

As the class headed up the stairs for the hallway door, Jeannie felt a hand slide under her arm. Jeannie turned to see Roe smiling at her. "Jeannie, we've decided to be your friends."

Jeannie shook her head slowly.

Cyra nudged Roe aside. "What Roe means is—in Bo's words—you're our hero. We want to be your friend." She sashayed a few steps back and said in a loud voice, "Did you see how she put that uptight ex-wife beatch in her place? She did; I say, she did!"

The next thing Jeannie knew she was in the middle of the Tri-Sigs being propelled toward the hallway door.

Roe leaned in to whisper, "Want to join us for talent rehearsal at Jeers tonight?"

"I haven't—" Jeannie began.

"Hell's bells, we loved your horsing around poetry. You can help us with our talents, girl! You come on over," Cyra said.

"I don't know what to say," Jeannie said.

"Just say what you always say," Cyra said. Then all together, they sang, "Da-dum!"

"I didn't know anyone was listening."

"We didn't know anyone was listening to our discussion about Professor Sherman, either," Roe said.

"It appears everyone was listening to everyone else, except whom we were supposed to be listening to," Jeannie said.

"And, that would be—?" Cyra said.

"Professor Sherman, of course," Jeannie said.

"Well, look at the man! He don't know he hasn't been listened to. I actually believe he thinks he's taught us something." Cyra stared at the dais where Sherman was still beaming.

Students from Sherman's Literature class rushed through the door to get to the hall before exploding with laughter. They passed around words like "imagination," "underwear," "nude,". coupled with "Bare Brent" and "Sexy Sherman" and "Pants-off Professor," making literary doggerel of them all.

Jeannie was thoroughly enjoying herself for the first time in a long time. She felt young, a part of the college crowd. She sensed she'd bridged a gap between herself, their Lit Professor, and her classmates.

Abruptly, their laughter died. The group became individuals again, as they stared at Officer Leland Leblanc and Officer Clint Anderson standing in the hallway outside the Lit room. "Watch it," Leblanc ordered as they entered Sherman's classroom.

A custodian stood on a ladder, snipping the rope holding the banner that read, "Vote for Rita, No One Sweeter." The banner slipped and fell to the hallway floor, just outside the Literature classroom.

"Fold it up and let's get moving," a second custodian urged.

Evidence of Rita Gibson's candidacy for Hale University Queen disappeared as quickly as the candidate herself.

Maximum Exposure's flashbulb was on the scene to record the fact that life was a harsh reality. Realization came as easily as a banner falling from its place in the hallway.

Chapter 35

"See you at Jeers around sevenish?" Roe asked. "Just wear hangout clothes."

"Bleep–bleep." Jeannie's cell phone battery was low. She plugged it in to the outlet in her bedroom, hoping to charge the battery before leaving for Jeers.

What was Roe's idea of hangout clothes?

From her Max days, Jeannie knew what he called hangout clothes: boobs overflowing skimpy tops and short-shorts blending thighs with buttocks. Or hip huggers showing pierced navels.

Tri-Sig's casual dress was probably designer jeans and logo tees.

Thirty minutes later, Jeannie's complete wardrobe lay on her still-messy bed, resembling a drop-off package for the Salvation Army. She shimmied into a faded pair of jeans with ragged holes in the knees. Cloie loved these jeans. Jeannie's mom threatened to mend them. Lying face up in the middle of the pile of clothes, Jeannie sucked in and gradually pulled up the jeans' zipper. She eased to a standing position and pranced around, distributing her assets in a hangout mode. Satisfied that she could breathe, she grabbed a tank top and pulled it over her head and almost down to her jean tops where a roll of skin plumped up.

Jeannie shuddered, wrestling on an oversized fishnet shirt to cover her "hangout." She surveyed herself in the mirror, shrugged, and picked up the guitar she brought home from Cloie's house. She grabbed an old, black cowboy hat she and Max bought at the state fair. She pulled it low on her head and glanced in the mirror again. Poking her stiffened index finger under the brim, Jeannie pushed the hat up and drawled, "Howdy, Partner! Let's go do some horsing-around lyrics in 'Low Places.'"

Inspired, Jeannie scooted a tall kitchen stool in front of the mirror and plopped herself on top of it. She leaned her head low over the guitar like Garth and strummed a few notes of "Low Places."

"Blame it all on true loves,

Handle them with kid gloves,

For a one night stand or a long time affair…"

The words were the same ones in her dreams the other night. How did the rest of the strange rendition of that song go?

Jeannie Day Jonson, you're cruising for a bruising, she told herself. Nodding, she slung the strap of the guitar over her shoulder.

Her cell phone rang just as she was heading for the front door of her apartment. Thank God for the reminder. The dang thing was still plugged into the charger. She unplugged her cell phone and took it with her. She'd plug it into her car charger.

Without glancing at the caller ID, Jeannie said, "Hullo?"

"Jeannie Jonson?" a male voice asked.

Opening the back door of the Explorer, she deposited the guitar. Sliding into the driver seat of the Explorer, Jeannie glanced at her caller ID only to see "Unknown Caller."

"Who's calling, please?"

"This is Roscoe Rayl, the bartender at Jeers. I'm also in charge of the talent show Saturday evening."

"Sure, you and Lynn Copper Sherman," Jeannie mumbled.

"Excuse me?" Rayl asked.

"Nothing. What do you want?" Jeannie asked.

"I received a list from Ms. Sherman. She indicates they plan to compete in our talent show Saturday night. Your name is on the list as one of the contestants, but it doesn't say what talent you'll be performing. Would you mind filling me in?"

"How did you get my cell phone number?" Jeannie asked, perturbed that Lynn had anything to do with her entry.

"All the names have complete information," Roscoe said.

"And just what does that mean?" Jeannie asked.

"Hey, I didn't call to play twenty questions, Ms. Jonson. I'm just trying to get the program filled out. Are you or are you not going to be in the talent show? And if so, what talent will you be doing?

Pretty simple question for a college coed, I'd say." Roscoe's voice had a sarcastic bite to it that set Jeannie on edge.

"Sorry, Mr. Rayl. Me and a bunch of the girls are coming over to your place this evening. We're going to get organized on our talent. Is it okay if I tell you then?"

"Why don't you just give me a hint. I'll write it in and you and I can talk about it later."

Jeannie sighed. "Just put down 'Low Places.'"

"You doing a solo?"

"Sure, so low no one can hear, I hope," Jeannie said under her breath. "You asked for something to put down. I gave it to you. We'll figure out the rest when we get there."

"Sure, how many coeds are coming?"

"Umm, I'm not sure, probably several."

"Your name sounds familiar, Ms. Jonson. Do you come to Jeers often?"

"Not recently. I used to come in with my ex, Max Jonson." Maybe mentioning Max would shut him up.

Rayl was silent for a moment as though he was digesting this information.

"I think I saw you Monday evening, Ms. Jonson. Have you ever been in one of our contests before?"

"No."

"Talkative little thing, aren't you? I think you and I have a mutual friend that we should discuss. Can we meet later?"

"Probably not. Goodbye." Jeannie closed her cell phone, irritated that a perfect stranger would have access to her cell phone number. "Mutual friend? I doubt that."

The little voice in Jeannie's head reminded her, *He's probably not perfect, Jeannie. The men in your life seldom are. He's just trying to do his job. And be honest: you're just mad because you're ill prepared for this talent show. And that Lynn is involved with it.*

Jeannie headed for the north side of town. She hit Kearney Street. Turning right, she started toward the 65 bypass.

Jeannie's cell phone jingled Max's ring.

"Hullo?"

"You're moving with a fast crowd, Bull Creek!" Max said.

"What?"

"College professor, Tri-Sigs, murdered coeds, and who knows who else at Jeers?" Max's voice was filled with trepidation.

"Talk about the pot calling the kettle black!" Jeannie hissed.

Max uttered a string of unrepeatables.

"Watch your language! What's your problem?"

"Check out your rearview mirror and you'll see the idiot that almost sideswiped me pulling in behind you."

Jeannie did a quick check of the mirror and saw a maroon BMW. "She's cutting it awfully close," Jeannie breathed into the phone as she sped up to keep from getting clipped.

"Now you've done it!" Max jibed. "Nobody pisses Lynn off and gets away clean."

"Not Lynn Copper Sherman?" Jeannie asked.

"None other. You know her?"

"Uh huh, I had the pleasure of meeting her earlier today."

The BMW was hugging Jeannie's rear bumper like newlyweds on their wedding night. In her side mirror, Jeannie could see Maximum Exposure hot on Lynn's tail. Both lanes were crowded with vehicles. A block ahead was a traffic light already changing from green to yellow. A semi was easing to a stop ahead of the Jeep Cherokee in the lane directly in front of Jeannie. The left lane was filled with sport cars racing through the traffic light ahead like it didn't exist.

'Uh oh!" Max's voice crackled over the cell phone Jeannie still clutched in her right hand. "Watch your driver's side. Lynn's out and around."

At the sound of Max's voice, Jeannie's gaze moved to the rearview mirror. She was surprised to find Max's van directly behind her. The sharp staccato of a car horn was accompanied by the squeal of tires on Jeannie's left. A cacophony of blaring horns trumpeting protest caused Jeannie to glance out her window about the time the BMW pulled further into the left lane. It edged into the center turn lane to pass a car on the wrong side. The BMW veered back right into the left lane just in time to scoot through the red light. The last thing Jeannie saw was personalized plates reading L-COPP-S.

"Man, she's high on something tonight!" Max breathed into the phone.

"Who in the hell does she think she is?" Jeannie braked about an inch from the rear bumper of the Jeep Cherokee. She acknowledged the bird the driver flipped her with one of her own.

"Lynn doesn't think–she knows—who she is. She's the sole heir to the Copper millions," Max said.

"Yeah, yeah!" Jeannie muttered. "It must be nice to have a million-dollar-daddy to pay your way."

The light changed and traffic inched forward.

"What do you mean, 'yeah, yeah'? It's the truth."

"I've heard this story before. So what does Miss Society do besides spend her inheritance on drugs. And strip in bars?" Jeannie asked, peering ahead at a flashing sign that proclaimed Jeers on the opposite side of the four-lane.

"You're a good one to talk about Monday night. I saw you turn your blinkers on for Tyler Vaughan, who jumped Rita's bones."

Jeannie's face flushed as red as the blinker light she pushed down to signal her turn into the center-turn lane by Jeers. Jeannie wondered what happened to Tyler Vaughan or "the blond hunk" as she chose to think of him after Rita ditched him to follow her.

"Bleep–bleep." Jeannie's cell phone battery was complaining again. Max pulled into the lane behind Jeannie. "You still there, Bull Creek?"

"Yeah, but my phone battery is low. I was thinking about the blond hunk, Tyler Vaughan. Wonder what happened to him after Rita walked me out to my truck."

"Rita walked you to your truck? When did you and Rita Gibson get so chummy? I missed that, I guess," Max said.

"You saw Vaughan hit on her and pass me up. But you didn't see Rita follow me out of Jeers when she saw I was upset?"

"Yeah, it was pretty hard to miss watching you make a play for Jeer's Bogus Boss." He chuckled.

"What do you mean Bogus Boss? You mean he owns Jeers?" Jeannie asked.

"Let's say it's a family venture. Bad boy Tyler is doing community service in Missouri while his big sister Tresa runs the family trucking business in Oklahoma. Word's out he's got a dirty finger in both pies. And Tyler's got the hots for chicks. But, hon, you were laying yourself open for a world of hurt trying to compete with a beauty queen. Even though there was more to Rita Gibson than her obvious assets."

A stab of pain wiped out everything but Max's evaluation of her and Rita. The painful sensation cut deep, letting Jeannie know Max could still hurt her. "And I'm just a little old country girl who doesn't have a clue how to land a stud like Tyler Vaughan?"

"Now, I wouldn't go that far, hon. You landed me, didn't you?" Max said in that cocky tone of his.

"Sure, but I threw you back about a year ago, hon. You weren't a keeper."

"Funny you keep score. It was 'bout a year ago when Lynn threw back that phony professor of yours. I guess he wasn't a keeper, either. You and him should hook up, Jen. You've both got a lot to learn."

She was silent a moment, waiting for traffic to slow so she could cross to Jeers. "Funny you know so much about Ms. Copper Sherman." Jeannie blinked back a blur of tears as she maneuvered the Explorer next to a Hummer. She gulped. "You didn't, you haven't, er, you weren't involved with—"

"Jeannie, Jeannie, I'm surprised at you. I may be a lot of things but kiss-and-tell isn't my style. Watch your step, hon. Don't get in over your head." Max hesitated. "And hon?"

"Yes?" She hadn't heard this urgency in Max's voice for a long time. Breathlessly, she waited.

"You still got the Davago pictures?"

"Yes."

"Take another look at them. I developed that roll of film on the run and stuffed envelopes in a hurry. I remember something else in the background of one of the films. I can't put my finger on it. You may have the last copy of that picture," Max said.

Jeannie had run the business end of Maximum Exposure long enough to know that couldn't be true. "Don't kid me, Max. We always had three sets of each film. You kept a numbering system."

"Good girl, you remember. But I may have slipped up on this one. Too many things going on."

"Like an overnighter at the Tri-Sig house?" Jeannie taunted.

Max's tone held a hint of laughter. "Yeah, that, too. Anyway, I seem to remember two people near the back of a vehicle embracing. Put on your glasses and see if Tyler Vaughan is one of the pair. I might still get some mileage out of that film." Max finished the conversation with a resounding click of his cell phone.

Maximum Exposure was Max's ticket into the most illustrious families in the area. Those mommies and daddies loved how he captured their families on film for posterity.

On the other hand, the same families had come to depend on Max to capture their little darlings' indiscretions on film also. And to hide those indiscretions for a price. Max was more than willing to accommodate. After all, business was business.

Jeannie tried to remember the vehicle in the background of the pictures. What was Max mixed up with now? If she had the pictures Max had given to Mic Davago, where were the other two sets of film?

Jeannie sorted out the information Max told her about Brent,-her professor…her fantasy lover.

What about Brent's ex-wife who was heir to the Copper fortune, Lynn's drug habit, her and Brent's relationship?

Rita Gibson: what had Max said about her? Mmm. He'd said there was more than met the eye with Rita.

And why would it matter if Tyler was embracing someone in the picture? Mmm. Why, indeed? She'd like to find the answer to that.

What did Max know? She had to find out. But first she had to get this blasted talent contest over.

Bleep-bleep. Her cell phone sounded like it was on its last bleep.

"What next?" Jeannie searched her bag for her car charger to no avail. "I don't need the blasted thing anyway." Jeannie punched the off button, putting her phone out of commission. She had been so involved with her cell phone, she'd failed to notice she had parked around to the back side of Jeers near the blocked off crime tape. The Hummer, Jeannie's Explorer, and a green van were the only vehicles in that area.

Jeannie slid out of the Explorer. She grabbed the guitar, slid the strap over her shoulder and started for the front entrance of Jeers. Shivers crawled up the nape of her neck, knowing this was the sidewalk where Rita Gibson had walked Monday night before her disappearance and death. Jeannie strode purposefully toward the entrance of Jeers.

"Jeannie, Mrs. Jonson, wait up." The masculine voice calling from behind Jeannie gave her a jolt, a high like no artificial stimulant could ever do.

"Huh?" Jeannie turned to see Brent Sherman hurrying to catch up with her. A feeling of unexplained pleasure swept over her at the sight of him. The crease in the legs of his faded blue jeans elevated them from casual to dress. They were accented by the white shirt he wore open at the neck. His sleeves were rolled up to expose a masculine expanse of wiry black hair that was unexplainably arousing.

"What are you doing here?" Jeannie blurted.

Brent's lopsided grin was directed at Jeannie alone. "I couldn't let my students embark on a literary adventure alone, now, could I?" Staring into Jeannie's eyes, he finished, "I wasn't sure that was you with a guitar on your back. But somehow it fits. Dashing! Later, we need to talk about a lot of things, all right?"

Dashing? It seems to fit. His words turned her insides to jelly. *For God's sake, get a hold of yourself, Jeannie.* Her thoughts were racing but unfortunately were losing out to the throbbing emotions claiming her body. "Professor Sherman, I—"

The lock of dark hair had fallen across his forehead. He brushed it aside. "Don't you think it's about time you started calling me Brent?"

Was she dreaming? If so, Jeannie hoped she'd never wake. "Yes, Professor, er, Brent."

They fell into step. His arm brushed hers. Their fingertips touched briefly, generating static electricity.

Jeannie suppressed a shudder of excitement.

Brent smiled and whispered something. Jeannie leaned closer trying to hear his words.

"Smile, we're under Tri-Sig scrutiny." Brent casually distanced himself from her.

"Well, it's about time you got here, Jeannie." Cyra smirked, looking toward Professor Sherman. "And, you brought your–guitar? Let's get this rehearsal on the road."

Roe and Gussie stood behind Cyra. A group of guys held the door to Jeers open, and they moved inside.

Somehow, Brent claimed Jeannie's hand. He tucked it beneath his arm as they moved forward. A supercharged atmosphere of laughter, music, booze, and God knows what else, carried them through the lobby.

Roscoe presided at the long bar.

On the other side of the room was an elevated stage where one bar stool stood sublimely alone in the glare of a baby blue spot light. Tables and chairs edged the small space used for dancing.

"Oh, my God!" The thought of standing alone on that stage made Jeannie feel faint. Only her arm laced through Brent's held her upright.

Shrill laughter rose to an hysterical level. It echoed through the room, squashing the jovial atmosphere like a giant fist. Jeannie found the source of the noise at the bar: Lynn Copper Sherman.

Brent must have discovered the source about the same time. Jeannie felt his arm stiffen and his body grow tense.

"For God's sake, not now." Brent stared at the bar where a petite young woman and the blond hunk, Tyler, were chugging drinks.

Lynn's slender legs were encased in skintight jeans. A figure-hugging, sky-blue summer sweater showed off her petite body. She turned and saw the party of people. Tilting her head back, she shrilled the ungodly laughter once more. "Tyler, I do declare. Look who's slumming—Professor Sherman." She paused staring in Jeannie's direction. "And his prize student, Mrs. Jonson. And, she's sporting a *guiiii-tar*." She drawled the word "guitar," sounding like a hillbilly. "This should be some talent show."

Jeannie suppressed the desire to yell "Hee-Haw" and advance on Lynn strumming a mean rendition of the *Deliverance* theme song.

Snickers ran through the crowd of Tri-Sigs, turning to giggles and finally to uncontrollable laughter. Tears ran down their faces, smudging their mascara. Each time one girl tried to regain her composure, she'd look at a friend and begin laughing again.

The laughter was contagious. Jeannie could feel her lips curling into a smile. Laughter bubbled up in her throat. She glanced at Brent, hoping to regain control, but he was smiling, too.

Cyra sashayed toward them. Bumping into a waiter carrying a tray of drinks, Cyra's arm encircled his waist to steady herself. The waiter did an exaggerated body twirl balancing the tray on his upraised arm. Cyra moved with him in perfect synchronization. Completing the turn, they separated to a spatter of applause from couples seated at the tables.

"Wow! With moves like that you guys should enter the talent show," Jeannie said.

Cyra giggled as she caught Jeannie up in a bear hug, guitar and all. Her finger tips rested on the guitar on Jeannie's back. She plucked a string--plunk, plunk, plunk. "Why I declare, Jeannie, you did bring your guiiii-tar."

Laughter overtook everyone again.

Groups sitting at nearby tables begin to laugh. The urge to laugh circled the room. Soon Jeers was filled with laughter.

Everyone seemed to be laughing but Lynn. She turned her petite back on the rowdy group. Lynn tilted her head back and downed the last of her drink. She pounded the bar. "Fill it up, Roscoe. This is going to be one hell of a long night."

Roscoe obliged. As he handed Lynn her drink, his arm hit a stack of JeersBerry inhouse cell phones reserved for JeersBerry banter and flirting on Singles Saturday night. Jeers provided the machines for their customers interested in trying to start a relationship without having to leave their table.

JeersBerrys careened in all directions.

Seeing Roscoe's scowl, Lynn's laughter joined the rest of the Jeers' crowd. She nudged Tyler, who encouraged her change of mood by laughing along with her.

"Sons of a bitch!" Roscoe yelled, glaring at Lynn and Tyler.

"Tyler, I've got orders piling up. You think you might help out a little?" Roscoe indicated the JeersBerrys littered on the floor.

Tyler's laughter faded and was replaced by a scowl. "It's your mess."

"I didn't mean to—" Roscoe began.

Tyler barked a short laugh. "You never mean to, but—"

"Forget it! You're nothing but a—" Roscoe broke off as Tresa Vaughan rose from a table at the far end of the room and began to walk toward the bar.

Tyler swallowed the remains of his drink in one swift movement. The look he directed at Roscoe indicated he'd take care of him later. Tyler moved swiftly to intercept his sister. Roscoe left his place behind the bar and began the task of gathering up the cell-phone handouts.

Lynn grabbed a JeersBerry. "Want a little help tossing these out?"

"No! It's not singles nights." Roscoe grabbed for the JeersBerry. It meant a lot of extra work for him reprogramming the JeersBerrys each night they were used.

"Party pooper." Lynn turned toward the group of people surrounding Jeannie, Brent, and the Tri-Sigs. She yelled, "Brent! Here's you a JeersBerry. You may need it to pick up another tart. Just turn it on, dial the strumpet of your choice and hook up."

Brent looked up just in time to see the small JeersBerry sailing his way.

"Look out, Jeannie!" Roe yelled.

Jeannie glanced up to see a JeersBerry sailing in her direction. Brent eased Jeannie's arm from beneath his and nonchalantly reached out a hand to capture the machine. She followed Brent's lead and soon had a flirting machine securely in her palm. Each machine had its own in-house telephone number. The JeersBerry was reprogrammed each night it was used with a new customer number. It made it impossible to hook up with the same person on a different night. Or for any personal information to be stored on the machine. Personal security was a big plus in a nightclub like Jeers. A JeersBerry relationship only progressed if both parties agreed to meet face to face or exchanged private information on their own.

Brent fingered the small instrument. "Do people actually walk up to each other in nightclubs and introduce themselves anymore?"

Jeannie shook her head. "That's a thing of the past." She held up her JeersBerry. "Today it's bold, brash words sent from one machine to another. No face, no name, only a number."

Despite Roscoe's bitching and moaning, the Friday night crowd joined in the fun. Soon everyone was snatching up the machines reserved for Saturday evenings when singles banter was served up RIM-style.

Brent caught Jeannie's hand and pulled her toward a secluded table. They collapsed into chairs, laughing. Many singles began socializing with the JeersBerry number of their choice. Soon couples began pairing off if they liked the message texted to them. If not, they chose another number and started up another flirtation.

Jeannie disentangled herself from her guitar. "I'll get rid of this until I need it." She placed it in a nearby chair. Glancing across at the JeersBerry lying by Brent's hand, she noted the number 8 emblazoned on the machine, personalizing it for the user. Casually, she pulled her JeersBerry into her lap and let her fingers do the walking.

Brent jerked upright when the small instrument on the table jingled. Frowning, he cautiously pulled it within reading distance. Then, he glanced at Jeannie and began to laugh.

"I never doubted you were a ten."

Grinning, she held her JeersBerry up to display the number 10. The message she'd sent read, "I always wanted to be a 10. Remember when it took more than a box to prove it?"

Jeannie's JeersBerry rang the minute she laid it down. She glanced at Brent with a smile. But his JeersBerry was on the table. She looked around the room to see patrons' fingers moving rapidly moving over the keys on their phones as they texted messages.

Brent raised an eyebrow in question. "You've got another admirer?"

The word "another" blushed color to her cheeks. She activated the JeersBerry. "You look as good as you did Monday night."

Her color deepened as she turned off the screen. "Nice pick-up line."

"What?" Brent asked.

Jeannie repeated the message.

"Well, you do, you know. You going to answer it?"

"Thanks, but no thanks." Jeannie laid the JeersBerry on the seat beside her.

As much as Jeannie liked Brent's company, she felt things were moving much too fast. How strange was it to be seated in a nightclub with her English Lit professor whose ritzy ex-wife was fraternizing with the bartender? Jeannie glanced toward the bar to assure herself of the reality of the situation. She almost choked on her drink.

Brent grinned. "So, you just noticed the odd couple have paired up?" He nodded toward the bar where Lynn and Max were engrossed in conversation with Roscoe. Jeannie felt a stab of jealousy. Then she reminded herself she was part of an odd couple, too. She wondered if Max had even noticed.

The bar seemed a popular spot this night. She was surprised to see Tresa Vaughan had parted company with her brother Tyler and was chatting with a distinguished gentleman, who looked vaguely familiar.

"Are you acquainted with the redhead at the bar?" Jeannie asked.

"She's the out-of-town owner of Jeers, Tresa Vaughan. She owns a trucking company in Tulsa."

Who's the dignified dandy she's talking to?" Jeannie asked.

"Gentleman is Bill King. I met him at a political rally Richard P. hosted at Hammond Towers. He's with the Department of Public Safety. Zip and I are acquainted with him through the Fire and Safety Division."

"Tresa has strange bedfellows," Jeannie said. "Who's Zip?".

"You'll meet him soon. He's my fireworks partner," Brent said.

Jeannie was drawing a mental picture of the man who had been with Brent in the woods the day she'd thought they were actually shooting punks and burying them. She nodded and swallowed hard. Had she ever told Brent she followed them that day?

"I can't wait to meet him and get to know about fireworks," Jeannie said. Her mind raced with possibilities as she recalled more about that day. Zip had said something about "If the Marshall gets wind of this ..." And "If we shoot the big one, we'll have to put it in the ground." Jeannie knew they weren't shooting people but things—fireworks.

"Check out the two plainclothes policemen at the other end of the bar," Brent said. "Officers Leblanc and Anderson paid me another visit this afternoon."

Jeannie glanced at the two officers who were talking to Tyler. They caught her gaze. Abruptly, they looked away and continued their conversation. Jeannie wondered if continuing her regular lifestyle included bar hopping with her English Lit professor.

"Interesting," she said. "Do you think they're questioning suspects in Rita's death?"

Brent considered and shook his head, laughing. "That's Tresa Vaughan's younger brother. He considers himself quite the ladies' man.

"I noticed him Monday night with Rita Gibson," Jeannie said.

"Tresa put him in charge of Jeers. Technically, he's boss but Roscoe runs the place. Rumor has it he was in some kind of trouble in Oklahoma." From Sherman's tone, one could tell he was not impressed by the man.

"Quite a lineup at the bar." Jeannie decided to steer the conversation back to Bill King. "Jeers seems a funny place for a state official to hang out."

"I guess it does," Brent considered. "Unless he's working with the ATC."

"The ATC?" Jeannie asked.

"Division of Alcohol and Tobacco Control."

Then, it hit her: Brent was talking about Rita's murder. "You think Rita was mixed up with drugs? I find that hard to believe," Jeannie protested.

"How well did you know Rita?" Brent frowned.

"Not that well. Of course, I'd seen her around campus, but I only met her personally Monday night," Jeannie said.

"Monday night? Of course. I remember her calling after you when you ran out the door. You'd just bumped into me while I was—" His voice trailed off as he remembered the circumstances.

Jeannie studied the scene at the bar. "Does Lynn know Bill King?"

Brent's lips curled into a sardonic smile. "I doubt she'd know him as a government official. She'd probably be more interested in him as a dignified dandy."

"Touché." Jeannie grinned. Brent hadn't missed her definition earlier.

"I doubt if anyone at the bar," he paused, "with the exception of your ex-husband, might recognize King."

Jeannie frowned. "Why do you think Max would know him?"

Brent reached over to clasp both of her hands. He leaned close to whisper, "My darling girl, your Max knows everyone and everything. You should know that better than anyone."

Jeannie's JeersBerry rang. She picked it up, activated it, and read. "I need to talk to you about something."

Jeannie's fingers raced across the keys. "Who is this?"

Immediately a message appeared. "Meet me in the parking lot where you were Monday night."

Jeannie turned off the machine quickly. She looked around the room trying to gauge who was texting her.

"You all right?" Brent asked.

A loud crackling of static silenced the noisy room.

"What the—?" Brent jerked back, dropping Jeannie's hands.

They looked toward the stage. Roscoe Rayl sat casually atop the tall stool. He spoke into the microphone. "Good evening, ladies and gentlemen. And I use the terms loosely." He waited for the laughter to die down.

"I'm Roscoe Rayl, better known as the bartender. Some of you know that better than others." Again he waited as drunken toasts were tossed his way.

"I'm also the director of JETS, better known as the Jeers Evening Talent Show." Roscoe drawled. "I'm delighted to have Ms. Lynn Copper Sherman helping direct the show. Her father, Richard P. Copper, graciously supplied the prize money of five thousand dollars. So tune up your talents, guys and gals. Three of you will be pocketing big bucks tomorrow night. Prize money stacks up this way: first place walks away with three thousand dollars. Second place receives fifteen hundred dollars. And, third place gets five hundred bucks. Not bad for a night's work, right?

Brent mumbled, "Yeah, yeah, Roscoe. Get on with the show.

Phrases from her visit to the woods itched at Jeannie's mind as she watched Roscoe play to his audience. The delivery man, Roscoe had claimed, "Trucking's not my only job."

It gave Jeannie an eerie sense of unease, realizing she knew things that Brent didn't know that she knew. She grimaced at the decline of her sentence structure. Pieces of a puzzle were falling into place—like Tyler, the blond hunk, being the brother of Tresa, the owner of Jeers. If he had been in trouble before, why was she putting him in charge of a place that served liquor and overlooked the casual use of drugs?

Jeannie's mind scrambled to put these pieces in the right place, but it was impossible when she didn't know the whole of the picture.

Brent tilted his head inquisitively.

She shrugged, returning her gaze to Roscoe's performance as static from his mike drew her attention to the stage. "Those of you who plan on being contestants in the talent show Saturday evening need to meet with me in the room adjoining the stage. Don't everyone come at once. Only the winners need to hurry." He laughed along with the patrons of Jeers as everyone who considered themselves potential winners hurried toward the designated room.

Cyra broke away from her sorority sisters long enough to sprint across the room. She grabbed Jeannie's hand. "Come on, girl! You're a winner!" Dragging a reluctant Jeannie across the floor, Cyra shouted over her shoulder, "You, too, Professor Sherman! And bring the lady's guiiii-tar with you."

"Da-dum!" Brent grunted as he reached across to fetch Jeannie's guitar.

A patter of light applause sounded from the bar where Lynn had resumed her position and was encouraging her drinking buddies to join her in ridiculing her ex-husband. She nudged Max, who had turned back to the bar and was nursing his drink. "Consider this: you just missed a great shot! Picture those two in the *College Review* with a caption stating, 'Professor and student make beautiful music together.'"

Max murmured something that sounded like, "If music is the food of love, play on."

Lynn stopped clapping, "What did you say?"

Max picked up a manila envelope with Maximum Exposure's

logo, ME, embossed at the top and slapped it down on the bar in front of Lynn. "Consider this," Max said.

Lynn clasped the envelope in one hand and saw her name scrawled across the front. She reached for her glass and clicked it against his. "Honey, you've got it bad. You just quoted Macbeth."

Chapter 36

Jeers' Friday night crowd dwindled as talent show stragglers discussed strategy at a table pulled near the stage. Other talents continued to rehearse.

Jeannie surprised them all with her rendition of "Low Places."

Most of the JeersBerrys had found their way back to the area where they were recharged, renumbered, and sterilized into anonymity. Roe, Cyra, and Gussie still used their machines to text remarks back and forth.

They weren't the only ones to still have a JeersBerry.

Someone had been trying to get Jeannie's attention all evening. She frowned as her machine played text music. Jeannie glanced at the words. "It's getting late. You know something I need to know." Jeannie looked around the room at the remaining crowd. Who was messing with her?

"What? What is it, honey?" Cyra tried to pull the instrument from Jeannie's unwilling hand. "Who's trucking with you, girl?"

Jeannie shrugged and laid the machine down..

Cyra had been smoking heavily all evening and was beginning to feel the effects. As she watched the last of the contestants preview their talent, she rummaged in her Jimmy Choo bag for another joint.

Swaggering like a drunken sailor, a black man built like a linebacker belted out risqué lyrics. "Oh, I'm Popeye the sailor man. I live in a garbage can. I like to go swimmin' with bowlegged women—"

"Mm-mm, too bad I didn't bring my bikini," Cyra sighed.

"How many does that make?" Roe yawned.

"Including us, there's fourteen." Gussie glanced at the professor. "Make that fifteen if our esteemed professor joins the competition."

Brent held up a hand as if to ward off further discussion. "Count me out. You girls represent our group very nicely."

"Oh, I'm Popeye the sailor man. I live in a garbage can. I like to go swimmin' with bowlegged women..." Cyra hammed up the song as she mimicked the linebacker's swagger.

"For God's sake, Cyra. That guy is coming over this way," Roe said.

Cyra giggled. "Good! I can tell him how much I like his—talent."

Popeye towered over Cyra. "Girl, you got something to say to me? Then say it to my face."

Cyra tilted her head back. She stared up at the giant. "Funny, I always thought Popeye was a white man."

The man glared down at her. "And I thought black girls had better manners."

Cyra's mouth dropped open and her stub fell out. "Flattery will get you everywhere, Popeye."

He glanced at Cyra with a forgiving smile. "Just call me Oscar, sweet thing. I can't wait to see you perform. The way you moved with that waiter earlier. Mm–mm! You got talents I couldn't even start to mimic."

Cyra simpered, "Why Oscar, I bet you could mimic my talent better than anyone."

Cyra's stub lay smoldering near Jeannie's JeersBerry. Music sounded, signaling a new message coming through on Jeannie's machine. Words raced across the tiny screen, "Sons of a bitch! You gonna tell me what you know, or not?"

Jeannie gasped and tried to cover the screen.

But Oscar had seen it. He thundered, "Who's the son of a—who's texting filth to this lady?"

The remaining patrons of Jeers stared at Oscar and the table of sorority girls, Jeannie, and the professor. It looked like a storm was brewing.

Roscoe moved quickly to the mike. "All right, boys and girls. Fun time is over. Toss the toys in the basket on your way out with no questions asked." He looked around the room with a scowl. "Or me and my buddy," he looked over at Oscar, "will hunt you down and throw you in the basket."

Oscar moved to stand beside Roscoe. The remaining patrons who had JeersBerrys formed a line and began tossing their instruments in Roscoe's basket, all proclaiming their innocence.

When Jeannie reached the basket, Roscoe held out his hand for the JeersBerry that she had used. "Hon, I'll take care of that one. Sorry about that."

Jeannie nodded, picked up her guitar and moved to join her group.

Roscoe motioned for Jeannie to wait. "Hon, I noticed your guitar strings need a little tuning. I'd be glad to help you if you'd like to stay for a while."

Brent was close at Jeannie's heels. "Jeannie, I'll get the head of the music department to fine tune it." Brent glared at Roscoe. "We wouldn't want anyone to think you're giving special treatment to one of the contestants."

Roscoe conceded. Turning to Oscar, he said, "She does do a mean rendition of our friend Garth's 'Low Places,' doesn't she, Oscar?"

Oscar grinned broadly. "Good enough that himself might want to hear it."

Jeannie flushed. She knew Garth Brooks had just opened in Branson over the weekend. She couldn't imagine him wanting to hear anything she might do. Especially her trumped-up version of "Low Places."

Overhearing the remark, Lynn said, "'Low Places' seems the right place for rural folks." Lynn's drinking had progressed throughout the evening, but she'd handled her part of the talent show professionally. She smiled at Jeannie, "Let me tell you, those original lyrics rate right up there with the classics."

Jeannie winced at the direct hit. Once more, she wished she'd never agreed to be in this blasted talent show.

Abruptly, Roscoe strode toward the stage and picked up the mike. "Don't forget to be here early tomorrow evening. I'll have a lineup posted." He waved his clipboard above his head. "Check out your time and be ready." The clipboard slipped from his fingers and hit the floor, scattering papers filled with notes and a large manila envelope with ME embossed at the top.

Customers scrambled to pick up the debris. Roscoe waved them off. "Okay, okay, I can handle it. Move along. We'll be closing shortly." He picked up the envelope with Roscoe Rayl scrawled across the front. Lynn reached to take it from him while he rearranged his notes. She laid the envelope on a table behind her where her notes and the envelope Max had given her lay.

Brent stopped outside the front door. "I'll see you ladies to your vehicles. And I'll expect a full report of the talent show for Lit class next week."

Oscar was Cyra's shadow. They beamed like children who shared a secret. He followed her outdoors, offering his arm. She steadied herself against the bulk of him. They moved out to the parking lot.

Memories of Rita Gibson engulfed the group when they remembered this was probably where Rita Gibson was kidnapped.

Gussie shivered. "The newspaper said this was where they found Rita's car after she was murdered."

"Why did we all come in separate cars?" Roe demanded. "I told you we should have all ridden together."

"Let's make a pact. We'll all walk together to our cars. Brent and Oscar will walk with the last girl. Then, we'll all follow each other until we're on the highway," Gussie ordered.

A rich, deep, voice bellowed, "Sounds good, but this young lady isn't in any shape to drive. "In fact," he reached down and picked Cyra up like she was a feather, "she's falling down asleep."

"Put her in my car!" everyone hollered at once.

It was decided Cyra would go in Roe's car with Gussie following. They would activate the alarm on Cyra's Jeep Cherokee and leave it locked up. They could pick it up tomorrow night. Brent would follow Jeannie home. They would all see Oscar at Jeers tomorrow evening, if not before.

Jeannie pulled up in front of her apartment, secure in the knowledge that Brent was right behind her. She shut off the motor, hopped out with her guitar, and waved at Brent.

Brent shut off his motor and stepped out. "Hey, I don't usually leave a girl on the sidewalk. My mom raised me to see a lady to the door."

He laced his arm through hers. They walked slowly to the front door.

"Give me your key," Brent said. "I'll unlock your door for you."

"I can—" Jeannie began.

"Shush! Don't argue with the teacher."

She handed him her key.

As he unlocked the door, he whispered, "I can hardly wait."

Jeannie felt her heart leap into her throat. It was too soon. She wasn't ready. "What? Wait for what?"

Brent laughed. "For summer. For fireworks season when we'll be working together all the time." He tilted her chin up and looked deeply into her eyes. "What else?"

"Ditto. I mean, of course, what else?" Jeannie liked the feel of his hand under her chin. When he removed it she felt like a part of her was gone. They had talked about business during the evening. It sounded like fun. But she was glad Brent was taking it slow.

"Goodnight. Parting is such sweet sorrow." He was moving down the walk away from her.

She whispered, "Till the morrow."

She waved from the safety of her doorway until his taillights were almost out of sight. They flashed like lightning bugs in the distance, echoing "till the morrow."

As she closed the door, she noticed the glint of a light nearby. Was it the porch light across the street? Or a neighbor turning out their house lights? Or—it didn't matter she was safe at home, locked inside. She drifted around the room, discarding her guitar, her fishnet top, and other garments.

Discovering her dysfunctional phone in her purse, she plugged it into her charger and turned it on. "Bleep–bleep," the phone complained. Checking it closer, she found she had several missed calls. She didn't recognize any of the numbers. And they didn't leave a message. So, she wasn't answering any of the calls.

Seeing the envelope of Davago pictures lying on her bed, she remembered Max's request that she look closer at the vehicle in the background. She wanted to get a closer look at Tresa Vaughan, the lady who owned Jeers and a trucking company in Tulsa, too. She must be quite a woman to charm Mic Davago and Bill King.

"She's a looker, okay." Jeannie picked up one of the photos lying on her kitchen table. She adjusted her glasses and held the picture closer to the light. The lightning was a scene grabber, but Max had focused on Mic and Tresa, who seemed to be walking across the back parking lot at Jeers toward a Hummer.

"Of course, she remembered the Hummer and the green van which belonged to Jeers were parked near her Explorer Monday night. She sorted through the pictures, hunting for one with a vehicle in the background. Deciding it must be the green van, she pinpointed what looked like two figures in an awkward position near the back of the vehicle. Squinting, she held the picture close to the light. One figure was a man wearing a ball cap. She recognized the red cap and long jean-clad legs, not of Tyler Vaughan, but of Roscoe Rayl. The other figure was of a woman in a Hale U jersey in a clench with Roscoe. Da-dum! It was Rita Gibson.

Questions raced through Jeannie's head. Why had Max expected the picture to have Tyler Vaughan in it? Maybe he thought Tyler and Rita had something going on and…what? Did Max think Tyler killed Rita?

When was the picture taken? If Mic and Tresa were walking in front of Jeers, it would have to be right after Jeannie left. She'd seen them near the entrance when she pulled out onto the highway. *Sure, because Max made it across town and picked up Cloie before I got there,* she decided.

Jeannie wished she could blow up the picture to see exactly what Roscoe and Rita were doing. Roscoe may have been the last person to see Rita alive. *Oh, my God! Roscoe might be the killer.*

For God's sake, she had to call Max! She dialed his number.

Jeannie's call to Max's cell phone went directly to his message, alerting her that he was using his phone. Probably with one of his bimbos. It still hurt to remember the sweetness of their beginning and the cruelty of their breakup. The fragile patching up of their relationship sustained the give and take of a brother-sister closeness.

Max might be an SOB, but he was her SOB.

Not far down the way, a street light flickered across a logo on the side of a black van highlighting the words "Maximum Exposure." A lone figure sat inside with head bowed over the steering wheel. Max Jonson toked up on the habit which kept him from crossing the street, knocking on the door, and asking the girl he loved to take him back.

"Jeannie. Why, Jeannie?" He could ring up any number of girls and they'd be here in a flash. Max started the motor of the shutter-buggy. His job here was finished. Jeannie was home safe. He'd watched her and Sherman tonight. He knew their relationship was becoming more serious. He'd seen Sherman walk her to the door. Had he kissed her? It was too dark to be sure.

"Damn it! Jeannie's my wife." He'd always think of her that way. He couldn't stand the thought of another man touching her. He remembered the softness of her skin as her body moved against his. The special spots he caressed to arouse her. The way they satisfied each other's needs. Max shifted uneasily redistributing his assets. Arousal was not what he needed right now. Business, he needed to think of business. He needed to call Jeannie about the Davago picture. He dialed her cell phone number. It was busy. What? She and Sherman hadn't been apart thirty minutes and they were already on the phone together?

Chapter 37

As Max drove toward home, he reviewed the two envelopes he'd given out at Jeers tonight.

Lynn Copper Sherman's envelope contained film he'd taken Monday evening as she stripped on the dance floor at Jeers. He'd labeled those photos 'For Daddy?' Gossip might reach the ears of Richard P. Copper concerning his daughter's actions in public, but a photo of the act was a different matter. Max had received cash gifts from Lynn before when he presented her with naughty pictures she didn't want her daddy to see.

The other envelope he gave out tonight was to Roscoe Rahl. It might cost Roscoe his job or maybe not. Max knew the value Roscoe put on his job at Jeers. He was more than a bartender. He did the job Tyler Vaughan was supposed to do. Why? Max had a hunch Tyler was Roscoe's contact to drugs. His hunch paid off when he followed Tyler and Roscoe early Monday evening. They'd driven the Jeers van to a nearby quarry where they met a Vaughan freight truck. Photos of Roscoe and Tyler helping transfer boxes from the Vaughan truck to the Jeers van were in the folder Max left for Roscoe.

Was it drugs? Max asked himself. Did Tyler have a dirty finger in both Jeers and the family truck line his sister was running? Rumor had it Tyler had been in trouble in Oklahoma. The family had sent him to Missouri to do community service at Jeers. If the delivery was legit, why didn't the driver deliver it directly to Jeers? Tresa Vaughan had been in town all Memorial Day weekend. Could that be the reason for the off-premise delivery?

And why would Roscoe and Tyler hurry to unload the stuff themselves under the back deck of Jeers into the cellar? And on a busy

Memorial Day weekend? Max wondered. He'd followed the two back to Jeers and captured their unloading effort on film there, too.

Those were the pictures he put in the envelope he gave to Roscoe tonight at Jeers. If it wasn't drugs they were smuggling to Jeers, the pictures might be of no value. If it was drugs, then Roscoe and Tyler might not want Tresa Vaughan to see the photos. Not to mention Bill King. Max knew the Division of Alcohol and Tobacco Control, ATC, would be very interested in the photos if the merchandise was drugs. In fact, that might be the connection to Rita's murder. If so, whoever did it was in bigger trouble. The ATC took care of their own.

Max discovered Rita was undercover for ATC when he was at her place taking publicity photos for Miss Hale University. He'd seen a business card with a series of numbers and letters on the back. He'd memorized the numbers. He tried several different combinations of the numbers and letters and did a little calling. One number led directly to Bill King's Missouri ATC private line. He'd wanted to offer his help, and then it was too late. It might be too late for Rita, but maybe his film could help find her murderer.

"Come on, Jeannie, answer your phone," Max said, as he dialed her number again.

"Max, I've been trying to call you." Jeannie sounded excited. Jeannie told Max in detail about the Davago photo, the van in the picture, and the two figures in the background in a clumsy embrace. "I'm almost certain the two people at the back of the van are Roscoe Rayl and Rita Gibson. If I bring the photo to your place, can you blow it up so we can be sure?"

"Sure, baby. But be careful. This is dangerous stuff we're messing with. Bring all the pictures, okay? I promise I won't use them on Mic again," Max said and started to hang up.

"Max, wait, don't hang up! You do still number your films and record which envelope you put them in, don't you?" Jeannie waited. This was a system she'd been very particular about when she ran the business side of Maximum Exposure.

"For God's sake, Jeannie! You still ragging me about that? Sure, I do—" Max stopped in mid-sentence. Of course, he could find out what happened to the two extra Davago pictures by checking the system. Thank God for Jeannie and her system of rules.

"You still there?" Jeannie asked. "There's a bunch of numbers on the back of this film. Which one do you need to check our system?"

"Give me the last three numbers." Max reached for a pen. He loved the sound of OUR system.

"Zero, twenty-two. Does that sound right? It's got five, twenty-six in front of it." Jeannie said.

"Sure, baby. I changed it a little bit. Fifth month—five, twenty-sixth day—Memorial Day. And zero, twenty-two shows what number the film is on the roll. Get it? Of course, you do; you started the system. Thanks for…a lot of things. Hurry over. We've got a lot of work to do." Max hung up as he pulled into his drive. He could hardly wait to get to his darkroom and Jeannie's system of records. And he could hardly wait for Jeannie to come back to OUR place.

Parked in a wooded section of trees on a lot adjoining Jeers, the surveillance team of Officers Leblanc and Anderson had their gaze focused on the back door of the nightclub.

"Jeers has been on the ATC list for some time. State moved some top dogs in. It won't be long, and we'll have enough to close the place down," Leblanc said.

Anderson whistled. "Selling drugs in Greene County must be a lucrative business."

"Yeah, marijuana is huge. Street cost on meth is pricy. Hell, coke is less. Meth lasts longer…" Leblanc said. "And getting meth into the system isn't hard."

"Any ideas on how this connects to the Rita Gibson murder earlier this week? You think the Gibson broad was mixed up with the drug scene?" Anderson asked.

"Word is there was nothing in her body. But who knows? Meth gets out of your system in three days and you can pass a piss test," Leblanc said. "Take it a step at a time, Anderson. Watch that door, and we'll see how many people come out. That should narrow it down to what? Liquor? Drugs? Who knows?" Leblanc let out a low whistle.

They watched as a classy redhead strolled toward the Hummer parked near the front of the building. The redhead climbed behind the wheel and drove the Hummer expertly out of the lot.

"License on the Hummer is issued to Vaughan Trucking Company out of Tulsa. Dame's name is Tresa Vaughan," Leblanc reported. "Report shows the deed to Jeers is in her name DBA Vaughan Trucking Company, out of Tulsa."

"Vaughan? Isn't that pretty boy's name at the bar tonight? Tyler Vaughan? Acts like he owns the place but hangs out at the bar instead of working."

"That's the dame's brother. He's got a record in Oklahoma for transporting. Makes him worth watching."

"Speaking of watching, someone's coming from the front lot."

A figure in an oversized windbreaker moved past the Jeep Cherokee parked near the front of Jeers Nightclub. Hesitating near the dark green van still parked near the rear of the building, the figure knocked on the back door. Light spilled out when the door opened. The figure disappeared inside.

"What do you make of that?" Anderson was excited to be on this stakeout. He was determined to do everything by the book.

"Could be anything." Leblanc shrugged. "Cleaning woman, night watchman or a late pickup for liquor."

"You don't think it has anything to do with the coed murder?" Anderson asked.

"Who knows? Let's just watch. That's why we're here," Leblanc said.

Ten minutes later, the door opened. The same figure hurried out, wearing a backpack.

Anderson was already on the radio, reporting the incident. "Track the suspect and report where the backpack ends up. Over."

Static filled the air. Then a terse voice reported, "Suspect is joining a second party in a BMW. They are just pulling away from the curb, heading west on Kearney. Over."

"Get a make on the license and the color of the car. Over."

"BMW. Hmm, five will get you ten it's the Copper Sherman lady's car and she's a carrier," Leblanc said.

The voice came over the radio, "Maroon BMW. License plate reads L-COPP-S. Over."

"Better write up your report and file it for future use. No use taking the princess in. She'd be out before you got your report filed. Over," Leblanc advised.

"One night we stopped Ms. Copper Sherman's car. She was drunk as a skunk. But by the time we got her car stopped, she wasn't driving," Leblanc said. "Switched places with the passenger while cruising over eighty miles per hour."

"Was the passenger sober?" Anderson asked.

"Yep, her current toy boy," Leblanc said. "Stud football player her father hired to squire her around."

"Why did her father have to hire the guy? From what I've seen she's a hot-looking babe," Anderson said.

"Who knows? After a thorough search of her vehicle, we found nothing but a pack of imported cigarettes." Leblanc shook his head. "Marriage and divorce weren't even a speed bump in her road. Everyone knows Ms. Copper Sherman is a user, but where does she get her stuff?"

"It's no scoop. Jeers is a hot spot. Undercover reports revealed waiters carry weed in their pockets," Leblanc said.

"To use or sell?"

Leblanc barked a laugh. His gaze was trained on the back door of Jeers, but his thoughts were inside the nightclub. "Did you watch those blatant chicks from the college cozy up to the waiters?" He laughed again. "Hell, the dame looks like she's flirting, but she's actually picking Jeers' pocket for a smoke."

"Compliments of the house?" Anderson grunted.

"What goes around comes around. Someone higher up will make a killing when the babe graduates to meth or worse."

"And the big dude is who we're holding out for, right?"

Leblanc nodded.

Static started up again. "Guess everyone is tucked in for the night. Sorority girls stumbled into their digs. We followed the college professor to his new girlfriend's house. What's her name? Johnson? Over."

"J-o-n-s-o-n! That broad was married to Max Jonson. The man about town with Maximum Exposure. Over." Leblanc said.

Static sounded on the line. The officer asked, "The society photo man? Big shots—too dumb to not party? Big shots—too rich to not pay? Over."

"Something like that. Over," Leblanc said.

"Say, isn't the Jonson dame the one that is connected with the Gibson murder? You guys do have your scrambler on. Over." Leblanc looked to Anderson for confirmation.

Anderson shrugged.

Leblanc could cuss like a sailor when the occasion called for it. "Blank, blank. Frickin' first thing they teach you in training school is not to transfer conversation live without a scrambler." He reached over and switched the radio to safety. "Over."

"Sorry," Anderson mumbled.

"Better keep that radio clean. You know half the town listens on these call-ins," Leblanc grunted.

Static confirmed a call coming through on the radio. "The Maroon BMW just pulled into a garage. We'll wait and see if they're here for the night or hitting the road again."

Leblanc clicked off. "Might as well make yourself comfortable, Anderson," Leblanc said. "It promises to be a long night."

Chapter 38

Static blared from a sleek chrome scanner attached under the dash of L-COPP-S's maroon BMW. Tyler glanced toward Lynn, who was reclining against the passenger seat door. She was the classiest slut he'd ever known. There was something about her that reminded him of his sister. Arrogant, he guessed, was the word. These women took what they wanted without considering the consequences. But as surrealistic as they both were, they couldn't compare with the woman he'd loved and lost, Rita Gibson.

Tyler wondered what he was doing chauffeuring Lynn Copper Sherman around town. Sure, it was a blast to his ego. But what he really needed was someone to listen while he spoke of his unrequited love. He'd only known Rita for a short time, but she had made such an impact on his life. He could have been all the things his family wanted him to be—for her. Her beauty, her charm made him her slave. He could have given up drugs, trafficking, illicit behavior. If he'd only had a little more time, he knew he could have won her love. But no, her life had been snuffed out. If he ever discovered who had killed Rita, he'd make that person wish they'd never been born.

"Lynn, there are things I need to tell you," Tyler began.

"Shhh! Listen to those cops. They don't even have a scrambler on." Lynn kept her finger to her lips for silence.

The scanner conversation continued. "Say, isn't that Jonson dame the one that is connected with the Gibson murder? Over."

"You guys do have your scrambler on, ten, four? Over. " Static, static—silence. The scanner went dead.

"See if you can dial them back up, hon. It was just getting interesting." Lynn swiped at her nose several times with the cuff of her windbreaker. She settled herself and began rummaging through her backpack, sorting through white envelopes.

"Where're we headed?" Tyler asked.

Lynn shook off her hood and shrugged her shoulders. "You need to talk? Tell me about it."

Tyler pulled the BMW away from the curb and headed west on Kearney. As he drove he poured out his heart to Lynn. "...and the last time I saw Rita was Monday evening. Roscoe and I were talking to her outside Jeers. Roscoe had to go back inside for a minute. It was actually the first time I'd kissed Rita. Then my sister and some guy came out of Jeers. I'd had an argument with Tresa earlier. I didn't want another encounter with her, so I slipped in the back door to avoid her. I had some appointments later. And, that was the last time I saw Rita. I'll never forgive myself for leaving her there like that. If I'd stayed, she might still be here today."

"Feel better?" Lynn said when Tyler finally stopped talking. "It helps to get it all out. At least, that's what my shrink tells me." Lynn pulled out a manila envelope. She turned up the dash light and peered at a name scrawled on the front of the envelope. "What the hell? He switched the envelopes!"

Tyler glanced sideways as they paused at a traffic light. He wished he hadn't told this woman his secrets. She listened, but she dismissed his deepest hurt like so much fluff. And what was she doing now? He couldn't make out the scrawled name on the envelope, but the return address read ME in bold script. He'd seen an envelope like this before...but where?

Inserting a manicured thumbnail under the envelope flap, Lynn ripped it open. Photos spilled out. Lynn gathered them up like a poker player rearranging her hand. She studied a photo as she held it closer to the light. She cast a furtive glance at Tyler. "Freaking-A? Who would have thought it?"

The BMW made a quick turn on National and another turn on the next street up. "Don't look now, but we've got company," Tyler said.

"Lose him!" Lynn kept flipping through the pictures, stopping to peer closer at some photos.

The BMW twisted and turned on side streets heading south. Tyler pulled out his cell phone to text a message as he cruised streets lined with quality homes.

"Beep." His cell phone sounded a return text. Tyler looked at the screen and read one letter, "K."

"Eat my dirt, buddy." The BMW turned into the drive of a home just as the garage door moved slowly upward. When the BMW was inside, the door closed. Lights came on in the garage. Directly ahead of them was another set of garage doors.

"We safe?" Lynn asked.

"Safe as a bug in a rug," Tyler said.

Lynn glanced at the driver. "That's snug as a bug in a rug."

"That, too," he said. "What's with the pictures? I thought you were picking up stuff."

Lynn nodded at the white envelopes. She crammed them inside the manila envelope. "Interesting photos. You might want to see them later."

Scooping up the pictures, she inserted them in the envelope, too. At the last minute, she pulled out a photo and stuffed it down the front of her jeans, mumbling, "Max knows all the secrets. But he screwed up this time. If I have Roscoe's envelope, he must have mine." She scratched through the name scribbled on the front of the envelope. Quickly she inscribed a name and post office box address. Rummaging in her jacket pocket, she pulled out a priority stamp and pasted it on the top of the envelope. "Let's get out of here. Head for the post office drop on Glenstone. We don't want to be picked up with this envelope in our possession."

Tyler looked at his wrist watch. "Give me two minutes."

Lynn pulled out a stack of papers from her back pack. She flipped through them. Satisfied, she placed them inside her backpack.

The garage door in front of them begin to rise. When it was at its peak, the BMW pulled out onto the next street over and headed toward Glenstone. Tyler chuckled. "Sit there and watch the door we pulled into all night, piggies. We're out and gone on the other side."

Later, across town, static from an incoming call jolted Leblanc and Anderson from an open-eye snooze. "Leblanc, you still watching Jeers? Over."

"Confirmed. Over," Leblanc answered.

"We just stopped a maroon BMW for speeding. We're running a check on license plate L-COPP-S. Two occupants. Passenger, white female. Lynn Copper Sherman. Driver, white male in his early forties. Tyler Vaughan. Over."

"Where did you stop the vehicle? Over," Leblanc asked.

"Heading south on Sixty-five toward Ozark. Over," the incoming call replied. "Passenger says she owns the car. Smells to high heaven, but she claims they aren't carrying. Over."

"Does she have a backpack? Over," Leblanc asked.

"Yep. Over."

"Check it out. She arrived at Jeers earlier and left with the backpack. Over."

"Checked it out. Ms. Sherman claims she's helping the bartender at Jeers, Roscoe Rahl, with a talent show. She picked up contestant information in the backpack to review. Over."

Leblanc gave Anderson a knowing look. "You might want to put in a call to the officers who have the BMW stakeout. Tell them their watch is finished. Over. "

Ten minutes later, static announced an incoming call. A police patrol voice droned, "Leblanc, you were right about that Copper dame. Cheeky broad pulled through a two way garage and slipped out the other side. We sat for a while before we noticed another car pull into the same garage and it was empty. Over."

"I guess you know the BMW was pulled over for speeding on Sixty-five south? Over," Leblanc asked.

"Yep. Thanks for giving us the heads up. One day that broad will get hers. I hope I'm around to see it. Over." The radio was silent.

"Ever had that garage caper pulled on you?" Anderson asked.

"Not yet, but I guess we better find out the address and be ready for it," Leblanc said.

Jeannie's cell phone rang. She grabbed an oversized, man-tailored shirt from her closet. She'd run the battery down on her cell phone talking to Max, and she'd hadn't plugged it back into the charger. Bleep-bleep.

Maybe it was Max calling back. Or maybe it was Brent. Self-consciously, she struggled into the shirt as though her phone had eyes. "Hello?"

"What did she tell you?" a slurred voice demanded.

Jeannie frowned, belatedly turning the phone to check the caller ID. "Unknown," she whispered.

"That's right, Ms. Jonson, unknown. But I need to find out what Rita told you." The man's pitch got higher. He stressed *Ms.* Johnson.

"What?" Jeannie gasped.

"You heard me. I know you were the last one to see her alive. I know she told you something. What was it?" the drunken voice questioned. Then, "It wasn't like I meant to hurt her."

Bleep-bleep. Jeannie's cell phone didn't have much power.

Jeannie moved toward the phone on her nightstand. If she could reach it, maybe she could call someone to—to do what? Her thoughts raced as she tried to stall. "My battery is low."

"I heard, Ms. Jonson. Just answer my question. What did the conniving bitch tell you?"

"I don't know what you're talking about," Jeannie said.

"Of course you do. Just think. Monday night at Jeers, Rita knew something was wrong. She had to tell someone something. She was talking to Tyler Vaughan when you started bawling. She followed you out the door. She talked to you all the way to your truck. What did she say to you in Jeers' parking lot?" He over-enunciated every consonant and vowel.

While she listened, Jeannie took the receiver off her bedside phone. Phone numbers popped into her mind.

Dad and Mom? Too far away. The lawyer, L.D. Stone? What was his number?

The police detectives? Business cards were in the next room. Brent? No. Max? She dialed the familiar number, which went promptly to his voice mail. Damnation, he was on the phone. Renee? She dialed the number quickly and left the receiver lying upright on her nightstand.

"I'm waiting...what did she tell you?" the voice asked.

"Who is this?" Jeannie demanded. "I want to know who's calling me on my cell phone this late. I want to know who knows so much about me and Rita Gibson. And—and what happened to Rita Gibson Monday night at Jeers' parking lot."

The voice took on a sing-song tone. "Well, well. The cat doesn't have her tongue. We need to talk. What do you say we meet somewhere?" the man asked, slyly. "Maybe at the scene of the crime?"

"I'm not meeting you anywhere," Jeannie cried. She hoped she was relaying enough information to Renee, who was listening on Jeannie's bedside phone.

Jeannie could hear Renee's voice coming through the receiver. "Jeannie? Jeannie? I can hear you. What's going on? Who are you talking to?"

The caller's voice was slowly losing the raspy quality. "You're just as stubborn as Rita was. I only wanted to know how much she knew. But she wouldn't cooperate. That's what happens when you try to play both sides of the fence. What could I do?"

Jeannie's brain tried to cope with the fact that she was talking to a murderer on her cell phone. If she could keep him on the phone long enough, maybe—

"Are you coming or not?" the unknown voice asked.

"Not! Tell me who this is." Jeannie knew this voice. Who was it? Jeannie unplugged her cell phone and walked into the next room. She reached for the stack of business cards and shuffled through the pile until she found the cards of lawyer L.D. Stone and Detective Leblanc.

"If I tell you who I am, you'll come?" the hopeful tone erased the varnish of drunken deception.

Jeannie could almost place the voice. Where had she heard it? "I might. Who is this?" She walked back into the bedroom where she could hear and be heard by her bedside phone.

Renee's muffled voice on the bedside phone was yelling. "No. You don't go anywhere, Jeannie! NO!"

"Ms. Jonson? This is your last chance. You want to meet me at Jeers parking lot? Or you want me to come to your place?" He snickered.

Jeers parking lot? Was that the scene of the crime? Or was that just the last place Jeannie had seen Rita Gibson alive? "Mmm, if I met you at the scene of the crime would it be Jeers parking lot?" Jeannie probed.

The voice on her cell phone said, "That may be where Rita's accident started but not where it finished. Want to meet me where it started or where it finished?"

The bedside phone was practically jiggling from the vibrations of the voice on the phone. "Jeannie, keep that person on the phone. Annie Leblanc is staying overnight with Cloie. She has an emergency number for her dad. She's calling him. We're on our way over to your place." Silence. The security of Renee's voice was gone.

"No!" Jeannie realized the bedside phone dial tone wasn't buzzing. They'd left the phone off the hook. At least they were on their way to help. And Detective Leblanc's kid was alerting him.

The voice on her cell phone dropped to a hushed whisper. "Hey, I didn't call to play twenty questions, Ms. Jonson."

There it was! The same voice had said the same words to her not so long ago. *Who?* Jeannie remembered driving to Jeers this afternoon. She's answered her phone to Unknown Caller, and it had been Roscoe Rayl. During their conversation, he'd became agitated and said, "I didn't call to play twenty questions, Ms. Jonson."

Oh, my God! It was Roscoe Rayl. Jeannie saw the packet of film on her bed. She remembered seeing him and Rita at the back of the van in the picture. He wasn't embracing her. He was attacking her. Jeannie decided to play a wild card. "I believe I know who this is. And I believe you attacked Rita in Jeers' parking lot at the back of Jeers' van. I think there are witnesses who can identify you. In fact there's a picture—"

"That's it! If you want to find out who I am, you'll have to meet me here in ten minutes with some answers. Be here or I'll find you. You'll never know when or where, but I'll find you. I will get answers." Click. He hung up.

"Bleep-bleep." Her cell phone was completely dead.

"Wait!" Jeannie screamed at both of the phones. Her cell phone's battery was dead. The phone on which Renee had been talking was left off the hook. Useless, both of them. Unless she could find her car charger for the cell phone. She raced around the room, grabbing clothes as she went, pulling open drawers, and shaking out purses.

The murderer's voice replayed in her mind. "Hey, I didn't call to play twenty questions, Ms. Jonson."

Of course, she knew who it was! How could she have been so stupid? She struggled into the pair of jeans left lying on her bed.

Ten minutes. As she passed the table by the front door, she spied it: the charger for her cell phone. She grabbed it, stuffed it in the pocket of her jacket with the Davago films and headed out to her Explorer. She'd call Max as soon as she was on the way.

Oh, God, I hope I'm not too late.

Max's cell phone rang as he finished pulling out the photo system record book. He hoped it was Jeannie. It was taking her long enough to get here. As he riffled through the pages, he checked the caller ID. Nope, it wasn't Jeannie. The caller ID read, Unknown Caller. Whatever. Maybe it was a customer. Unknown's money was as good as the next guy. "Hullo?"

"Why in the hell did you give me a packet of pictures with the Copper dame stripping?" Roscoe Rayl asked. "Give them to someone who gives a damn."

Max was dumbfounded. Why would Rayl have the envelope with Lynn's pictures in it? Trying to make sense of the conversation, Max's fingers found the correct page in the system book. May twenty-six. He traced a line down the numbers showing where the pictures had been placed.

Stalling, Max said, "Hold up, buddy! The envelope I gave you was a damn sight more interesting than Lynn Copper Sherman's pictures. I think a lot of people would be interested in seeing just what you and Tyler Vaughan loaded from a Vaughan freight truck at the Quarry and unloaded Monday evening at Jeers."

"Sons of a bitch!" Roscoe paused, as if considering what might be on the film.

Max continued his search for the film. Fifth month—five, twenty-sixth day--Memorial Day. And zero, twenty-one shows what number the film is on the roll. And there was the record for the three pictures. One of the pictures was put in Roscoe Rayl's folder. The other two pictures were still on file.

"Why'd I put that picture in Roscoe's folder?" Max whispered. There must be some mistake. Jeannie had the Davago pictures, and she'd seen the picture with Roscoe and Rita at the back of the van. If that was right, how could the other two prints still be in the file?

"Damnation!" Max blurted. What were the numbers Jeannie had read off the back of the photo? Fifth month—five, twenty-sixth day—Memorial Day. And, zero, twenty-two was the number of the film on the roll.

Twenty-two! Sure, the number was twenty-two, not twenty one. And there it was—three pictures! One was labeled Davago. One film was still in the file. What the hell? Where was the other picture? Max peered at the film as he held it up to the light.

As Roscoe listened to Max's mumbling, thoughts swirled in his head. If he had Lynn's folder, she must have his. He shouted into the phone, "If that Copper woman has my file, a lot of shit will hit the fan."

"Whoa, back up. I handed each of you the right folder. How'd you and Lynn mix them up?" Max said, as he held the two pictures up to the light. Twenty-one and twenty-two looked like the same photos. He pulled out his magnifying glass and peered closer.

"Well, I'll be goddamned." Both pictures had Tresa Vaughn and Mic Davago in the foreground. Both pictures had the girl wearing a Hale University shirt, who was Rita Gibson. But in film twenty-one, Rita was in an embrace with someone who looked a lot like Tyler Vaughan. In film twenty-two, Rita was being dragged by a man wearing a Cardinal ball cap. That had to be Roscoe Rayl. Max read the name of the envelope where the third picture had been sent. "Lynn Copper Sherman, son of a—" Max whispered. If Roscoe had Lynn's envelope, he not only had the pictures of her stripping at Jeers, he had a picture showing Rita Gibson being attacked—by him, Roscoe Rayl.

Roscoe's mind flashed back to Jeers where he'd dropped his

clipboard after rehearsal. His notes had scattered and the envelope had dropped to the floor. He had picked up the envelope, handed it to Lynn, and she'd laid it—where? Of course, on the table behind them, with another envelope that had to be the one Max had given her.

"Stupid!" Roscoe was bitching and moaning. *I've got people on my back. Boss lady's in town checking on Tyler. Tyler's got it going on but has lost his head over Rita's death. And you wonder why I can't concentrate? If this film is what I think it is—* "What kind of dough you asking?" Roscoe demanded.

Max decided to go for it. "Roscoe, did you look closely at all the pictures in Lynn's folder?"

"Huh?" Roscoe was obviously leafing through the pile of photos again. "Sons of a bitch!"

Max knew Roscoe had found the picture of him and Rita at the back of the Jeers van. The one where he was not embracing her but attacking her. The picture Max had mistakenly put in both Davago and Lynn's envelope. When the folders got mixed up, Roscoe had Lynn's envelope, and it had a picture of a murder in progress, and the murderer was Roscoe Rayl.

"I see you found the photo, Roscoe. Lightning flash lit up the scene well. I'm sure you must have seen your boss lady, Tresa, and Mic Davago when they crossed in front of the van. Question is, just how much did they see? Did you and Rita show up as well for them as you did for my camera?"

Roscoe's voice was deadly. "Does this mean the Copper Sherman bitch has the pictures of me and Tyler loading shit? And a copy of this…?" He paused as though putting the puzzle together. "I suppose you passed one of these out to Mic Davago and Tresa?"

Max thought fast. "Davago didn't know what he had. He was just worried about being seen with Tresa. We got those photos back. The one in Lynn's folder was a mistake." A very big mistake. If Lynn saw the picture, she might mistakenly think Tyler could be the last person to see Rita alive.

Roscoe chuckled. "You slipped up, Max. Very unprofessional of you."

"Everyone makes a mistake sometime," Max said. "Maybe Lynn hasn't looked at your envelope yet and—"

"It's not Ms. Lynn I'm talking about. You said WE got the photos back. 'We' must mean your ex, Ms. Jeannie. I just got off the phone with her. She talked about this very picture. I was just too dumb to know what she was saying. But Max, you laid it out for me."

Jeannie talked to Roscoe on the phone? Max couldn't believe his ears. Why? What? "Let's get the folder back, and then we'll talk," Max said.

"I got me a date with your ex. She's hurrying over here right now to tell me what she and Rita talked about Monday night." Roscoe chuckled.

"Roscoe, you're in enough trouble. Don't make it worse. Where are you? I'll come over, and we'll work something out." Max was already out the door and in the Shutter-buggy.

"You do that, Max. But no need to hurry, Miss Jeannie should be here any minute. I wouldn't want to hurry our talk up none." Roscoe hung up.

Immediately, Max's cell phone rang again. It was Jeannie's ring. He breathed a sigh of relief. "Hi, baby. Talk to me."

Max listened intently. "We've got some lethal information." Quickly he brought Jeannie up to date on everything."

"Max, if Lynn is out and about, she could be in trouble. She's a sitting target for Roscoe carrying that envelope."

"You're the sitting duck, baby. He thinks Rita told you something. Did she?" Max asked.

"Nothing as important as you just told me, Max. I can't believe she was an undercover person for the ATC. No wonder Jeers was crawling with state officials like Bill King," Jeannie said.

"Thanks for mentioning him. I'm going to notify King. He'll want to be in on this. I'm on my way to Jeers, baby. You say Cloie's friend is calling her detective dad? You stay out of danger, Jeannie. I mean it. Don't go in Jeers. I'll call you back. Be careful." Click.

Then Max picked up his cell phone, dialed, and whispered, "God, don't let it be too late."

Chapter 39

Leblanc nudged Anderson as the BMW cruised into the parking lot at Jeers. The driver pulled to the back of the lot and parked near the green van. Lynn Copper Sherman and Tyler Vaughan got out. Lynn waited while Tyler unlocked the back door of Jeers. Both entered the building.

"I'm going to the little girls' room, Tyler." Lynn was hoping to get a minute alone to get a better look at the picture she'd kept from Roscoe's folder. Jeopardy was sobering. Was she in the company of a man she should be afraid of?

"Sure. I need to take a leak, too." Tyler headed across the hall. "The van's here. Roscoe must still be around."

Tyler finished up and headed for the bar. He could see Roscoe talking on his cell phone. Tyler walked behind the bar and poured himself a shot of whiskey. Roscoe must still be doing business. He edged closer to listen.

"...like I said, I've got an important date. Can you hang out for—" While Roscoe listened to the caller, his gaze swept the bar area and saw Tyler. Hurriedly, he said, "No problem. I'll be there in about twenty minutes." He ended the call and turned to Tyler.

Tyler snorted, "You? Got a date? Who'd hook up with you, Roscoe?"

Roscoe's face flushed. "You think you've got the market cornered, Vaughan? Ever since you laid claim to the Gibson broad, you think your shit don't stink. Well, get a clue: she wasn't interested in you. She was milking you for information she could give to Mr. Bill King, head of ATC. You think she wasn't watching us Monday evening before and after we got back from the Quarry? She was pumping you for her report, and all you could think about was touchy-feelie."

Tyler slammed down his empty glass on the bar. He picked up the first thing his hand closed on, the whiskey bottle, and advanced on Roscoe. Rage fueled by the events of the past week caused his eyes to narrow to virulent slits. "You sicko, what do you know? And what were you doing sneaking around watching us?"

Roscoe moved back a step. He'd heard of Tyler's high-risk rage but he'd never witnessed it. "Sons of a bitch! Put that bottle down. You out of your freaking mind?"

Tyler raised the bottle higher as he followed Roscoe's retreat. "You think I didn't see you watching Rita? Jealous, that's it. You were jealous because she chose to be with me. Not you, Roscoe, me!"

"You're nuts. Your tongue wagged too much. She lapped it up so she could run to Bill King, big dog at ATC. I just needed to talk to her and find out how much she knew—"

"What else did you do, Roscoe? Did you come back Monday night after I left Rita outside by the van? Did you—" Tyler edged closer, backing Roscoe against the back bar.

"It wasn't like I planned to hurt her. Shit! We could do time for what we were doing, man. And there you were blabbing to her."

Roscoe pushed away from the back bar and began to edge Tyler backwards. "I just wanted to talk, but Rita went berserk! Then I heard someone coming and had to shove her inside the van so they wouldn't see. And then, blood, there was so much blood." Roscoe shook his head as if to clear bad memories. "Served the bitch right if she was connected with the ATC."

Tyler stared at Roscoe. The bottle was suddenly heavy in his upraised hand. "You killed her—you killed Rita—"

"I pushed her. The next time I looked, she was dead." Roscoe glanced toward the front of the bar. "Now put down that bottle. Your sister will have both of our heads."

Tyler lowered the bottle and glanced around, expecting to see Tresa still in the building. The next thing he felt was a bottle crashing against his skull. Liquor mixed with blood gushed down his head, soaking his clothing as he slumped to the floor behind the bar. "Sorry, buddy. Looks like you're tending bar tonight." Roscoe walked toward the back door.

Outside Jeers, Anderson was on the radio with the scrambler reporting the arrival of the BMW. LeBlanc's cell phone played the music reserved for a call from his daughter, Annie.

"Shit!" LeBlanc said under his breath, pulling out the phone. Annie would never call him unless it was an emergency. And she was staying over with a friend tonight.

"Annie, what's up?" LeBlanc asked.

"Jeannie needs your help, Dad." Annie repeated what Cloie's mom had heard on Jeannie's phone. "You can help her, can't you, Dad?"

"Yes, Annie. Tell Cloie's parents if Jeannie comes anywhere near Jeers, we'll know it," LeBlanc said.

"Thanks, Dad. We're on our way to Jeannie's house. I'll keep you posted. Bye."

"What! Annie, I don't want you going anywhere near Jeannie's house. Do you hear me?" LeBlanc was yelling into a dead phone. Annie had hung up.

Lynn washed her hands, checked her makeup. and reached for the photo she'd secreted in the front of her jeans earlier. She put on the eyeglasses she never wore in public. Peering closely at the photo, she noted Tyler's sister, Tresa, and Madam Davago's husband, Mic, with a van parked in the background. Two figures stood near the back of the van. On closer examination, she identified Tyler. Noting the Hale University jersey which Rita wore Monday evening, Lynn confirmed what she'd expected. The woman was Rita Gibson.

"I've been driving around with someone who could be a murderer," Lynn whispered. She picked up her cell phone and called the only man she trusted completely.

When Richard P. Copper answered his phone, Lynn told her father the circumstances. Ironically, she received the same advice Jeannie had received earlier. *Trust no one. Do what is needed, but be safe. I'll alert Bill King and bring the local authorities.*

As Lynn started for the bathroom exit, her cell phone rang. "Lynn, this is Max. Somehow the folders I gave you and Roscoe were switched."

"I know."

"If you've examined the photos, you may have discovered you're in dangerous company."

"I just called my father with the information about Tyler, Max." Lynn repeated what her father had advised her to do.

"Lynn, it's not Tyler you need to be afraid of—it's Roscoe. The picture you saw is Tyler and Rita embracing. The envelope I gave to you earlier, the one Roscoe has now, contains a picture taken a few minutes later with Rita being attacked by Roscoe. He must be the murderer. Where are you now?"

When she told him, Max let out a low whistle. "Since you're there, find out what you can, but be extremely careful. You sound sober; are you?"

"Completely sober, Max. And I intend to stay that way. I don't want my body to be found in a shallow grave."

"If Jeannie shows up, do you two think you can work together?"

"I can if she can," Lynn retorted.

"Both of your lives depend on it. So knock off the bullshit." Max's voice was dead serious. "I'm on my way. Are you sure Roscoe is in the building?"

"No, but I know Tyler is. I'll keep you posted." Lynn closed out Max's call. She thought for a minute and dialed Brent's number. If she could just hear his voice, it would give her strength. She knew their relationship was ruined, but he was still a potent force in her life.

The phone rang, rang, and went to message mode. "You have reached Professor Brent Sherman. Your assignment is to leave a brief message. I'll answer soon."

Lynn sighed, "Brent, I need you. And," she hesitated, "your Ms. Jonson needs you." Brief message be damned. Resolutely, she poured out all the details of the night. Lynn clicked off as she heard what sounded like Tyler calling her name.

Lynn moved out of the ladies' room. In the light filtering through from an open door at the end of a hallway, Jeannie could make out the bar area. "Tyler? Hey, I've got a lot of questions that need answers." She clutched the picture as she walked toward the bar.

"Tyler is manning the bar," a voice whispered from somewhere behind her. Before she could turn around, she heard a swishing noise and felt a blow to the side of her head and sensed herself falling.

"LeBlanc, what do you make of this? It looks like Roscoe the bartender is leaving in the green van," Anderson said.

"Get on the radio and report we're tailing the green van. If they want someone watching this place, they need to send in replacements. Tell them Tyler Vaughan and Lynn Copper Sherman are still inside." Leblanc started up the motor.

"I'm on it," Anderson said, reaching for the radio mike.

The green van left Jeers parking lot and turned east on Kearney.

A few minutes later, the police car eased out to join the traffic headed east on Kearney.

In his rearview mirror, Anderson caught a glimpse of a car pulling into the turn lane as they sped past. Looking back, he whistled between his teeth. "Busy place, that parking lot. A black Explorer just turned in."

"Shiiit! Better get on the horn, again. That sounds like the Jonson babe's vehicle." Leblanc followed the green van through the light at the exit for I-44. "What the hell? Where's Roscoe Rayl headed?"

"Nothing much out this way unless he's heading cross country," Anderson said.

"Shit!" Leblanc glanced at Anderson. "Get back on the radio. Annie just called and said the bartender was harassing Jeannie Jonson on the phone."

"Huh?" Anderson said.

"Annie's staying overnight at the Jonson dame's sister's house. She's good friends with her daughter, Cloie." Leblanc finished relaying the story as he slowed to keep a distance between himself and the green van. "Here's the kicker. Annie said they were on their way over to Jeannie's house."

Anderson whistled, "And, the Jonson dame just pulled into Jeers."

"You got that right." Leblanc braked as taillights on the cars in front of him glowed. Ahead, the green van was turning into the entrance of the old quarry road. "Get a look at the road as I go by. I can't chance just pulling in blind. We'll have to turn around at the next drive and come back."

"Not much out there. Quarry dugout was made into storage space. It's lit up like a Walmart parking lot. You can drive right into the side of the hill. And, that's what the green van is doing," Anderson reported.

"Remember which hole the rat crawled into. We'll try to flush him out," LeBlanc said. "Check on what's going on back at Jeers. And, better call for back up at both places."

"I'm on it," Anderson said.

Jeannie pulled into the center lane to turn into Jeers. The green van that had been parked at Jeers earlier had pulled out and into the lane headed east. Immediately, a black sedan pulled out from the next lot west of Jeers and also into the lane headed east. Jeannie wheeled her Explorer into the parking lot. It was deserted, except for Cyra's Jeep Cherokee. Then, she saw Lynn's BMW parked near the back door.

Oh, my God! Who's driving the green van? What's Lynn's BMW doing here? She checked her watch. *It took me fifteen minutes to get here. No way could I have made it in ten.* She reached for her cell phone and plugged into the charger just as it rang.

Roscoe was livid. *Why is it nothing I plan ever goes right? My funds are getting tight. Things are closing in on me. I've got to get out of Halesville. The extra money I've made using Jeers' van to help transport fireworks is small change compared to the shipment of drugs being delivered to Tyler at Jeers. Why should I do all the work and take all the changes and let Tyler get the credit?*

Roscoe reviewed events of the evening. He'd set up a rendezvous with the Jonson woman, hoping to find out what Rita Gibson had told her Monday night.

Then he'd found out the envelope Max Jonson gave him had been switched with the one Max had given Lynn Copper Sherman. In the envelope was a photo Max had taken Monday night of Mic Davago and Tresa Vaughan with Rita Gibson in the background.

He'd told Max he was going to meet with Jeannie, hoping to get him out to Jeers where he could deal with him, too.

Tyler had arrived at Jeers with Lynn Copper Sherman.

Roscoe had received a call from the driver of the truck from Vaughan Truck Lines, who had delivered the shipment of stash Monday evening. The driver was at the Quarry with another load and couldn't find Tyler. Roscoe decided to deal with the driver himself and cut Tyler out. Things were getting too risky. If he could handle this delivery and distribution, he'd have enough to hit the road. As he was making arrangements to meet the driver, Tyler had pussy-footed up to the bar, helped himself, and sneaked a listen to the end of the conversation. Tyler had gone berserk, and Roscoe had to take him out.

Roscoe grinned as he thought of taking out the Copper Sherman broad. *Prissy bitch had it coming.*

He packed up a few things and split. Just as he thought he had it made, he'd caught sight of the Jonson woman pulling into Jeers. Should he call her?

Jeannie sat in her Explorer in Jeers parking lot trying to decide what to do. Her cell phone rang. She grabbed her phone. "Roscoe, what kind of an idiot—"

"Jeannie, Jeannie? Are you all right? Lynn left a mixed-up message on my cell phone." Brent's voice was a mixture of emotion as he poured out the story Lynn left.

"Oh, my God, Brent! Everything she said is true, but the picture I saw had Roscoe Rayl in a clench with Rita Gibson, not Tyler. Of course, Max had said there were two pictures. She must have the one of Tyler," Jeannie rambled.

"Stop, Ms. Jonson." Brent emitted a shaky laugh. "I mean, Jeannie. Where exactly are you now?"

"I'm getting out of my Explorer in Jeers parking lot. Lynn's BMW is parked at the back," Jeannie said.

"I'm in my car heading your way."

"Don't go in. If you value your life, and their lives, don't go in. I'll be there as fast as possible. I tried Lynn earlier and she didn't answer. I'm going to try again. Bye."

Crash! A noise near the back door of Jeers startled Jeannie. She watched as a pack of dogs fought over food spilling from a large garbage can they'd just knocked over. One dog bashed against another, slamming into the back door. The door swung open.

"No way!" Jeannie exclaimed. She was out of the Explorer and headed across the parking lot. She extended her keys toward her truck and pushed her lock button. Her truck honked in response. At the same time, the Jeep Cherokee alarm sounded. The shrill warning device scattered the dogs who had been standing their ground to guard the spoils.

"Great, I've created my own security alarm. 911, pay attention!" She peered in the open door. "Lynn? Mr. Vaughan?" Hearing nothing, she stepped inside.

Ramey, Renee and the girls arrived at Jeannie's house to find the front door locked, the windows dark, and Jeannie's Explorer gone.

Ramey looked inquiringly at Renee. "What exactly did you hear on the phone?"

Renee repeated the conversation.

Annie piped up, "That's exactly what I told my dad, Mrs. Allen. He said if Jeannie showed up at Jeers, they'd know it."

"So, what are we doing sitting here, Dad? Let's head for Jeers," Cloie urged. "Annie, you should report to your dad that Jeannie's not at her house." By the time Cloie finished her sentence, Ramey had his car in motion, and Annie was calling her dad.

"Do you think I should call Mom and Dad? Or the lawyer?" Renee grabbed hold of the dash as Ramey turned the corner on two wheels.

"I wouldn't bother your folks until we know something for sure. And save the lawyer if we need to bail Jeannie out," Ramey said solemnly.

When all three females gasped, Ramey chuckled, "Just kidding, just kidding. Hold on ladies, we're headed for Jeers."

Annie hung up her phone. Quickly, she dialed again. "Hi, Mom?" She listened. "Of course I'm okay. It's just that—" Annie repeated the story again. "I'm fine, really. I'm in the car with Cloie's mom and dad. It's just that I tried to call Dad back to report that Cloie's Aunt Jeannie wasn't home, and I can't get him to answer." Annie listened. "I know he's probably busy—but he always answers my calls, no matter what. I'm worried about him."

Chapter 40

Jeannie paused inside the back door of Jeers, trying to adjust her vision to the darkness. Ahead, she saw the glow of light from the front part of the nightclub.

"Lynn? Ms. Sherman?" Jeannie yelled. "Mr. Rayl? Roscoe? Tyler? Mr. Vaughan?" ?" It suddenly occurred to her she had given away her position. She moved forward toward the light and stumbled, falling over something on the floor. Groping, she tried to attain leverage to push herself up.

She screamed as she felt the softness of a body beneath her fingertips. Jeannie jumped up and ran toward the light beyond the door.

In the dimness of the main room, Jeannie was drawn to the more vivid light illuminating the bar.

"Anyone here?" she called.

Someone moaned.

Where had the sound come from? Jeannie tilted her head and strained to hear. Nothing. Looking around, she noticed the room was pretty much like it was when they left earlier. So, who was the body in the back room? Where was the light switch for the back room? Should she go back? Should she take a chance that whoever had left the body there was still there?

No, use your head. Stay in here until someone comes. Jeannie moved closer to the lighted bar. Surely, Max was on his way. Brent was on his way. For certain, the alarm from Cyra's vehicle would cause someone to come. Jeannie moved to the back side of the bar. The smell of whiskey was overpowering. She started to step backward when a hand closed around her ankle.

Jeannie screamed, kicking wildly to free herself. Her foot came free straightaway, causing her to tumble sideways. She rebounded off the back bar and fell sprawling over another body.

She screamed again, scrambling off the muscled feel of a male form. Jeannie pushed upward with her left hand and forearm. Shards of glass from the broken whiskey bottle pierced her palm and arm. She shrieked and clutched her throbbing arm to her chest, wondering which way to run.

The figure moaned.

Jeannie kept screaming.

Suddenly, lights came on, blinding Jeannie.

"Jeannie? Where are you? Are you okay?" Max's voice called. He hurried to her as the room filled with people. Renee, Ramey, Cloie, and Annie were coming toward her, too.

Police officers and paramedics filled the room.

Jeannie blinked and looked down at the blood-stained body of Tyler Vaughan, who moaned again as paramedics began their examination. The thought crossed Jeannie's mind, *It must have been Roscoe in the green van.*

Jeannie stumbled forward into the arms of Max, who held her close. He patted her shoulders, comforting her while sobs racked her body. Her family surrounded her, moving in for a group hug.

A sharp pain in her left hand caused Jeannie to pull away. She examined her palm where a large sliver of glass was lodged in the soft flesh by her thumb. She reached to pull it out.

"Stop it, Jeannie. Let the medics take care of that," Renee scolded.

"Oh, Aunt Jeannie, you got glass all over your arm. It's bleeding through your sleeve!" Cloie cried.

Jeannie stared at her left arm and hand that were covered with blood. She swayed against Max, who caught her to him. "Oh, my God, Max, I got blood all over you, too!" She giggled hysterically.

From further away, Jeannie heard Brent's voice calling, "Lynn, Lynn, are you all right?"

Max kept an arm around Jeannie. He led her towards the back exit where medics were continuing to arrive.

Jeannie gasped as she stared down at Lynn Cooper Sherman on the floor. *This must be the body I stumbled over.*

Blood discolored Lynn's beautiful blue sweater. Tangled locks of blonde hair tinted red with blood lay in disarray. A gash on the right side of her head continued to bleed. Fragments of glass littered the area around her. The remnants of a broken beer bottle lay nearby.

Paramedics moved in to examine Lynn as Brent Sherman continued to call her name.

Lynn Copper Sherman awoke to bright lights. A voice kept saying her name, "Lynn, Lynn. Wake up."

She struggled to sit up, and fireworks went off in her head as she was helped into a wheelchair. She whimpered. Squinting, she looked at the figures standing over her.

Her dad stood with Tresa Vaughan, Bill King, and some men in uniform, who were scribbling in a notepad. Richard P. Copper glanced toward his daughter, "You all right, Lynn? I'll just be a minute. We're finishing up here."

Lynn was used to her dad putting business first. She was just glad he was here. "Where's Tyler? Is he okay?"

A familiar voice from behind her said, "They just took Vaughan to Cox South Emergency. They said he'd be okay, but he needed stitches on his head." Brent moved forward and looked down at his ex-wife. "Try to remain still, Lynn. Your head wound is still bleeding. They're going to take you in for some stitches, too."

Lynn looked up at Brent. She was really glad he was there. "What happened to Tyler's head?"

Max and Jeannie Jonson, Renee, Cloie and Ramey Allen, Annie LeBlanc and two of Halesville's finest, came from the bar area and joined the group. Jeannie, bandaged arm in a sling, answered Lynn's question. "The consensus is the bartender wasted a good bottle of whiskey on Vaughan when he smashed it against his skull." Jeannie belatedly realized Tresa Vaughan was still at Jeers. "Sorry, I—"

Tresa smiled. "I couldn't have said it better myself, my dear. He was in his element."

Richard P. gave Tresa an understanding smile. "Ms. Vaughan, your brother was very cooperative in giving evidence that helped the local authorities apprehend Roscoe Rayl." He patted her arm and glanced toward his daughter. "It just takes some of our children longer to grow up than others."

Tresa returned his smile. "Thanks, Mr. Copper. Please call me Tresa. I've about decided I've sheltered Tyler a little too much. This time I'm going to let him face the music. Maybe I'll find out if he's adaptable or if he's going to be tone deaf forever."

Richard P. gave Tresa a speculative look and nodded. "Likewise. Call me Richard. They say you can't teach an old dog new tricks. But Tresa, I think you may have just taught this old dog a very important trick." His gaze rested on his daughter and her ex-husband. He realized Brent Sherman had been listening to their conversation and unconsciously nodding along with their words. He may have misjudged this young man.

"Was Tyler conscious when they took him to the hospital? There was a picture I wanted to show him," Lynn said.

"Conscious enough to suggest Roscoe might be in the vicinity of the old Quarry storage area. Luckily, he'd heard enough of Roscoe's conversation to realize what Roscoe was planning to do." Bill King answered Lynn's question but his words were directed at Tresa Vaughan.

One of the officers with Max and Jeannie spoke. "We alerted this little lady's father." He patted Annie on the head.

Annie smiled but shrugged away from the officer's hand. "I'd already warned my dad on the cell phone earlier. He and his partner, Anderson, were on the scene at the Quarry."

The officer smiled. "That's correct, Miss Annie. You are to be commended for the way you handled your information." This time the pat on the head did not follow. "And your father and his partner are to be commended, too."

Cloie joined hands with Annie. She whispered, "I just wish we could have been there when the police made the drug bust and caught that Roscoe murderer."

Annie grinned. She whispered, "And I bet your aunt gets her watch bracelet back now."

The two girls blushed when they realized the room was quiet, and everyone had been listening to their conversation.

Max walked to stand beside his niece. He hugged her and started to pat Annie's head. Remembering her reaction earlier, he extended a hand for a handshake instead.

Cloie returned her uncle Max's hug. In a loud whisper, she asked, "Where's your camera? You're missing a lot of awesome action shots."

Max shrugged. In his haste to get inside and be sure Jeannie was safe, he'd completely forgotten his camera.

Soon the whole room was applauding and congratulating everyone on their part in the apprehension of Roscoe Rayl. Tyler would soon be joining his cohorts in the jail, including the now-jobless truck driver, who delivered drugs mixed with legit deliveries through Vaughan Truck Lines.

Richard P. stepped over to Max. "Young man, I've heard a lot about your photography." He glanced at his daughter. "And I've seen some pretty revealing shots."

Max's gaze locked with Lynn's. They knew he must have seen the photos that ended up with Roscoe, which should have been Lynn's envelope.

Both flushed, aware that if the circumstances had been any different, they might be paying the penalty for drug use. It was a huge incentive for rehab.

Richard P. was unaware of the silent communication between ex-spouses. He continued, his question directed to Max, "You're aware that I own a cruise line?"

Max nodded and looked at Jeannie inquiringly. He knew she was hellbent on going to Mexico with the Spanish club this summer. Maybe Richard P. was offering a job on a cruise ship. He'd been offered stranger things in connection with Maximum Exposure.

Richard P. said, "I've been hunting an on-ship photographer whose proficiency will compliment my customers on tour. If you're interested, drop by next week and we'll talk about it."

As the group moved toward the back door, Richard P. leaned closer to his daughter. "Thanks for the confidence call earlier. It took you a long time to realize your old dad is there for you when you need him."

Lynn looked up and smiled. "I've always known that. It's just that you're really busy sometimes." Seeing his frown, she continued, "And after Mom's death, you taught me to be independent."

"Maybe too independent," Richard P. murmured. "But we'll try to rectify that." Turning to Brent, he extended his hand for a handshake.

Brent had moved further away while Lynn and her father talked. Now, he moved forward to accept the long awaited man-to-man handshake. "Mr. Copper—"

Richard P. turned the handshake into a gentleman's hug when he pulled his ex-son-in-law to him. He'd heard Sherman was Lynn's protector, even though they were divorced. He watched how Sherman had moved away from Lynn when Jeannie Jonson and her ex-husband had come into the room. Regretfully, he realized there was a spark that kindled when Ms. Jonson and Brent's gaze met. Hindsight nearly always dealt a fatal blow. But for now, he needed to make amends. "Son, I've got a cruise ship that needs a cruise director the last of July. You'd be doing me a great favor if you'd accept the responsibility."

Brent glanced at Lynn. If he wasn't mistaken, that was the cruise she generally managed. Two years ago, they'd served as co-directors.

Lynn blinked. "Daddy, if you're talking about the Copper Four, that's my ship directorship, isn't it?"

"It was. This year you're going to have something more important going on." He looked at Tresa Vaughan and winked. "This old dog has a new trick called rehab that we both need to explore."

"Daddy, I've tried—" Lynn began.

"The key word is 'I'. This time it's 'we'...we are going to not only try, we are going to accomplish it." He glanced at Max and winked, "I'm actually going to instigate a rehab program on board the cruise ship for those interested."

Max peered at Jeannie. She had moved closer to Renee and her family and was staring, open-mouthed at the proceedings. He'd seen that look. It was her what-about-me look. He felt for her. She'd wanted to go on a summer vacation, and now, here was the owner of a cruise ship tossing free passes right and left but not in her direction.

Lynn gaped at her father. It had been a long time since she'd heard him use this parental tone with her. It had been a long time since she'd felt so protected and confident in his love.

"Yes, Daddy. I think, together, we can do it."

Richard P. cleared his throat. "Now, young man, do I take that silence as a yes?"

Brent was in shock. "I've got fireworks—"

"Do you think I don't follow your careers? Your fireworks venture will be well over by the time you'll need to report for the cruise duty." He finished softly, "I really need your help, son."

Brent looked at Lynn inquiringly.

She nodded.

He glanced at Jeannie, sensing her feelings. He shot her a reassuring look.

Jeannie shrugged and smiled. Her little voice was pouring on the pity party. *Well, looks like that accounts for everyone but the person who really wants to go. And that would be— shut up! I still have a summer job. I can earn my own way. And, who knows? Maybe I'll win the talent show.*

As if reading Jeannie's thoughts, Lynn said, "Dad, I've got a proposition for you."

Richard P. grinned. That was his daughter, even with a gash on her head, making lemonade out of a lemon tossed her way. "And, that would be?"

"Jeers has a talent show scheduled for tomorrow night." She checked her watch. "Actually, it's tonight, now. Roscoe was in charge." She glanced at Tresa. "With Tresa's and your permission, I'd like to be in charge. I've been helping Roscoe, and I'd hate to disappoint everyone." She turned to Jeannie and smiled. "Ms. Jonson and a lot of her friends are counting on it."

Jeannie clutched her throbbing arm and hand to her chest. She blinked and smiled back reflexively. Was this really happening? Was Lynn Copper Sherman smiling a genuine smile at her? Was she really thinking about a talent show after all this had happened and she was getting ready to have stitches put in her head? Had she been wrong about this woman? Da-dum!

Jeannie said, "Hey, Lynn, if you can manage the talent show with a hole in your head, I can surely manage to strum my guiiii-tar with one hand."

Tresa walked over to Lynn and patted her on the shoulder. "I see that Copper shining through, Miss Lynn. I'd be happy for you to manage the show, if you're able. I understand your daddy is furnishing the prize money. It would be a shame to have that money go to waste." She winked at Richard P. "Of course, I'll expect the financier at my table tonight."

Richard P. nodded. "My pleasure."

"Well, let's get this place closed. I have a crew coming to clean up the mess and open in a few hours," Tresa said. The responsibility of ownership rested heavily on Tresa's shoulders now that her brother was in jail.

Richard P. said, "Of course, Lynn. Let's get you to the ER. Our doctor is meeting us there."

"Tresa, may I speak to you a minute?" Lynn said.

Tresa nodded and followed as Richard P. pushed Lynn's wheelchair to the exit. By the time they reached the door, Tresa threw back her head and filled the room with laughter, "You're kidding me, right?"

Lynn smiled, "I kid you not. He actually said he would try to be here. And to save him a table in the corner. Preferably in the shadows."

Brent took Jeannie's arm as they moved toward the door. "I'm so glad you're all right. I was worried."

Jeannie nodded toward Lynn, "I noticed."

Brent glanced at Max, who was staring openly at them.

"Et tu, Brute! That makes two of us noticing," Max grumbled.

"The devil can cite scripture for his purpose," Jeannie quoted sweetly.

"But love is blind, and lovers cannot see the pretty follies that themselves commit." Brent was gazing into her eyes, determined to not lose the ground they had gained in the last few days. He caught her good hand in his as they moved side by side.

Jeannie nodded wearily, "I'll see you tonight, okay?" She indicated the room of people, who seemed bigger-than-life. "All that glitters is not gold." She returned the squeeze to her hand as Sherman let go. She added, "Sometimes, it's copper."

Chapter 41

The crowd at Jeers on Saturday night was unusually lively. Due to the circumstances of last night, the curious had turned out in droves. Media coverage of the drug bust and arrest of Roscoe Rayl, Tyler Vaughan, and Lester Moore made front page:

> Two suspected primary players in a drug ring which operated in Halesville, Missouri were apprehended early this morning by Task Force Supervisor Bill King of the Missouri Drug Task Force, aided by local officers, Leland LeBlanc and Clint Anderson, who had staked out Quarry Road where the arrests were made.
>
> Taken into custody were Roscoe Rayl, 38, of Halesville, Tyler Vaughan, 35, of Tulsa, Oklahoma and Lester Moore, 50, of Tulsa, Oklahoma. Arrest warrants have been obtained for six other suspects on felony drug violations.
>
> King said the ring, which dealt in cocaine, marijuana, and meth, had been under surveillance for some time. The arrests were made without incident. No firearms were found on the men, but stash worth $5,000 was recovered from a truck carrying freight for Vaughan Truck Lines out of Tulsa, Oklahoma. Also, a quantity of crack cocaine with a street value of $50,000 was confiscated.
>
> Rayl will be arraigned before District Judge Cody Scott Monday morning. A preliminary

hearing will be held June 10 in connection with the death of undercover deputy Rita Gibson, who is thought to have been murdered while investigating the drug ring.

Vaughan and Moore will have separate hearings.

Alec the Great was ruling with finesse at Jeers bar. He'd cleaned all traces of drugs from the premises. Waiters were straight. "No Smoking" signs were posted with an emphasis on no toking.

Tresa kept watch from her table where Richard P. Copper and company ruled. Because of the trouble with the Jeersberrys the night before, the machines were not handed out.

Jeannie knew without a doubt the person harassing her had been Roscoe. The language was definitely Roscoe. From the beginning, his usage of plural "Son" in "Sons of a bitch" had been a red light, if she'd been paying attention.

Lynn sported a new hairdo which completely covered her bandaged head. She posted a listing of talent contestants and their time of appearance on stage. Those competing could watch others perform from tables near the side of the stage if they were ready to perform when it was their turn. Lynn had added critique judges who were seated near the stage. However, the audience was the final judge. Ballots were available for voting, and all were encouraged to participate. Lynn enlisted Bo Hankins and the football jocks to collect the ballots after each performance. Tabulators were available to tally the results.

Jeannie favored her right hand when she played but gingerly used her left when she could. Cloie and Annie designed a black elastic bandage with diamond studs to cover Jeannie's bandaged left arm and hand. It actually added a bizarre touch to her costume.

In the tiny dressing room offstage, Cyra was antsy as a cat on a hot tin roof as she bustled around the small dressing room. She busied herself getting into her Marilyn Monroe attire, the white halter dress with wide skirt, stiletto heels, and a marvelous blonde wig. When her makeup was applied, she turned to Jeannie. It wasn't Cyra who asked the question; it was Marilyn. "Do you think we have a chance? Be honest, Jeannie."

"Honey, everyone has an equal chance. It doesn't hurt that Sherman's Lit class is here in force. We're all assured votes from our friends." Jeannie was amazed at the image Cyra conveyed and wondered what facet of Marilyn would be portrayed by Cyra.

Jeannie was surprised at the confidence she, herself, derived from her attire. She'd donned her black, rhinestone-studded jeans and fringed leather vest that covered her jeweled bustier, for which Max aptly took credit. He'd already sneaked in to snap a million photos.

Cloie and Annie were allowed to come to Jeers to watch because they were to be seated with their parents. Renee and Ramey seemed to be enjoying the company of Leland LeBlanc and Annie's mom, NezAnne.

The girls joined Jeannie in the dressing room where they helped pull and tug her black boots until the soft leather finally slipped comfortably in place. Cloie brushed her aunt's hair to a sheen. Both girls helped attach the hoop earrings that added an emphatically sexy appeal. Then Jeannie lifted the black felt cowboy hat and dropped it on her head. She adjusted it to a jaunty angle, poked a stiffened finger beneath the brim, pushed it up, and peered out from beneath. She winked at the girls with her expertly-applied-mascara lashes.

"Aunt Jeannie, you're a winner." Cloie hugged her aunt. Annie rushed to join the group hug before Jeannie was ready to step out and join her friends at their stage-side table. Jeannie returned their hugs and sent them to their seats.

Jeannie hoisted her guitar over her shoulder and made her way to the dressing room door.

The room lights had been lowered, and the pale blue spotlight was trained on the performer on stage as each performed their talent. Their friend Oscar was the tenth competitor. Jeannie was number twelve. And Cyra was last, number fourteen.

Oscar, in his Popeye attire, was seated with Brent and Gussie and Roe, who had finished their performances. Two chairs were empty at the table. Oscar looked up as Cyra and Jeannie emerged from the dressing room. His eyes lit up when he saw Cyra, resplendent in her white dress that hugged her curves like her counterpart, Marilyn. He motioned to the seat next to him.

Brent was shaking his head from side to side slowly as he saw Jeannie and mouthed, "Wow!" He started to rise but realized he'd be blocking the view of the stage. He motioned to Jeannie to come sit by him.

Jeannie looked to where Max was flashing pictures of the talent show.

He caught her glance and smiled. Without missing a flash, he gave her the thumbs-up signal.

Jeannie looked from Max to Brent.

She winked at Max and moved to sit in the chair beside Brent. Lynn announced the next performer would be Oscar Denver performing as Popeye, the Sailor Man.

Oscar reached down to drop a kiss on Cyra's cheek. "For good luck, okay?" he said.

As Oscar started for the stage, he looked toward a table in the far corner where a figure sat in the shadows. Oscar stopped and bent at the waist in a deep bow. Then, he unsheathed the long sword from his side and raised it over his head, pointing it at the figure. Those seated close by heard him exclaim, "For you, buddy."

They strained to see who it was that Oscar was posturing for.

Cyra's gaze never wavered from Oscar as he made his way on stage, swaggering as he went. The shy smile on her lips spoke of secrets she and Oscar shared. Without a doubt, she knew who the figure was at the table in the shadows.

Applause resounded as Oscar finished. Grinning, he returned to the table, tossing a saucy salute in the direction of the table in the shadows.

"Oh, yeah!" shouted a male voice from the shadows.

The next two performers sang and danced their way through applause.

At the mike, Lynn announced, "Ms. Jeannie Jonson will be performing her original lyrics of 'Low Places,' a song made famous by a Country favorite who is performing in Branson this weekend, Mr. Garth Brooks."

As Jeannie picked up her guitar and prepared to move to the stage, Brent reached out to clasp her fingers and gave them a quick squeeze.

Jeannie looked into his eyes and drew confidence from his words, "Though this be madness, yet there is method in't."

Jeannie leaned down to whisper, "I, dear Polonius, am completely mad."

Jeannie stepped onstage to a round of applause and cat whistles from Bo and the jocks.

"Thanks, boys. I appreciate that more than you know," she said as she arranged herself on the tall stool bathed in the baby blue spotlight. Positioning her guitar, she strummed an introduction.

"You sing it, baby!" Cyra yelled.

Oscar hollered, "Do it for Popeye, honey. And make the man proud."

From somewhere in the corner of the room, a voice yelled, "Yeah, make the man proud."

With her index finger, Jeannie pushed the black cowboy hat up to peek at the audience.

She grinned at Max.

She gave Cloie and Annie an exaggerated wink.

Jeannie strummed the guitar once more and began to sing the strange rendition of "Low Places." The original Jeannie lyrics were the ones Garth Brooks had sung to her in her dreams one night when she was at one of the lowest place in her life.

"Blame it all on true loves.

Handle them with kid gloves.

A one night stand or a long term affair.

He'll be the first one to go.

You'll be the last one to know

you two are no longer a pair."

Jeannie couldn't sit still. She was off the stool moving to the edge of the stage. She was singing to Max with all the hurt in her voice that came from being cheated on. It made the song a heartbreaker.

"So don't be surprised

If he has roving eyes

After he's drunk too much champagne.
And when he starts telling you
It's just a stage I'm going through
You can bet he's mixed up with some dame."
Jeannie strummed the guitar, playing to the audience. Then she blasted into the next lines.
"And she'll have curves in all the
Right places.
She'll be an easy score when she freebases
She's fine stuff and chases
his blues away."
A flash of light reminded her that Max was still on the job. She knew that he knew the feelings they had shared were something special. But it required TLC—tender, loving, care. Jeannie knew Max had loved her, but other things had been more important than their relationship. The fire had burned out. Maybe it still smoldered. If fanned, one day, it might return to prove that love is a blast. But for now, they moved in different directions. She smiled at Max as he flashed another picture.
Then, Jeannie turned her gaze in Brent's direction, and sang with gusto.
"Then, he'll be okay.
Cause he's a womanizer without social graces.
He's an easy mark for pretty faces.
Oh, I lost him to low-ho places."
Jeannie was back on the stool when she finished with her head bent over the guitar. Again, she pushed her index finger beneath the brim of the hat and raised it up to wink at the audience. She sang the last line one more time.
"Oh, I lost him to low-ho places."
Through a blur of tears that threatened to ruin her perfect mascara, Jeannie took several bows before the audience let her leave the stage. The spotlight followed her back to the table where she found Cloie and Annie seated in Cyra's and Oscar's chairs. They ran around to hug her, telling her how great she'd been.

Lynn announced the next talent, number thirteen. As the performer moved to the stage, the spotlight shifted. It lingered at the table in the shadows where Oscar and Cyra were talking to a man whose face remained in the shadows. As the spotlight returned to the stage, Jeannie caught a glimpse of the man in her dreams who'd sung to her one night.

"No way!" she said, looking at Brent, who nodded and smiled.

As number thirteen finished her talent, Cyra and Oscar returned to the table.

Cyra bent to brush her lips against Jeannie's cheek. "Pardon the Marilyn lipstick, honey, but I just wanted to remind you we got friends in low places."

Jeannie hugged her.

Lynn was announcing Miss Cyra, or is it Miss Marilyn? Cyra sashayed over to claim the stage.

Oscar moved to a place below the stage and switched on a fan which caught Cyra's white skirt. The wide skirt billowed up. Cyra did a pretty pout and placed her hands, Marilyn-style, in the right place to hold the skirt positioned to show her shapely legs.

While Cyra swayed slightly toward the audience, revealing her Marilyn cleavage, she crooned a medley of tunes made famous by Marilyn. And, suddenly, she was Marilyn.

"A kiss on the hand may be quite continental,

But diamonds are a girl's best friend…"

Cyra held out a dainty hand covered with jewels. Placing the hand over her lips in mock surprise, she gasped a Marilyn gasp. She moved to the edge of the stage, still holding her skirt. She motioned for the spotlight to include Oscar, who hunkered out of sight at the fan. The baby blue spotlight found Popeye and returned to Cyra, who was luring her man onto the stage with the tip of a sexy finger, gesturing and re-gesturing to him. The crowd broke into laughter as he lumbered up the stairs to join Marilyn, AKA Cyra, who immediately broke into the lyrics:

"I wanna be loved by you, just you,

And nobody else but you,

I wanna be loved by you, alone!
Boop-boop-de-boop!"

With Oscar playing the male buffoon, Cyra postured and preened as she continued to sing.

"I wanna be kissed by you, just you,
Nobody else but you,
I wanna be kissed by you, alone!"

As Marilyn grabbed her man and bent him backwards for an exaggerated kiss, the audience stomped and cat-called their approval. She put her hands on Oscar's chest and lightly pushed him from her, primly. Then, she moved back to claim the spotlight alone and finished by belting out the final lyrics:

"I wanna be loved by you,
Ba-deedly-deedly-deedly-dum-ba-boop-bee-doop
Boop-boop-a-doop!"

The spotlight faded as the crowd went wild. When the light came on again, the stage was empty, except for a banner reading:

"They've tried to manufacture other Marilyn Monroes and they will undoubtedly keep trying. But it won't work. She was an original." ~ Billy Wilder

Jeannie and the people at her table crowded around Cyra and Popeye, congratulating them.

Lynn claimed the mike to announce the end of the show, thank everyone, and explain there would be a brief intermission while the votes were collected, counted, and the announcement made as to winners. "Then comes the payoff!"

"Aunt Jeannie, Aunt Jeannie!" Cloie exclaimed. Annie grabbed Jeannie's good hand. "Come over to our table." Pulling and tugging her along, they moved toward the table where Renee, Ramey, and Leland LeBlanc sat with Annie's mom, NezAnne.

"Sis, I couldn't believe it was you! You were great!" Renee's excitement was contagious. Soon, everyone at the table was adding their comments on a first-name basis.

"So, Jeannie, what are you going to do with all that prize money?" NezAnne asked.

Conversation stopped at the table.

Renee, Cloie, and Jeannie replied in unison, "Go on a cruise with the Spanish Club to Mexico."

NezAnne laughed along with Leland and Annie.

"I see you've given it a lot of thought," Leland said. "And what if you don't win?"

NezAnne gave him a playful shove. "Leland's a laugh a minute."

Jeannie grinned. "Maybe he should have entered the talent show."

Cloie piped up. "Aunt Jeannie doesn't have to win the prize money. She's going to run a fireworks tent. And I'm going to help her. That's how she's going to make money to go on the cruise."

"Fireworks!" NezAnne exclaimed. "I love fireworks. Can I help?"

Leland scowled. "You can't sell fireworks, You've got a job."

"Hey, I'm due for a vacation," NezAnne said.

"Yeah, Mom's due for a vacation. And, I can help, too." Annie nudged Cloie.

Cloie nodded. "Yep, we can all help, can't we, Aunt Jeannie?"

"Well, I will need some help." Jeannie paused, looking around the table. It would be worth hiring Annie and her mom just to watch LeBlanc's reaction.

As though reading Jeannie's thoughts, Renee said, "What about me? I can use some extra spending money."

Jeannie shrugged her shoulders. "We'll see. I've got a lot to learn about this business before I start hiring help. But Annie, you and your mom will be at the top of the list when I do hire."

Renee gave Jeannie a forsaken look.

"Et, tu, Brute."

Thirty minutes later, Lynn moved onto the stage with envelopes in hand, to a spattering of applause.

"I'd like for my father, Richard P. Copper to join me on stage." Lynn smiled into the spotlight as groans of protest came from Tresa Vaughan's table.

Tresa's brassy tones carried easily over the turmoil. "Get on up there, Copper; it's not like you haven't done this before."

Laughter accompanied Richard P. as he joined his daughter on stage. "To what do I owe this privilege?" He inquired.

Lynn hugged him and whispered, "I need a little support. In lieu of something more potent, I guess you'll have to do."

Her father hugged her back and motioned for her to continue.

"Without further ado, I'd like to call the top three contestants on stage. I'm calling the contestants in the order in which they performed, not as they are ranked. Remember, this is the decision of the audience."

Lynn was drowned out by the audience giving themselves a round of applause.

Lynn continued, "Oscar Denver, Jeannie Jonson, Cyra Butler, please come to the stage."

Yelps of excitement, moans and groans, and a "hee-haw" from the corner table in the shadows accompanied the excited finalist to the stage.

Jeannie left her guitar at the chair. Her heart pounding, she followed Oscar and Cyra on stage.

Brent's words followed them, "You all were great!"

Lynn shook hands with each of the finalists as did her father, who held the winners' envelopes.

"All right, let's find out who wins the big bucks," Lynn said, amidst a flash of light as Max took another picture.

"I'll start with number three. And, will the winners please stay on stage for pictures following the presentation? May I have the envelope, please." She turned to her father, who handed her the envelope.

"Winner number three, who receives five hundred dollars, is Ms. Jeannie Jonson." She smiled a genuine smile as she handed Jeannie an envelope. "Would you like to say anything, Ms. Jonson?"

Jeannie accepted the envelope and stammered, "Thanks to all my devoted fans." She stopped as the crowd applauded. She blushed, and continued. "As you could probably tell, I'm not used to performing before an audience. I was a contestant in the Miss Bull Creek pageant and came in fourth." She paused, "Hey, you can't beat that, I moved up to third this time."

Shut up, motor-mouth, Jeannie told herself. *Next thing you'll reveal is there were only four contestants in the Bull Creek pageant.*

An echo of her thoughts came from behind a blinding flash as Max yelled, "Way to go, Bull Creek."

Lynn hugged Jeannie and whispered. "You're a winner in more ways than you know, Jeannie."

Lynn continued, "The winner of second place and fifteen hundred dollars is Oscar Denver, better known as Popeye." She handed him an envelope. "Anything you want to say, Oscar?"

Oscar grinned broadly and tossed a salute to the far corner table. "First time I bested himself." He turned to Jeannie and gave her a hug. He whispered, "I didn't best you, darling. I just had to give myself a hard time." Aloud, Oscar said, "Turn up the fans, boys, and let's give Marilyn a hand."

Lynn shouted over the crowd, "Oscar, you beat me to the first place announcement. The winner of three thousand dollars and first place is Cyra Butler."

Cyra's skirt bellowed upward. As she grabbed for it, she babbled out her thanks and hugged Oscar, Jeannie, and others who were coming onstage.

Lynn's voice came over the mike. "Please, let's give our winner a chance to speak." She handed the mike to Cyra.

Cyra held the envelope over her head and waved it Marilyn-style. In a throaty voice, she spoke into the mike. "John Hudson once said this about my idol, Marilyn Monroe, 'It's a terrible pity that so much beauty has been lost to us.'"

The crowd settled as Cyra continued to speak, "I agree with him. And, this week we lost another lovely young woman, who lived and worked among us. Her beauty inspired her peers to choose her as a contestant in the Miss Hale University contest."

The silence was complete as the crowd drew a collective breath of regret for the loss of one of their own.

Cyra continued, "Rita Gibson attended Hale University. She was also affiliated with the ATC and was killed in the line of duty."

Gasps from parts of the audience spoke reality into existence.

Cyra held her envelope out to Richard P. Copper. She said, "I'd like to present my prize money to a member of the board of Regents at Hale University in memory of Rita Gibson. I hope this will be the start of a scholarship in her name."

Oscar immediately handed his envelope to Richard P. "Very nice, Miss Cyra. I'd like to follow suit. I pledge my prize money to the scholarship fund, too."

Thoughts had been racing through Jeannie's head. *I won five hundred dollars.* As she looked at the upturned faces in the crowd she saw Renee, to whom she owed at least one hundred and fifty of the five hundred dollars. Da-dum, the money was already slipping through her hands.

She saw Cloie, Annie, Max, and, Brent, who were smiling congratulations to her.

She grinned at Annie and her mom, who wanted to work with her in her fireworks tent. And Leland LeBlanc, who might become a friendly adversary. Jeannie knew their thoughts as well as her own. *You finally have some cash to put toward the Mexico trip.*

But Cyra's words and Oscar's words and actions spoke to Jeannie in a language she knew and admired. As they handed their prize money to the University representative in memory of Rita Gibson, Jeannie knew without a doubt what she would do.

"And mine, too," Jeannie said, as she handed her envelope to Richard P. Copper.

The silence of the crowd was broken by a low chant coming from Bo Hankins and the Hale University jocks.

"Rita Gibson, yessss, yessss,yesssss!

Hale yes! Hale U! Hale Yes!"

As the crowd moved restlessly, expecting dismissal, Richard P. Copper handed another envelope to Lynn.

Lynn stepped to the mike. She cleared her throat. "Please, may I have your attention. First I'd like to express appreciation to these three contestants for their generosity in pledging their winnings for a memorial in memory of the late Rita Gibson. My father and I plan to add to this generous gift."

Murmurs of approval throughout the crowd spoke of other contributions to come.

Lynn turned to the three winners. "Thank you. There's one more award I'd like to present. Earlier, my father and I discussed an award for Best Style in Performance, which would be decided by the critique panel." Lynn motioned to the tables where the critique panel still sat. "The ballots are in on that award. I'd like to announce the winner, Ms. Jeannie Jonson." Lynn extended an envelope to Jeannie.

Jeannie blinked against the flash of light which could only mean Max was recording this moment. What award had Lynn mentioned? Style of Performance? What a night! She'd placed in the top three of the talent show and won five hundred dollars. Of course, she'd promptly given it away.

Jeannie's dad's voice joined her on stage. *That's my Jeannie— always passing the buck.*

Granted, Dad, but it was for a good cause. Now, she was to receive a certificate for best style in performance. "What a night!" Jeannie voiced her thoughts, moving to take the envelope from Lynn as she expressed her thanks to both Lynn and her father.

Richard P. Copper winked at Jeannie and smiled.

Lynn spoke into the mike once more. "This award is contingent on the acceptance of the winner's utilization. If the winner is unable to use the award, it will revert to the second place winner in that category. Will you be able to use this complimentary ticket for a cruise aboard the Copper Cruise Lines, Ms. Jonson?"

As Lynn was speaking, Jeannie was trying to sort out her announcement. How would she not be able to use a Certificate of Recognition? She would frame it or put it in her scrap book.

"Say what? Cruise?" She replayed the last sentence in Lynn's presentation. "Will you be able to use this complimentary ticket for a cruise aboard the Copper Cruise Lines, Ms. Jonson?"

Jeannie clasped the envelope tightly. "Will I ever!" She said it not as a question but as a statement. How long had she been trying to make some big bucks for a short-term job to pay her way on a Mexican cruise with the Spanish club? And, now she held the ticket for that cruise in her hot, little hands.

"Thanks, thanks so much," she kept saying as she hugged Lynn, her father, anyone within hugging distance and made her way off the stage and to the table to collect her guitar.

Heading for the dressing room, Jeannie heard someone call her name. She turned and was immediately caught up in a hug by Brent Sherman.

"Well, well, Ms. Jonson, it looks like you've achieved your goal. I guess you won't be needing that fireworks job with me after all?" Brent said.

Jeannie returned his hug. "Of course, I'll need the fireworks job. It'll mean working with my favorite people."

Brent grinned. "Thank you very much."

"I meant Cloie, Annie, and her mom, plus my sister, Renee. They all want a job, too," Jeannie teased.

Brent pouted a little boy pout.

"And, you, of course." Jeannie squeezed his hand. "Besides," she indicated her performance attire, "if a girl is going on a cruise she needs a new wardrobe." Jeannie tugged her vest closer over her bustier.

Brent pulled Jeannie close and gazed into her eyes. "Is there no space where a man can find some privacy to," he reached to strum a string on Jeannie's guitar, "tune a guitar?"

"What, exactly, did you have in mind, Professor?" Jeannie asked, trying to disentangle herself from the guitar.

"I've been wanting to do this all evening," Brent lowered his lips to hers for their first kiss.

Max dropped his camera to his side, not wanting this moment to be immortalized on his film as he watched another man kissing his woman. Looking away, he caught Lynn starring at Jeannie and Sherman, too.

Lynn hastily wiped a tear from her eye as she saw Max watching her.

Max placed a finger under his chin and tilted it upward motioning for her to do the same as he mouthed the words, "Keep your chin up."

Lynn knew Max well enough to know the words he spoke were not of defeat, but of encounters yet to come. Lyrics from a Robert Frost poem flashed through her head. It worked for herself and Max, too. " ... for we have promises to keep, and miles to go before we sleep."

When Max determined Jeannie and Brent's kiss lingered too long, he picked up his cell phone. As he dialed the familiar number he made a promise to himself. "Love can't die this easily. It may fizzle, but love can spark if there's enough fuse left to light."

Jeannie's cell phone rang. Still staring into Brent's eyes and with the kiss on hold, Jeannie clicked open her phone. "Yes?"

Max's voice came through loud and clear, "Turn your head a little to the right, Jen. This is going to make one hell of a picture."

Brent's eyes lit up with the humor of the moment. Misquoting King Henry IV, he said, "Shall we give the devil his due?"

Jeannie raised her lips to his, murmuring from Romeo and Juliet, "'Not stepping o'er the bounds of modesty,' are we?"

As Brent's lips lowered to hers, he responded, "Tempt not a desperate man."

A blinding flash captured Jeannie and Brent's monolithic moment where for the two pictured there, love was a blast!

Sonnet 18
"Shall I compare thee to a summer's day?
Thou art more lovely and more temperate:
Rough winds do shake the darling buds of May,
And summer's lease hath all too short a date."

The End

Jane Hale Bio

Jane Shewmaker Hale resides on the Hale family farm in Buffalo, Missouri. She combines family, business, community, alumni enterprises, and the promotion of area authors   through Ozark Writers, Inc. with her addiction to writing.

Jane, better known to the pyro world as the Firecracker Lady, is an active partner in family businesses, Hale Fireworks and Hale's Crossing Mall. She helped establish the Dallas County R1 Alumni Association and has served as president since 1971. She is a charter member of Ozark Writers, Inc., President 2010-2011; Springfield Writers' Guild, Vice President 1997; Ozark Writers League; and Missouri Writers' Guild, Vice President and Conference Chairman, 2003-2004, President, 2004-2005.

She is a columnist, photojournalist, author of children's and adult mysteries, gift books, and short stories in anthologies.